DOORBELLS AT DUSK

DOORBELLS AT DUSK

EDITED BY:
EVANS LIGHT

ASSOCIATE EDITORS:
GREGOR XANE
JASON PARENT
ADAM LIGHT

CORPUS PRESS
HORROR & WEIRD FICTION
CHARLOTTE, NC

Doorbells at Dusk

"Many Carvings" © 2018 by Sean Eads & Joshua Viola
"The Day of the Dead" © 2018 by Amber Fallon
"A Plague of Monsters" © 2018 by Charles Gramlich
"Offerings" © 2018 by Joanna Koch
"The Rye-Mother" © 2018 by Curtis M. Lawson
"Masks" © 2018 by Lisa Lepovetsky
"Trick 'Em All" ©2015 by Adam Light
"Rusty Husk" © 2018 by Evans Light
"Vigil" © 2018 by Chad Lutzke
"Adam's Bed" © 2018 by Josh Malerman
"Keeping Up Appearances" © 2018 by Jason Parent
"The Friendly Man" © 2018 by Thomas Vaughn
"Between" © 2018 by Ian Welke
"Mr. Impossible" © 2018 by Gregor Xane

Cover by Mikio Murakami.

Proofing and interior formatting by Lori Michelle of
The Author's Alley.

For more information about Corpus Press, please visit:
www.corpuspress.com

TABLE OF CONTENTS

A PLAGUE OF MONSTERS

Charles A. Gramlich

GUS KREBS GNAWED at his thumb while looking down at the unconscious monster strapped to the work table in his basement. He didn't know what it was but it looked . . . piggish. Nor did he have any idea where it came from.

He'd been watching *Wheel of Fortune* when his doorbell rang. He'd just solved a puzzle before the actual contestants and the thrill of that unusual occurrence made him forget normal caution. Carelessly opening the door had revealed this "thing" standing there. It carried a small glowing axe, and at sight of the weapon, Gus reflexively punched it twice.

It went down easily, maybe because it was small, and he'd dragged it into the house before any of the neighbors noticed. Because he often used power drills and saws while building furniture at home, his basement was soundproofed. Even if this thing woke up now and screamed, it wouldn't be heard.

Gus picked up the creature's axe. It appeared to be made out of some hard plastic. Like a toy. But Gus figured it wasn't any toy. The light inside had gone out when its owner lost consciousness. Maybe it was some kind of mind controlled laser. Would the little monster still be able to activate the weapon when it woke up and found itself a prisoner?

Gus had to take precautions, do something, fast. He grabbed

1

a hammer from his tool chest and smashed the weird weapon into smithereens, then threw its mangled remains into the trashcan.

Needing a moment to think, Gus went back upstairs and poured himself a cup of coffee with a dollop of whiskey to calm his nerves. The burnt scent of the coffee reminded him of his long dead daddy and immediately the odor started to soothe him. He was blowing on the coffee to cool it when the doorbell rang again. He jumped, spilling blistering liquid down his chin onto his shirt. Cursing, he set down the cup and grabbed a towel to mop himself.

The doorbell rang twice more and its incessant demands forced him out of his kitchen into the living room. He crossed to the door and peeked out through the spyhole. Nothing. Taking up the baseball bat he always kept handy against potential intruders, he cautiously unlatched his door and opened it.

Two monsters waited outside. They were smaller than the first but they also had laser weapons. These even looked like Sci-Fi blasters and they whined as they lit up. In a panic, Gus bashed both creatures over the head with his bat and quickly dragged them inside.

As he slammed his door, he realized his front porch light was on and wondered if it were attracting these grotesque things. Maybe they were like moths that way. He flicked off the light and double locked the doors, then hauled the two monsters down into the basement. Neither of them appeared to be breathing but he bound them to stout chairs anyway.

Once more he returned to his kitchen and poured himself a cup of coffee. Pacing and sipping, pacing and sipping, he tried to figure out what was happening. Finally, he went to the front of the house and eased back the window curtains to look outside. He quickly slapped a hand over his mouth to keep from crying out. The sidewalk along the road that ran past his house had become a monster freeway.

Dozens of the horrible creatures scampered along beneath the streetlights, with normal people intermingled among them. He saw attractive Mrs. Broussard from next door and Mr. Demby from down on the corner. Two small monsters tugged at Demby's hands as they urged him along; Demby laughed as if it were glorious fun.

Gus backed away from the window, then quickly opened the closet and took out the shotgun he'd bought a few years back for home defense. He'd never had to use it but that might soon change. Fumbling around on the closet's shelf, he found the shells and began pushing them into the gun's magazine.

The doorbell rang.

Gus jumped and almost pulled the trigger on the shotgun. He moved cautiously to the door, weapon ready, and peered out through the spyhole. Two police officers, a man and a woman, stood outside. He breathed a sigh of relief.

"Uhm, just a second," he called. "Hang on."

Sticking the shotgun back in the closet behind some coats, he returned to open the door. As he was about to warn the officers about the monsters, he noted that plenty of the nasty creatures still wandered along the street. The police didn't seem to notice or care. That scared him.

"Yes?" Gus asked warily.

"Mr. Krebs," the policewoman said. "I'm Officer Benton and this is my partner, Officer Reynolds. Sorry to bother you but we've had a report of a missing child. Cory Olsen. We were wondering if you'd seen him? If he'd been here trick or treating? He was dressed as an orc."

Gus had no idea what an "orc" was, but he wanted to shout, *Well, of course you've got missing children. You've got a town full of monsters. What do you expect?*

Then something else Officer Benton had said registered.

Gus repeated the phrase. "Trick or treating? But it's not Halloween."

"No, no," the woman said. "But you knew the town council voted to change the date this year, right? Because of the big parade to honor our returning veterans? They're coming back on the 31st. Can't have that and Halloween on the same day." She smiled.

Gus's mind did a back flip inside his head. Did that mean that he . . . Could he have made a horrible mistake in identifying the monsters? Were they just . . . *No!* He wasn't crazy. He knew what he'd seen. And even though he never celebrated Halloween, there'd been no vote that he was aware of to change the date. The police were lying.

In the next instant, he figured out why. Whoever or whatever was behind this monster plague must have planned it for Halloween—the perfect cover. But something had gone wrong. Things had started too soon and the forces behind it were scrambling for excuses. Anyway, he knew to keep such doubts and questions to himself. If they could lie, he could lie.

"Uh, well, yeah. I mean, I completely forgot to get candy. Because of the date change. So I've just been leaving my porch light off. The Olsen kid, you say? I'll certainly keep an eye open for him but I doubt I'll see him. I'll call you guys if I do."

The female officer, Benton, was smiling, but her male partner, Reynolds, was busy looking over Gus's head into the house. Gus didn't like that. What if they wanted to come inside? Even if they didn't check the basement, the baseball bat was still behind the door. He hadn't cleaned it after knocking out the last two monsters. Did it have blood on it? Other stuff? He started to take a deep breath to calm himself, but thinking that might be suspicious he quickly turned it into a cough.

Reynolds frowned. Benton kept smiling and said, "Do keep

an eye out. I imagine he's just off somewhere binging on Halloween candy. But his parents are pretty worried."

"I will. Certainly I will, officers." Gus forced a smile of his own.

The officers turned away and Gus shut and locked the door behind him. He grabbed up the bat, which *was* discolored around the tip with what might be drying blood. He rushed downstairs with it.

Once in the basement, Gus paced back and forth muttering to himself. "The police. They didn't care about the monsters on the street. So maybe *they're* monsters. Or at least they're following the orders of the monsters. That means they aren't looking for Cory Olsen. They're looking for. . . " Biting his lip, Gus turned toward the three creatures he'd captured.

Looking for them, he thought.

He had to do something, get rid of the things before the police came back and looked harder. He strode over to the first monster he'd captured and stared down with revulsion. The thing began thrashing back and forth on the table. Gus let out a little scream and jumped back. But he still had the baseball bat in his hands and he began whacking, whacking until the thing went still again. A lot more blood coated the bat this time.

Then Gus noticed something else.

"My God, my God!" he muttered.

The monster's face had sloughed to the side as Gus hammered at it. Beneath the hideous piggishness was a second face. One he recognized. Little Cory Olsen.

Can't be! No! I couldn't have killed . . . His thoughts stopped for a moment as he studied the remains of the thing. He saw it then, enough to convince him that he wasn't crazy. His thoughts restarted. *No, no, no. It's growing another Cory Olsen inside. A false Cory Olsen. I see parts that aren't human. The other two monsters I've*

5

got down here must be like this one. But the adults. The parents. Are they the same? Already . . . molted maybe?

Gus dropped the bat with a clang and backed away from the horror on the table. He kept backing until his legs struck something behind him. Startled, Gus spun around to see nothing more than his band saw squatting in its accustomed place. The solution to his problem shouted at him. He rushed upstairs to fetch towels and a bunch of black trash bags. Then he set to work cutting the three monsters into pieces and fitting them into the bags, which he tied off tightly and wrapped with strips of electrical tape.

The band saw was frightfully efficient. Within an hour, Gus finished his chore. The basement had a sink with running water and another hour saw the blood and gore cleaned away and the stuffed bags tucked into the darkest corner of the room. Gus pushed his bloody clothes into yet another bag, then went upstairs to take a hot shower.

After exiting the shower, he wiped away the condensation on the bathroom mirror to study himself in it. His reflection tore a gasp from him. His face! It was subtly altered. Not dramatically. Not yet at least. But he could see the differences.

The blood! he thought. *I had on clothes and gloves but it got on my face. I'm starting to change. It must be like an infection. It grows on the skin. First it takes you over. Controls you. Then another you hatches out from within. Not the real one, though. A modified one. One of them!*

Quickly and in desperation, using cotton balls and rubbing alcohol, Gus began to scrub at his face. He scrubbed and scrubbed, until his skin burned and tingled, until the fumes from the alcohol watered his eyes and made him feel faint. Only when his face was—as his daddy had always described it—pink as a freshly spanked bottom, did he quit.

Maybe, he thought. *Maybe I've stopped it. I hope I've stopped it.*

The doorbell rang once, then again.

Gus wanted to ignore the sound. He wanted to get into bed and bury himself under the covers until the world was shut out. But the bell rang a third time. And a fourth.

He finally shouted out, "I'm coming!"

Through the peephole, Gus saw the same two cops again. He thought about the bat, cleaned but forgotten in the basement. He thought of the shotgun in the closet. He dared not use it. If he did, the whole street, the whole town, would be on him in an instant. He'd have to bluff them again, then run as soon as they were gone. Surely there was another town he could escape to. The monsters couldn't have taken over everywhere yet.

Forcing himself to breathe steadily, he slowly opened the door. "Hello again, officers," he said. "Sorry it took me so long. I just got out of the shower." They could see his wet hair; they'd know he was telling the truth.

The policeman, Reynolds, still looked suspicious, and now the policewoman, Benton, was no longer smiling.

"Mr. Krebs," Benton said. "I'm afraid we've had two more children reported missing. We've been instructed to go from house to house doing a search. Is it okay for us to come in and look around?"

"Uh . . . well you don't think that I—"

"It's not a matter of thinking anything, Mr. Krebs," Benton interrupted. The whole police force is out. It's just our job to search every place where children might hide." Her eyes seemed to glitter. "Or where they might be held."

"Well, okay. Of course. I mean, I want to do my part. Come on in. You won't find anything here though."

Gus stepped back from the door to allow the two in. They quickly split up and began their search. Reynolds took the upstairs. Benton stayed downstairs to inspect the living room, kitchen, and laundry room. Gus trailed her, staying far enough away to avoid giving any impression of a threat.

There came a heart-stopping moment when the policewoman opened the closet and shoved things around. But if she saw the shotgun leaning against the back wall in the shadows, she said nothing. Of course, lots of folks had guns in Coleman, Louisiana.

Gus hoped the woman wouldn't even think of the basement. Few houses down here had them because of the danger of flooding. But this woman was thorough and eventually asked him point blank if he had one. He couldn't lie. How could he be sure she hadn't already noticed the obscure door and was just testing him?

He pointed out the bamboo screen he used to cover the ugly, unpainted door into the basement, opened it, flipped on the light, and went down the steps ahead of her. His eyes were wide as he scanned for any droplet of blood or unusual stain he might have missed. Everything looked clean. He could see the trash bags with the severed monster parts in them against the back wall but nothing indicated that they were filled with anything other than common trash.

Benton looked around rather perfunctorily. "Lot of equipment," she said.

"Yes. I make furniture sometimes. You can ask anyone."

She nodded, then shrugged. "All right. Nothing here." She looked at Gus. "We'll get out of your hair, Mr. Krebs."

"Sorry I couldn't be more help," Gus said, as the policewoman turned toward the stairs. "Wish I could."

A rustling came from the corner of the basement where the trash bags sat. Gus spun around in time to see what looked like a leg kick at the black plastic of the bag that wrapped it. He quickly moved in that direction as the woman turned toward him with a frown.

"Damn rats!" Gus said. "Can't keep 'em out of here. Don't know how they're getting in."

He pretended to look around by the bags, as if searching for a rat, then returned his gaze to Officer Benton. She was watching him and he smiled.

She smiled back. "I know the problem. We've got them down at the precinct, too." She went up the stairs then, and Gus followed after giving the offending trash bag a surreptitious kick.

Officer Reynolds awaited them in the living room. "Nothing," he said, sounding disappointed.

"All right," Benton said. "Let's get out of here."

Gus felt a smile coming on and fought it down.

As he closed the door behind the officers, a fresh banging came from the basement. Gus's smile disappeared and he quickly glanced out through the peephole to see if the police had heard the noise. Reynolds had stopped to look back at the house with a frown, but Benton was already striding down the sidewalk. After another moment, the policeman followed his partner.

Gus continued to watch, and was glad he did as Reynolds stopped at the end of the driveway and several other people joined him. Gus's eyes widened as he recognized Jim and Kathy Olson, Cory Olson's parents. There was another woman with them that Gus didn't know, and another couple that he did—Dwayne and Tina Lamont. Dwayne was a district attorney. Tina was a real estate agent. She'd tried several times to get him to sell his house but it had belonged to Gus's daddy. The Lamont's had a boy a year or so younger than Cory Olson. Gus had met him—*Terry*!

As Reynolds stood in deep conversation with the other five people, Gus wondered if one of the monsters he'd killed could have been growing into Terry Lamont. He was mulling that over when Reynolds and the others turned suddenly to look toward Gus's front door. Gus jumped back from the peephole, afraid they were reading his thoughts. Who knew what powers these things had.

They're onto me. They know I know. That means they'll be coming. I've gotta get out of here. Quick.

Possible escape routes suggested themselves—and were discarded. He couldn't go out the front way. They'd be watching even if they didn't seem to be. And the back was no good. He'd put an eight foot privacy fence around his backyard to keep out the kids and to make sure no nosy neighbors could look in on him. That fence had no gate and he'd have to use a ladder to get over it.

Too much noise.

There was one other way. When this house had first been built there'd been a coal fired furnace in the basement. Gus had long since converted to electric heat and removed the furnace. But the door to the coal chute was still there. He'd bolted it shut but had the tools to open it.

He'd have to leave with nothing but what he could stuff into a gym bag and with the money he had in the house. Fortunately, he'd never trusted banks so a cubbyhole in his basement wall hid most of his slender fortune, enough to take him a long way from here.

Rushing upstairs, he grabbed a gym bag he hadn't used for years and stuffed it with a toothbrush, a couple of changes of underwear, some shirts and socks and a pair of jeans. It was little enough for the forty-plus years he'd spent in this house. But he'd never married or had kids; he had no keepsake photos and had never attached himself to material objects other than the house itself. He was glad of that now.

After taking a last pee, he headed downstairs. A glance through the peephole in his front door showed a nearly empty street. Nearly everyone was probably taken over by now. If any real people remained in the houses along the road—or in the town—it didn't matter. He couldn't risk trying to identify any humans who were left. He had to save himself. *And . . . And. . . .*

For a moment he couldn't capture the thought he wanted. It finally came to him.

Warn the rest of the world.

With his mind a jumble, Gus opened the basement door, then paused. The lights were on; he could have sworn he'd turned them off. Was he getting forgetful as well as confused?

"Losing it," he muttered to himself.

Had to be the stress, he imagined. He started down the steps, froze at the bottom. *The coal chute door*! He'd planned to unbolt it and sneak out that way. It already hung open.

Impossible!

The scrape of shoes on concrete sounded behind Gus and he spun around. The policewoman—Benton—stepped out from the shadows beneath the basement stairs. A lit flashlight filled one of her badly trembling hands; the other held her service revolver, which pointed generally in Gus's direction. Vomit splattered the front of the woman's blue, uniform shirt.

"My God, Krebs," she muttered. "My God!"

Gus chewed at his lip. He looked over to where he'd stacked the trash bags full of body parts. They'd been torn open. A small arm hung from one, blackish blood dribbling down the ghastly gray fingers. Gus looked back at Benton. He held up his hands, spread them.

"You don't understand," he said. "I know what this must look like. But those things aren't *human*!

Benton retched, wiped her mouth on the back of the hand that held the flashlight. Her bloodshot gaze locked on his. Her lower lip quivered, then stiffened.

"I know," she said. "I saw . . . saw them. Some parts. I don't know what they are. And . . . then, sometimes pieces move. They should be dead but they move. My God, what are they?"

Gus swayed as he heard her words. Relief almost made him

pass out. "Monsters," he finally answered. "I don't know what else to call them."

"Monsters. Yes, monsters. How many? Are there more? Do you think?"

"A whole lot more, I bet," Gus said. "I'm sure the *parents* of these three things are. Maybe most of the people in town, judging from how many were on the streets earlier. I thought . . . *you* were. And your partner."

"Reynolds," Benton said. "I think you're right about him. He's been . . . weird."

Gus strained to focus his thoughts. His head buzzed. His bones seemed to rattle inside his body. "We've got to get out of here," he finally managed. "That's why I came down here. I've got money. Hidden. I was going to slip out the coal chute. You can go with me."

The woman wiped her mouth again, then slowly straightened as her training reasserted itself.

"Yes. We'll get out. But not through the coal chute. I told my partner I'd noticed something odd in your basement before, when you mentioned rats. I pried open the chute to slip in. He's outside. Waiting. He won't wait long."

"We can't go out the front door," Gus said.

"We can. We'll have to. I'll take you to my cruiser. Put you in the back like I'm taking you to headquarters for questioning. Then we'll just leave town. Find somebody to report this thing too." She stared at him hard for a moment. "I'll need to put you in cuffs. Temporarily. To make it look good."

Gus's heart pounded. He didn't want to be in cuffs. If the things came for him, he'd be helpless. But he couldn't think. He had to . . . trust Officer Benton.

Or give up, the thought came. *Let them have me.*

He shook his head in negation of that thought. "Okay. Just let me get my money."

Benton nodded as she moved toward the stairs. "Hurry!"

A hidden catch in the back wall of the basement opened a small cubby. Inside were stacks of bills and rolls of quarters, dimes, and nickels. Leaving the coins, Gus scraped the bills off into his gym bag and returned to Officer Benton. She led the way up into the house and they hurried to the front door.

Benton flipped the latch and had just started to turn the knob when the door thrust open and Reynolds bulled his way through. He held a baton, and as he swung it brutally toward Benton, the woman shoved her pistol into her one-time partner's chest and pulled the trigger twice.

The nightstick struck Benton's left shoulder and her sharp cry of pain was louder than the reports of the shots muffled by Reynolds' body. Reynolds lost control of the baton as he stiffened from the shock of the bullets. His eyes blinked. Then he grabbed his chest and slid slowly to the floor. Benton leaned over him, pressed the fingers of her gun hand against his throat. She looked up at Gus, shook her head. He nodded.

"Stay here," Benton said. "We'll have to do it differently now." She picked up Reynolds' cap where it had fallen and handed it to Gus. "Put that on. Your shirt's dark already. I'll get the car. Drive right up to your house. Hop in fast. Try not to let anyone get a good look at you."

Again, Gus nodded.

Benton holstered her pistol and went out through the door, favoring her injured arm where the baton had struck. Gus stepped forward, pushed the door but didn't latch it. He heard a squishing sound and looked down. Blood from the dead policeman soaked the carpet; tendrils of it had spackled his shoes and seemed to writhe even as he stepped back from the body and began wiping his feet off on the rug.

Nauseated and repulsed, Gus backed farther from the body. The blood seemed to follow him, swirling into crimson patterns that almost had meaning. The buzzing in his head had grown louder. His eyes throbbed in their sockets. Something made him step around the blood and kneel beside the dead officer. He unsnapped the strap that held the man's service revolver in its holster and tucked the gun into his gym bag among the piles of cash. Almost as an afterthought, he added the policeman's taser as well. Then his thoughts cleared. He rose again and waited for his ride.

When Gus heard the police cruiser pull up outside, he rushed out. Benton had the passenger side door open and he dove in. She immediately threw the cruiser into reverse and squealed out onto the highway.

"Slouch down," she said. "If we're lucky, they'll think you're Reynolds."

Gus noticed that Benton still wasn't using her left arm much, but it didn't seem to hurt her driving. "How are we leaving town?" he asked.

"Highway 23. It's the fastest route to the I-12. Plus, it's just past headquarters so it'll look normal for us to head in that direction."

"What happens once we pass headquarters?"

Benton glanced over at him. "We run for it."

Gus nodded. Then: "This thing. With the monsters. It's some kind of infection. Passed through bodily fluids. Like blood. It makes me wonder . . . "

"Wonder what?" Benton asked.

"Wonder how you weren't taken over? I figured they go after the police first."

Benton frowned at his comment, then gave a small gasp. "Bodily fluids. Or maybe food contaminated with such fluids? A few days ago, one of the officers brought in some cookies. I ate some. I think everyone did. That night I got very sick. Headaches. Nausea. I thought I was dying. But it passed quickly. I thought it had to be the cookies. Food poisoning. But the next day, none of the other officers admitted being sick."

"They'd been changed," Gus said.

"Yes." Benton nodded. "But it didn't take with me. For some reason." She glanced again at Gus. "Maybe I'm immune. Maybe you are too."

"Maybe," Gus agreed.

They passed Coleman's police station and turned onto Highway 23. A half-mile down they'd find the on-ramp for the I-12. From there they could get to New Orleans, Baton Rouge, Jackson. It wasn't going to be that easy, though. Benton slammed on the brakes as she saw what stretched across 23 ahead of them.

A double-thick line of people covered the road behind a barricade of sawhorses and yellow police tape. Most had guns, though some held axes and hoes and other garden implements. As the police cruiser rolled to a stop, the crowd began filtering through the barricades and moving toward the car. There were men, women, and some kids still in their "Halloween" costumes, though Gus figured none of them were really men, women, or kids anymore. Then Gus became aware of a low, moaning sound arising from the crowd. It stirred him in his seat.

"They know," he said. "It's no use. We better give up."

Benton shook her head. "No. Brace yourself. We'll ram through."

Gus watched the policewoman wince with pain as she forced her left arm up to grasp the steering wheel. She revved the engine but let off the gas when he pressed the pistol he'd taken from Reynolds against her neck.

"Don't make me shoot you," he said.

Benton turned her head very slowly. "What are you doing?" she protested. "You're not one of them. You killed those three monsters at your house. You're human. I know you are!"

The crowd was close now, close and watching. In another

moment the police cruiser would be completely surrounded. Gus shook his head at Benton, then opened his mouth and began to moan in synchrony with the approaching monsters.

Benton slapped at Gus's pistol with one hand while her foot smashed down on the accelerator. Gus had been expecting the attempt and he shot her with the taser in his other hand. She cried out, wilting over the steering wheel. The car lurched forward, then stalled and died.

The crowd's keening fell silent as they reached the car. Half a dozen tore open the driver's side door of the vehicle and pulled out Benton. She moaned at first, then began to thrash . . . and finally to scream.

Gus waited until they'd dragged the policewoman off into the darkness. Then he got out of the car as well. The crowd began to disperse, except for the children who'd completed their metamorphosis. Those began climbing up on the car, or onto anything else that would get them off the ground. Gus recognized several of them as kids he'd seen around his neighborhood. They looked almost exactly as they had when they'd been human—except for the dragonfly wings.

One by one, as Gus watched, the younglings spread their wings and took to the sky in a hum. Some flew south, others north, east, west. Gus thought of the towns they'd soon visit. Covington, Abita Springs, Hammond, Slidell, New Orleans. He thought of the new swarms that would soon be raised. And he wondered:

How long could he pass for a monster?

THE RYE-MOTHER

Curtis M. Lawson

AVID PRESSED HIS fingertip into the jagged edge of the school bus's torn vinyl upholstery. There was a sharpness to it, but the thin material gave way and folded over before it could cut into his skin. He wished the upholstery was made of tougher stuff—something that might lacerate his fingertip and cloud his mind with physical pain.

Other children laughed and hooted in their Halloween costumes. In the context of the day, their pageantry was normal. The wizard robes, clown wigs, face paint, and superhero capes had become temporarily commonplace, leaving David to look like a madman in his wool sweater and khaki pants.

Only one other child, a Muslim boy named Bahir, was dressed as mundanely as David. The religious beliefs of their parents forbade either boy from celebrating pagan rites such as Halloween. This shared misery had made them temporary allies, or at least bus buddies for the ride home.

"So, how come you aren't dressed up?" Bahir asked, trying to spark a conversation with David, who had a reputation of being quiet and antisocial.

"My parents are Jehovah's Witnesses," David remarked. "We don't do anything fun."

"Oh," Bahir responded. "We're Muslims."

David didn't respond, but rather stared out the window at the passing houses, decorated in cotton webs and crawling with plastic spiders. He admired the jack-o'-lantern grins that stared at him from porches, the sinister and the silly alike. Tomorrow they would be smashed, most of them anyway, their day having come and gone. There was a kind of beauty in that, or at least poetry, David mused.

He wondered how much candy, and what kinds, where hidden behind the doors of these houses. It was his belief, which had been aided by the mutterings of other kids, that the better decorated the house, the better quality candy they gave out—stuff like Snickers, Twix, or Reese's cups. The houses that didn't decorate, he had heard, were more prone to handing out whatever was on sale at the drugstore.

David would have jumped at the opportunity for any of it. Sweets, like Halloween itself, were not welcome in his parents' house. Instead, they might allow him a box of raisins tonight as a concession for robbing him of the magic outside—magic they saw as sin.

The bus turned the corner on to Route 2, leaving the school behind. Single and split-level ranches yielded to stretches of forest and the occasional gas station or fast food joint. David looked out the window with a steadfast gaze, not at the passing commercial banality, but through it and toward something that lay beyond—something he could feel in his soul.

"My mother lets my sister and I each pick out two chocolate bars from the store," Bahir added, after a long pause. "I guess she feels bad about us missing out, so that's her way of compromising."

"The candy would be nice," David responded, eyes still pinned to something beyond his field of vision.

The candy would indeed be nice, but David's concern was deeper than sugar, or even costumes. His interest in Halloween could not be explained in the limited vocabulary of man. To him, it was simply magical.

The bus wound past a tiny strip of businesses featuring a liquor store and a bait shop, and on to some side road. A half mile down, Gingham Farms came into view, though it wasn't a real farm like they have out in the Midwest, but a tourist trap. Rather than cows and grain silos, Gingham Farms was a glorified pumpkin patch with hayrides and a "haunted" corn maze.

The corn maze.

Something within it beckoned David. He'd felt its call every year, but only on Halloween. He never understood why until a few months back when he'd read a book on holidays in the school library, and learned the true nature of Halloween. On this last day of October, the veil between this world and the other—literally called Otherworld—is at its thinnest, and spirits, fairies, and all other manner of creature may travel from fairy hollows. David felt with every fiber of his being that the corn maze held such a hollow.

That book had led him to another, and this one had taught him about changelings—fairy babies swapped out with mortal young. The young fairies were then abandoned in the human world, left to wander in states of sickness or insanity. While he wasn't sick per say, an allergy to iron rich foods did complicate his health.

"Yes, the candy and the costumes would be nice," David repeated, "but the corn maze is what I'd really like to do."

And he would. He wasn't sure how, but he would go there tonight. Some of the other kids had mentioned this might be the last year for Gingham Farms. A big company wanted to build a soulless mega-store there, and the land was worth more than the farm could pull in. Tonight might be his last chance.

"I wish I could get dressed up. I think I'd be something scary, like Jason or Jigsaw," Bahir replied. "What would you be?"

"I'd be myself," David said, his hand pressed up against the window.

"Who's ready for Taco Tuesday?" David's father asked, with an exaggerated excitement and a preternaturally white grin.

His mother raised her hand and jumped up and down in the kitchen, feigning the same enthusiasm. Or perhaps it was real. David couldn't ever be sure with such things. He had a hard time reading other people and even greater difficulty relating to them. His psychologist had called it narcissistic personality disorder, not to his face, but in loud whispers to his parents. There were other issues the doctor had brought up, but this was the most troubling, or so David had overheard.

The doctor had put him on meds—little magic pills that subjugated his nature, like a whipped mutt. It worked for a while, but he eventually found ways around the soul crushing medicine. Some nights it was unavoidable, but most of the time he'd hide the pills under his tongue or palm them before they reached his mouth. His parents didn't understand that he had no desire to be "better". David did not wish to change.

David wondered how often they considered upping his dosage or putting him on something stronger that would turn his brain to mush. It was clear they didn't understand him, and regarded him as a broken thing in need of mending. At times, it seemed they tried extra hard to like him. Much harder, he suspected, than other parents tried to like their own children.

At least they gave it a shot, however. The kids at school and most of his teachers didn't bother. In some ways he preferred their honesty, but it did occasionally feel nice to see people delve to amazing depths of self-deceit just to make you feel wanted.

Sometimes a nice lie was preferable to the truth. But not tonight. Tonight he needed something genuine, something his parents could not offer.

Brooke, David's baby sister, looked up at him from her high chair. She was too young for tacos, but her tiny fists shook with the contagious excitement of their parents. Looking into her dull, brown eyes, David wondered if that was to be her lot in life—absorbing the emotions and passions of others, like human tofu. He supposed, in an introverted way which belied his age, that all people were something like tofu. Why should he expect Brooke to be special?

He had hoped that she would be different—an odd duck like himself. It would be nice to not feel so alone. Even if the eleven year age gap between them would remain unbridgeable, their shared strangeness would make the world much more bearable. It seemed that wasn't in the cards.

He felt something out there tonight however. An ethereal weirdness that perhaps leached out from the hidden fairy hollows at Gingham Farms and into the drab world of man. It turned children into monsters and myths, and implored rational adults to fear the dark. That was, after all, why jack-o'-lanterns glowed in front of all the houses, save his own—to scare off the dark spirits adults claimed not to believe in.

Father urged David to take a seat across from Brooke. He did, and began assembling a taco from the ingredients spread across several bowls and trays. In lieu of beef, he used chicken. The family rarely ate red meat, what with David's problems with iron. This particular medical issue had always bothered the young man, until last winter when he learned that fairy folk and other magical creatures were also harmed by iron. Now it felt something like a badge of honor.

Mother placed a plate of squashed avocado in front of Brooke, while father assembled tacos for her and himself. David waited patiently, knowing he dared not take a bite before his father led them in grace. A few moments later, once all the plates were made up, his father began their mealtime prayer.

"Thank you, Father, for this feast . . . "

With closed eyes and folded hands, David pretended to listen. Instead his mind wandered to the haunted corn maze and the fairy hollow he knew must be there. He wondered what manner of strange things walked within the rows of corn.

Father's voice cut out, and David and followed the cue to say "amen" before opening his eyes. The family began eating and a few moments passed before David worked up the nerve to speak.

"Maybe after tacos, we could drive over to Gingham Farms and check out the corn maze?" David used his most practiced "normal" tone as he posed the question.

His father raised one eyebrow. Mother glanced back and forth between the two of them, waiting on her husband to arbitrate.

"Come on now, champ. You know we don't do Halloween."

Champ. David hated that nickname. He'd never been champion of anything, and it felt condescending. Despite this, he wore a casual smile.

"It's not really a Halloween thing," David countered. "More like a fall thing. They keep it open through November."

"Then we can go after Halloween," father said with a smile. David had misspoken, and now the argument was lost. Anything else he said would fall on deaf ears. He took a bite of his chicken taco and glared at his plate.

Shouts and laughter penetrated the glass and the bars of David's bedroom window. His parents had the bars put in after he tried to run away last year, and they served as a reminder that he dwelled in a prison rather than a home.

It was fitting, he supposed, that bars of iron—the bane of fairy kind—would block his way from the magic of the night and of the corn maze at Gingham Farms.

Instead of focusing on the last bit of homework on his desk—some mind-numbing geography assignment—David looked down at the street. Through the bars he saw a group of teenagers in costumes consisting of little more than black hoodies and plastic masks, carrying bulging pillow cases. They passed a gaggle of younger children, all decked out in proper costumes, trailed by smiling grownups. A black lab with a pair of bat wings strapped to its back trotted along aside them, occasionally sniffing the ground for fallen candy.

David smiled, but there was no happiness in it. He envied those kids, but he also pitied them. For all the fun they were having, it didn't seem that any of them truly understood the rare quality of the night. Candy and costumes were all well and good, but Halloween was about that breach between the worlds and the magic which poured in.

Then again, maybe they did get it, he thought, somewhere deep within. Why else would they brave the cold night, scouring the town for candy that could be bought at half price tomorrow? Ever precocious, he pondered that perhaps there were things that could be understood by the soul, even if they never registered in the mind. He hoped that was the case, for their sake. While he found trouble relating to most people, he generally wanted the best for them.

He closed the shade and looked down at the map of Europe on his desk. The assignment was to label each outlined area with the proper country. It seemed a pointless task to David. His father had mentioned that countries in Eastern Europe change names and borders like clothes. What was the point of learning where Serbia was if it was going to merge with Bulgaria in five years? It was all so artificial.

A better use of his time—of all their time—would be to learn about the constants of geography. What locations had been regarded as sacred throughout history? What parts of the ocean connected to other worlds, like the Bermuda Triangle?

Where were the fairy hollows in the British Isles? Those were questions worth answering, not what flag flies over some arbitrary chunk of land.

David closed his eyes and let his pen hover over the map. He imagined himself as Volund, King of the Fairies, flying high above Europe on wings forged of steel, rather than the butterfly look of a Disney movie. He was looking for a way home—a fairy hollow that would lead him to Otherworld.

A magnetic force drew David's pen to the paper, startling him from his daydream. The tip of his pen had pierced the map, just east of the French/German border. David pulled the pen away. Burning within the pinhole poked through his homework was an intense, amber light, as if someone were holding an LED against the underside of the paper. Confused, David flipped the map over, and saw no strange light—nothing but the tiny hole.

With a bit of hesitation he turned the paper around once more, and held it straight on front of him. The needle of light pierced through the German landscape with brilliant intensity. David stood up from his desk, and moved the map around. No matter which way he turned, or how high or low he held it, the light continued pouring forth.

With a trembling hand, David pressed a finger against the needle of amber light. It was warm. It felt pleasant. He pressed harder, forcing the pinhole to expand beneath his touch. Pale, orange illumination poured out from the tear in the map.

The hole was large enough to see through now. David brought the map close to his face and peered into the hole. On the other side he could see his bedroom, or more accurately a place that looked something like his bedroom. The windows, the door, were in the same places, but the walls were rough, hewn from natural stone rather than smooth, painted drywall. His floor was a patchwork of dirt and tree roots. The cool blues and greens of his real world bedroom gave way to bright, earthy tones in the world which lay on the other side of the hole in the paper.

To David, the other world beyond the paper seemed more real than that which he had known all his life. It was like opening his eyes from a dream for the first time ever. When he pulled the map away from his face and looked around his room—his real world room—everything felt dull and washed out by comparison.

He picked up his pen again and jabbed a second hole through the page, roughly two inches from the first. David forced the plastic body of the pen through to make the hole wide enough for viewing, then pulled it back, but no eldritch light poured out. Even with his eye pressed against this new tear in the map, only his washed out, mortal world room lay on the other side.

Placing the map back on his desk, David considered this conundrum. One hole, the one just barely past the French border in Germany, shined with Amber light and revealed a surface of grainy, golden oak beneath it. The other, which had been bore through the cellulose likeness of some Eastern European nation David had not identified, gave off no illumination, and beyond it lay only the vinyl laminate of his IKEA desk.

David closed his eyes again and let instinct guide his hand, rather than poking an arbitrary hole. He could feel the magic pulling at the ballpoint tip of his pen. It stabbed into the paper, and David felt that the pen was more in control than he was.

When he opened his eyes, his pen had pierced through somewhere in the southern U.K. Lines of orange-yellow light crept out of the pin prick in his homework and up along the plastic shaft of the Bic. A wild smile crossed David's lips and he used the pen to carve an eyehole, working out from that tiny, glowing tear. Just as with the first hole, when David looked through this one, the world was a Day-Glo negative of the earth he knew.

"What are you doing there, champ?" Father's voice called from behind.

David turned around, his glance darting back and forth between his father and the glowing paper.

His father's expression betrayed no acknowledgment of the fairy fire burning from the holes in the paper.

"Um . . . just some extra credit for art."

His father smiled and tapped his wrist.

"Wrap it up. It's almost bedtime."

"Sure thing, Dad."

Once his father was gone David glared at the door before turning to the window. He pressed the map to his face and found that both magical rips lined up perfectly with his eyes. He scanned the room through the magical filter of the map and beheld the Otherworld version of his bedroom. While its size and shape were similar, no iron bars blocked his path while he peered through the hollows on the map.

A soft song drifted through his window. It was impossible in its beauty, yet eerily familiar. David couldn't quite place it, but it evoked a rare, genuine smile. The tune cut in and out, getting lost beneath the festive noises outside.

David placed the paper face-down on his desk and reached past his "word a day" calendar for a box of crayons. A green face of angular features began to take shape around the two eye holes.

The wind battering the paper mask David had fashioned from the map was deafening in his ears.

The sidewalks were empty around him, and will-o-wisps glowed where there should have been street lights.

He pushed the makeshift mask up above his head and the knot to the shoelace holding it to his head caught in his hair. With the mask off, David could see that he was not alone on the street at all, but surrounded by trick or treaters and mischievous teens. Left to only his own senses, the neighborhood looked dull and monochrome, save for the bits of Halloween magic—a fiery carpet of brittle, dead leaves, bits of rainbow candy strewn across the ground, and the wavering illumination from jack-o'-lantern flames. The veil between worlds truly was thin, and wonders could be gleaned by those with eyes to see.

David was not sure what he hoped to find on this night, but he knew where to look.

Gingham Farms was a bit of a walk, and though he didn't mind it, he figured it prudent to grab some food for the road. He ignored the more pedestrian houses—those bare of decorations—save for those where people waited on porches or stoops with buckets of candy. He was eager to find the fairy hollow at Gingham Farms, so he only knocked on the doors of houses with the most elaborate decorations. What he'd heard was true: the better embellished the décor, the better the candy given out. He'd even scored a full size snickers from a house where the fog bellowed out from the front door and obscured red glowing eyes beyond the threshold.

After a handful of houses, five candy bars, and an hour's walk, David could see Gingham Farms ahead and to his right. The corn stalks glowed faint silver beneath the moonlight, though to credit their soft radiance to this reality seemed too terrestrial. Surely the light they gave off emanated from the magical portal deep within the corn maze.

David crossed the street and stepped onto the grounds of the farm, his paper mask sitting atop his head. Even through the soles of his shoes, he could feel the power leaching through the soil, beckoning him to Otherworld. He wondered if he was the only one who heard the call.

Wondered if he was the only one to recognize it as such.

A line of teenagers, families, and twenty-something couples stood in line outside the maze, waiting to pay for the chance to get lost in the twisting rows of corn stalks. David had no money. He also had no intention of paying to get into the maze, or waiting in line.

As he had done to slip past his barred windows, he pulled the homespun magic mask back over his face.

Through the eyeholes, no one stood between him and the entrance to the maze. With deliberate steps, he approached the mouth of the labyrinth. Even from feet away he could feel heat from the corn stalks which, through his fairy vision mask, appeared to glow with golden light rather than silver.

A whisper—words too soft to comprehend—wound through the rows of corn. To other children—if they heard it—the words might have seemed foreboding, but something familiar to David lived in the soft voice. It beckoned to him, and feeling more confident than he had been about anything else in his short life, he entered the maze.

An orange radiance, far more intense than the general amber glow of the mask's vision, burned a trail in the ground. David likened it to a river of magma glowing just beneath the surface, and he followed it from the entrance of the labyrinth and down every branch that it snaked.

Wind coursed through the stalks from everywhere at once, and David thought of the magnetic repulsion that occurs when two forces of the same polarity come together. Was this further proof that he belonged there, in Otherworld? Was his spirit made of the same stuff?

The wind pummeled the paper mask, but he dared not lift it from his face and risk losing the radiant trail marked out on the ground for him. Nor did he wish to suddenly be caught in a crowd of terrestrial souls who could only sense the magic of this place on the most basic level. It was better to suffer the cacophony of wind against paper and press on, and so he did.

The magma glow meandered through paths cut between the luminescent grain. With each step the wind pushed harder against David, and with each step, the magic of the hollow compelled him more fully to move forward.

David turned right at an intersection and came to a dead end. The trail of magic below the soil continued on, beyond the wall of corn stalks. Reaching out, he parted the corn with both hands, and stepped through.

The light was nearly blinding, the spectral luminescence of each stalk amplified by the light given off by its neighbors.

Vertigo and nausea overtook him, and he feared that all the chocolate and sugar in his belly might escape through his mouth.

Stumbling through the corn stalks, eyes squeezed shut against the blinding light and ears deafened by the angry wind, David reached for his mask. It was too bright and the magic was too much for him, but in trying to tear off the mask to shut it out, he tripped on a root and tumbled into a circular clearing.

David opened his eyes. The glow here was less intense than it had been within the row of corn, and his vertigo subsided. Still, the soil burned with the same consistent orange as the trail through the maze had. The wind continued its assault with wicked fury, but here it whipped forward in a circuit around the clearing, kicking up a whirlwind of soil, rocks, and debris. The cracking sound of the paper mask being attacked by the weather grew nearly unbearable.

Stranger than the cyclone in the clearing, or the fairy glow of the earth, was the creature which stood at its center.

It was female, David could tell from the midnight breasts sagging down to her waist, and the thick patch of grey hair between her legs. But she was not human. An elongated nose hooked down over lips that stretched too far across. Calloused ears, riddled with coarse, gray bristles reached up into fine, pointed tips. A mane of hair, mostly white but mixed with occasional streaks of glowing amber, stretched from her head down to the soil.

"Eldon?" She asked. Her lips peeling back to reveal teeth like broken glass.

Eldon. That was right, he thought. Eldon was his name, not David. Eldon had always been his name.

"Why, to the hollow, has my child roamed?" The creature asked in a musical voice, incongruent with her nightmare visage. He was amazed that her words carried above the raging wind.

The voice brought back a flood of memories. Songs, sung to him in infancy. Songs in a beautiful language he had forgotten existed. And then memories of terrible quiet. Not the complete silence reserved for the dead or the deaf, but the muted sounds that a drowning man hears when cast from the world of light above and into the frigid darkness of the world below.

"Mother?" David . . . no . . . Eldon asked.

A clawed hand with knuckles like splintered obsidian reached out. Eldon took the hand of his forgotten mother. She pulled him to his feet and dusted him off.

"To come here was solecism," the dark fairy scolded. "What good does this pilgrimage, either of us do?"

The boy looked into the monster's luminescent eyes, and found in them a love and a passion which he'd never seen in those of the woman who masqueraded as his mother in the world of man.

"It called me," he replied. "You called me"

Leathery fingertips caressed his cheek, and a sadness overcame the cartoon features of the woman-thing.

"I want to come home," Eldon said.

"Too unripe you are, my little love," Mother—his real mother—added, with a sad undertone to the natural harmony of her voice.

Tears formed in Eldon's eyes. They dripped down his face and soaked into the paper of his mask.

"Please," he implored. "I hate this place and these people. I can't stand the washed out colors of their world and the washed out magic of their souls."

The wide lips of the mother-thing curved down her chin. Shimmering, metallic tears carved wet lines down her face.

Her hand trembled atop his.

"Oh my dear, Eldon, complete is the trade. By blood and by word it is bound. There is no coming home, not until you are grown."

The wind grew stronger around them. Sticks, and pebbles bombarded them both, but neither seemed to notice or care.

"No one understands me here," he said. "I'm so tired of being alone."

"The trade has been made," the mother-thing said. "Rules are rules are rules. I say it thrice."

"To hell with the rules," screamed Eldon.

He rushed toward her, but the cyclonic winds pushed against him, knocking him off balance and tumbling him to the soil.

Loose dirt and detritus swirled around her—his real mother—as he looked up pleading from behind his mask.

"Spirits of chaos, that is man. Phantoms, to them, are rules and law. Tangible are they, to us. Bound to our oaths are the fey, Eldon."

Corn husks broke away from stalks as the wind's intensity

increased. Angry gusts drummed out a timpani roll against Eldon's mask and in his ears. The fairy woman's hair whipped about, a thousand tattered ribbons in a helter-skelter color-guard display.

"Please!" Eldon cried out, tears soaking through the saturated, deteriorating paper of his mask.

"Slaves we are to our word, but you needn't be alone. Other bargains there are to be made." Her voice was quiet, but clear despite the cacophony of the gale.

"What bargains?"

Before she could answer, the cruel wind ripped the mask from his face. The magma glow of the soil vanished, as did the Amber radiance of the world at large. Corn stalks stood still and dark, barely reflecting the glow of the silver moon above. No gale force winds kicked up the dirt or stirred the rows of corn.

In front of David stood a shabby scarecrow. Washed out straw served as its hair and stretched down to the brown soil. A gnarled piece of tree root stuck out as nose from the middle of its dirty, burlap face. It curved over a lunatic smile painted ear-to-ear.

A sign post was hammered into the ground before the dismal scarecrow. Scrawled across the wooden placard in black spray paint was the word *Rye-Mother.*

David or Eldon, or whatever the hell is name was scanned the clearing for his mask. He needed it. He needed to know what manner of bargain they might strike, but the mask was lost to the rows of corn, just like he was in this gray, mortal world.

The boy stood and touched the scarecrow. Her face was coarse beneath his fingertips and there was no trace of life in her burlap flesh. No magic shined in the black button eyes he gazed into.

"Please . . . tell me . . . "

She didn't.

Eldon, as he now thought of himself, lay in his bed, staring at the ceiling. His parents—or the human things his real mother had given him to—berated him for sneaking out.

Do you know how dangerous, blah , blah, blah . . . What were you thinking . . . bullshit, bullshit, bullshit . . .

Why had the mother-thing given him up? Why had she swapped him with some mundane, human animal? What kind of bargain had been made?

Eldon thought of posing that last question to his human mother and father, but thought better of it. They might not even realize a deal had been struck. Such was the way with fairies.

"David, you look at me right now!" His father demanded. Eldon turned toward the voice, a blank expression on his face.

"How could you do this?" Father continued. "What do you have to say for yourself?"

Finding no words that wouldn't upset his supposed parents, Eldon chose silence.

"Answer your father!" his mother, exclaimed.

Eldon shifted his eyes to her. She stood behind father, balancing little baby Brooke—his alleged sister—on her hip. The tiny child gazed stupidly at him with brown, bovine eyes. She clearly belonged here in this tepid reality, just as she clearly belonged with these lukewarm people. Eldon hated her for that.

His parents scolded him further, but he tuned them out. Instead, he found his gaze focused on poor, stupid, baby Brooke, with whom he would never have anything in common, and that was when the Rye-Mother's words came back to him.

She was right. He needn't be alone, and as he gazed at Brooke's soulless expression, he realized that other bargains could be made. Halloween wasn't over, after all.

THE DAY OF THE DEAD

Amber Fallon

LOS CALAVERAS CANTINA was not a good bar by any stretch of the imagination, but it was *our* bar. The beer was cold and cheap and, well, we probably wouldn't have cared if it was cold or not, as long as it was cheap and plentiful. It was also close to the office, which was a great added benefit. It meant we could walk there and back and, if we got completely sauced (which happened from time to time) there were plenty of comfortable conference rooms in which to sleep it off before the boss man arrived. They had food . . . kind of. The menu was pretty much limited to chips and salsa or guacamole, and occasionally nachos when the mood struck the owner/bartender/cook, a friendly guy named Arturo, but it was cheap (much like the booze) and pretty tasty for what it was. We certainly weren't going to complain.

Arturo was a fun guy, but he could be a tad on the eccentric side. It wasn't at all unusual to come into the bar and find signs up everywhere advertising some new promotion he'd cooked up. Everything from "lucky" green (half-priced) tequila shots on St. Patrick's Day to Valentine's Day shooters filled with cinnamon hearts. So, it was hardly surprising to see a sign announcing a Day of the Dead celebration one day in late October.

JOIN US FOR A FESTIVAL OF THE DEAD! HALF PRICE DRINKS FOR ALL IN COSTUME! A MÍ LA MUERTE ME PELA LOS DIENTES!

Tiny skulls and maracas, obviously clip art, decorated the borders of the home-made sign.

"Day of the Dead? Huh." Marlene cocked a teal-polished thumb at the sign stuck to the front door with beer bottle labels, "You gonna dress up?"

"Um, hello? Half-priced drinks!" I rolled my eyes as we made our way to our usual table. "You're not going to come in costume? I asked my friend and longtime drinking buddy.

"Yeah, no." she said, shaking her head as she munched on a corn chip, "It seems a little morbid, you know? Dressing up as a skeleton." She shuddered.

"Yeah, okay, says the girl who came to the office as a slutty vampire last year. Suddenly you've got morals."

She threw a chip at me, "Something about it just seems . . . wrong somehow."

I flicked the chip off my lap and it skittered towards the bathrooms. "Suit yourself. I'll be enjoying my even cheaper beers, makeup and all."

Arturo arrived with our drinks a few minutes later. Soon the conversation was lost, all but forgotten amid the bustle of the after work crowd and the tinny mariachi music the bar always played once things got going.

Due to my planning brilliance, and the fact that Halloween actually occurred *before* Day of the Dead, I arrived at work the morning of Arturo's event fully prepared and patted myself on the back. Not only would my drinks be half off, but my makeup was, too! I had picked up a set of cheap face paint crayons at my local pharmacy on my way in to work, along with a big bag of

50% off chocolate bars. What? The only thing better than candy is cheap candy!

The workday passed as workdays often do: slowly. By the time the clock struck 5, I was ready to tear my hair out. I don't know why I was so excited to go to a place I'm at 5 or 6 days a week anyway, but I was. Maybe it was the half-priced booze, maybe it was the idea of a bunch of people dressed as skeletons drinking together, maybe I was just bored. Whatever the reason, I felt as giddy as a kid on Christmas Eve.

With that same enthusiasm, I darted into the office bathroom to apply my makeup.

I'm certainly no great *artiste* but I think I did okay for someone who hadn't done anything like this since high school drama class. I smudged the white gunk all over my face, somehow managing to get it to look vaguely even with the help of some rough textured paper towels. Foundation applied, I circled my eyes in black, drawing it out towards the edges of the sockets, then did a little upside down V on the end of my nose and teeth over my lips. On a whim, I added a curlicue mustache for good measure, then I tossed the rest of the makeup in the trash and headed out.

"That's cultural appropriation, you know." Robin from human resources scowled at me as I made my way down the hallway to meet Marlene.

"Die in a fire." I muttered, not knowing I'd come to regret those words.

Out on the sidewalk, I posed for Marlene, grinning like the skull I'd painted over my features. She swallowed distastefully as she stubbed out her cigarette. We walked over to Los Calaveras Cantina in silence.

As expected, Arturo had gone all out. He was wearing a velvet suit with elaborate embroidery and sequins sewn into it, along with a matching sombrero. Below the brim of his hat, his face had been turned into a work of art with swirls of paint and glittering embellishments. He smiled when he saw us and handed me a cold bottle of beer with a lime wedge stuck in the neck.

"First one on the house, *mi compadre!*" he crowed, "and one for the party pooper, too." Marlene reluctantly accepted the drink he handed her. She was definitely in the minority, uncostumed as she was.

The bar was busier than usual. We were surrounded by costumed patrons who had put various amounts of effort into their ensembles. Some, like me, had simply smeared on a little paint in vaguely appropriate shapes and called it done. A few had even gone a step lazier and wore flimsy cardboard or paper masks. Some had gone all out and decorated themselves similar to Arturo. All of them were laughing and drinking and eating chips and salsa when we sat down.

Marlene snickered, pointing to a pair of young girls in normal clothing in the corner who were taking pictures of everyone and giggling.

"Think they're old enough to drink?" she joked.

"Think Arturo cares?" I answered, carefully shoving a salsa laden chip into my mouth, to avoid spoiling my makeup.

Marlene laughed and took another chip. I was glad to see her relaxing somewhat. I'd been worried that her reservations would spoil my fun.

Arturo started the music, something slower and less cheerful than the stuff he usually played. It seemed almost somber, despite the rhythm. I shook it off and ordered another round of drinks, having finished my complimentary beer. Margaritas, this time. I liked those better and since everything was half off, why not?

Two drinks in and the girls in the corner were face down in their chips and salsa.

"Guess they couldn't handle their liquor." I laughed. Marlene smirked.

"See?" I said, gesturing with a chip, "I told you it wouldn't kill you to have a little fun."

Marlene slumped over, playing dead to punctuate the joke. I laughed for a moment, but she didn't lift her head up. One arm remained outstretched across the table, neon purple fingertips floating above the bright tile floor.

"Marlene?" I shook her a little, "Cut it out. That's not funny."

I got out of my seat and shook her harder, panic rising in my chest like a frightened dove. Marlene wasn't responding.

Someone screamed.

Outside the bar, someone else laid on a horn, long and loud. The sound ended with a crunch of metal that drowned out the screamer.

I shook Marlene even harder, desperate to wake her. Her head lolled on a neck which seemed suddenly devoid of bones, flopping backwards so that she was looking up at the ceiling, eyes staring sightlessly, mouth slack.

I didn't realize I was screaming myself until I felt something in my throat tear painfully. Hands shaking, I dug my phone out of my pocket and dialed 9-1-1. After seven rings, it went to voicemail.

The bar had descended into chaos. My friend was dead, as were the two giggling girls we laughed at earlier, the young busboy, and a handful of others. There was another crash from outside, the sound instantly identifiable as a car accident and a bad one at that. I hung up and dialed for help again and again, until eventually all I got was a busy signal.

People were shrieking and sobbing, some cradling lifeless bodies, others tearing at their clothing or ripping out their hair. It might have been comical, seeing all those skeletons freak out like that, were it not for the dire circumstances which caused it.

That weird music was still playing, providing backdrop to a chorus of wails. Arturo had taken off his sombrero and was hysterically shaking the busboy, who I assumed was a relative of some sort.

I looked at Marlene again. I couldn't bring myself to touch her. I knew she was beyond help, but I had no idea what to do about it. 9-1-1 was a dead end and I didn't know who else to call.

A woman ran into me, smearing makeup from the bones she'd painted onto her arms all over my shirt.

"They're dead . . . " she said. Her eyes were rimmed with tears and her once impressive face paint had been smudged and smeared into oblivion. Before I could react, she stumbled away, repeating "They're dead." over and over again.

Forcing myself to look away from the corpse who had once been my drinking buddy, I stared at my surroundings, hoping someone would come help us.

No help came, but I did locate someone I recognized and sort of new. Nina, from accounting. She was holding her head in her hands, staring down at Arturo and the dead boy. She looked up when she saw me approaching.

"What the hell do we do?" she sobbed, skeletal face crumpling into a mess of black and white tear stained grease.

"I don't know," I said, taking her arm, "but I think we should get out of here." The bar was starting to feel claustrophobic, which wasn't helping the adrenaline racing through my system. I needed air, and I wasn't sure I wanted to be hanging out in a place where a bunch of people had mysteriously dropped dead, anyway. Seemed like a surefire way to tempt fate into taking me, too.

I shoved my way past a bunch of sobbing people dressed like skeletons, dragging Nina with me. She didn't resist at all, choosing instead the path of least resistance and following me like a zombie.

Things weren't any better outside. The crashes from earlier had been fatal. We made our way around what remained of a blue sedan that had plowed head on into a brick wall. Blood pooled beneath the wreck on what had been the driver's door. I tried to pretend I didn't notice the top of a child seat in the back.

Some kind of work truck was wrapped around a pole across the street. The guy behind the wheel had been thrown through the windshield, leaving a trail of blood and broken safety glass in his wake. A few feet away, a teenage boy lay half on the sidewalk, half in the street, still clutching a leash. The dog I assumed he'd been walking was nowhere to be seen.

Working on autopilot, I brought us back to the office. Truth be told, I wasn't sure where else to go. We made our way inside, past the bodies of a few of our coworkers. Nina gasped and sobbed at each one we came across. I had started to feel numb to the death around us. Shock can do that to you, I suppose.

Whatever the hell had happened, it wasn't isolated to just the bar.

I dug my phone out again and tried calling my sister. No answer. The pit in my stomach grew as I began to wonder just how widespread this event was.

Surely it couldn't have gotten all the way to her place, three states away . . . could it?

I don't know if Nina was wondering about her friends or family members. She didn't seem to be thinking much of anything, judging from her blank expression.

We got into the elevator for the most troubling and awkward ride of my life, and that's saying something. I still didn't know why we were there or what I was going to do. Nina didn't, either, so at least I was in good company.

The elevator stopped at our floor and the doors opened in that old familiar way, revealing Robin, propped up against the doors leading to our area of the floor. I swallowed hard as I remembered my last words to her; "Die in a fire." echoed in my ears as I looked at her lifeless body. What the hell had happened? And why weren't Nina and I dead, too?

Something set Nina off and she started all out bawling. She pulled away from me and rushed through the front doors to the receptionists' desk. She grabbed a handful of tissues and began blotting furiously at her eyes. I stood there, helpless, not sure what to say.

"*Whyyyyy?*" she howled, "Why us? Why did we live?" she seemed to be demanding answers from me, but I had none to give. I shrugged, then struggled under the weight of an epiphany.

"We're in costume." I whispered. Nina stopped, staring at me, her mouth hanging open inside the rim of teeth she'd painted over her lips. She gawped, trying to find words.

"That's it. It has to be. Marlene wasn't in costume, and she's dead. Same with those teen girls. And the people outside the bar. They all died and we didn't, because we're made up like skeletons."

Nina swallowed so hard I heard the click of her dry throat. She held the wad of tear and greasepaint stained tissues out to me.

"So what happens when we take off the makeup?" she asked.

RUSTY HUSK

Evans Light

THE MAN WAS closer to heaven than he'd ever been, hung up high on a pole in the middle of a vast cornfield. Probably the closest he'd ever get to those pearly gates, he figured. Even though the burning sun rising before him was a reminder of where he was most likely headed, the warmth of it on his face was a pleasure far greater than any he'd experienced in the previous year.

A leather strap was looped under his armpits, holding him tight, allowing him to take in the rolling brown pastures spread out below. It was the last thing he'd ever see, he knew, but was satisfied.

A vulture landed with a flutter on his shoulder, drawn by the rotten stench of his flesh. The man remained motionless, unblinking, as the bundle of glistening black feathers shuffled closer to his face, long pink neck craning forward, a single beady eye hungrily examining his own.

He braced himself, waiting for the thin veil that separates the world of the living from the darkness beyond to be torn away. He wasn't afraid. Fear had long since lost its power. After the pain and suffering he'd endured, he yearned for his soul to be unfettered from this rotting husk of flesh.

The ravenous bird, unable to restrain itself any longer, began to peck at his eye with agonizing insistence. As the man's vision failed, suffering dissolved into relief. At last, he would be free. Death was close at hand and he welcomed it with open arms. Other vultures circled above, hissing excitement.

The world was swallowed up in darkness as the bird on his shoulder plucked out his remaining eye. Whether the warm viscous fluid streaming down his cheeks was blood or tears, the man didn't know and didn't care.

He only wanted it all to end.

"How do you do it?" neighbors asked. "It looks so real! Like it could jump right up and grab you."

The rocking chair scarecrow was the crown jewel of Mr. Rusty Husk's menagerie of Halloween decorations, one that struck fear into the hearts of children and adults alike. Halloween was his absolute favorite holiday, and each October for the last decade Rusty had made a new scarecrow.

He took extreme pride in his handiwork. A menacing jack-o'-lantern head perched atop its shoulders, this year's scarecrow was dressed in a traditional manner, sporting farmer dungarees and a plaid flannel shirt stuffed to bursting with hay. Its wrists and ankles were bound to the rocking chair with metal shackles. Thick chains wrapped around the scarecrow's torso completed the illusion that any visitor would experience a swift and certain death if the monster wasn't forcibly restrained.

Rusty hated to end his annual scarecrow tradition, but this year was to be the last. Having recently celebrated his fiftieth birthday, Rusty thought it time to quit while he was ahead.

After weeks of anticipation, Halloween finally arrived. As the fat autumn sun vanished below the horizon, clusters of costumed children began to roam the sidewalks. Bucket of candy in hand, Rusty was ready for them.

His house was always a draw, and that night was no exception. Scores of trick or treaters stopped by to beg for candy and endure his scarecrow — some reacting with frightened squeals, others with nervous laughter. His infamous rocking porch scarecrow seemed to rattle even the bravest among them.

Rusty took his sweet time, letting them shiver beneath the scarecrow's dark glare. He figured the kids enjoyed being scared, even if they didn't know it. The frightening moments he provided could very well be the most vivid childhood memories they'd have in old age. Those would be gifts *he'd* given them.

His neighbor, Luther, an elderly man whose gravelly voice made him sound like a pack-a-day guy even though he claimed not to smoke, eventually stopped by to inspect the final scarecrow, as he did every Halloween.

"Ever thought about putting yourself in that rocking chair, dressed up as the scarecrow?" he said with a sandpaper drawl. "Sit real still and then jump up and grab people when they least expect it? I saw somebody do that once. Scared the shit out of me."

Rusty had never done that cheap trick, and had told Luther as much, many times and in no uncertain terms. Yet Luther asked him that same question every year, and eventually the conversation had become an annual ritual between them.

As evening became night, the number of trick or treaters dwindled until, eventually, the doorbell ceased to ring at all. Rusty shook the cauldron-shaped bucket, pleased to hear a few remaining Halloween treats sliding around inside. He cocked a smile at the scarecrow chained down in the rocking chair.

"Just enough left over for you and me, Bertha."

The scarecrow didn't respond, of course. Its carved-pumpkin

eyes stared straight ahead, dark and unseeing. The rocking chair, firmly bolted down as a deterrent to pranksters, sat motionless.

"Fine, be that way. More for me." Rusty said.

Neighbors often asked why he didn't simply reuse his scarecrows, since each was so perfectly creepy. He'd never answered these questions directly, preferring to dodge with a smile and an oft-repeated story: Every morning after Halloween, he'd go onto the porch to take his coffee and the scarecrow would be gone. "Split for the cornfields, I suppose." He'd chuckle in a genial way, and that was the end of that.

The truth was, after trick or treating was done, he'd turn off the porch light, unlock the chains and swiftly pull it into the house. There, behind tightly-drawn curtains, he'd wrap it up tight, drive it down to the abandoned lots on Shady Lane for a one-way trip through the chipper, the same one he used to mulch the neighbors' Christmas trees in winter. He'd gotten the scarecrow's disposal down to a science over the years, and the process hadn't failed him yet.

Rusty glanced at his watch as he stood on the porch, sucking a Tootsie Pop. He scanned for stragglers, but the block was empty and the night silent. Deciding that Halloween was officially over, he called time of death as 10pm, flipped off the light and stepped inside, kicking the door closed behind him.

He went to the garage to fetch the clean-up equipment. Sometimes the slightest niggle of worry would strike, but it hadn't this year. *So what if I allow myself one little thrill? Is that really so bad?* he thought while digging through storage bins for a tarp and some duct tape. *Anyway, this was it, the last one, the very last scarecrow.*

He went into the living room and dropped the duct tape and tarp onto the sofa. After pushing the coffee table to one side to clear space in which to work, he started towards the front porch but ended up in the kitchen for some coffee instead.

He was procrastinating. Getting rid of the scarecrow was the single thing he hated about Halloween. Once he finished his coffee, Rusty grabbed his keys and headed to the front porch to unlock the scarecrow from its display.

The doorbell rang as he touched the front door, the unexpected chime jolting him as if the knob was electric.

Who could possibly be visiting this late?

He was irritated by the intrusion. The porch light was off, and that was a cardinal rule of Halloween: lights out, no more candy, end of story.

He decided it was best to simply move the late visitor along, so he grabbed the candy bucket and opened the door. "You almost missed out," he said, wearing his friendliest smile.

No one was there.

A haunted soundtrack of anguished moans and howling wolves floated across the yard from the speakers he'd hidden among the decorations in his front yard. Flashing lights painted the fog purple and orange as it billowed from the machine and rolled down the stairs.

Rusty stepped onto the empty porch, into the autumn night. The darkness was still as death. He frowned. Something felt wrong. Invisible fingertips crawled along his back as he turned towards the scarecrow.

The rocking chair was empty. A mess of scattered straw littered the floor where the scarecrow had been.

It had been on his porch for weeks. Seldom had an hour passed without him checking on it. With all the bolts and chains, no one could have absconded with his scarecrow without raising a holy ruckus.

But the chair was empty all the same, as if the scarecrow had just gotten up and walked away. As Rusty pondered what to do, a shuffle from behind drew his attention.

He spun about and found the scarecrow's dark jack-o'-lantern eyes waiting for him. It was taller than he remembered, the formerly hay-stuffed body grown thick and burly. Cords of muscle flexed beneath flannel sleeves, stretching the seams as the pumpkin head loomed above him.

An enormous hand clamped over Rusty's mouth before he could make a sound. The fingers of the scarecrow's other hand coiled around his neck, lifting him from the ground and thrusting him through the front door with a single violent shove.

The scarecrow clomped inside behind him, slamming the door closed. Rusty lashed out, frantic, fists pummeling the pumpkin head, smashing it into a pulpy mush. Pieces fell away as the pair moved into the living room.

Rusty dug his fingers into a slimy chunk of pumpkin flesh, taking it with him as the scarecrow hurled him to the floor, the impact with hardwood knocking the wind from his lungs.

He pushed himself up on his knees, discovering that his assailant was no supernatural being, no scarecrow come to life, as he'd subconsciously feared. It was only a man, a giant hunk of a man, whose beard was covered in strands of gooey pumpkin guts from the makeshift helmet he'd worn during the brief confrontation. The man's eyes burned with a fury brighter than any jack-o'-lantern Rusty had ever seen.

As Rusty struggled to his feet, a fist pounded into his face, sending him back down in a shower of stars.

Rusty felt hands on him, his arms twisted so hard behind him he feared they'd be wrenched from his body. Gritty carpet fibers pressed between his lips. Duct tape ripped loudly, the tightness of it felt first around his wrists, then his ankles. Then around his head it went—one, two three times, the tape sealing his mouth.

The man kicked Rusty onto his back, bashing his head against the floor. The intruder snatched the tarp from the couch, spread it out and dumped Rusty onto it.

The man dropped to his knees, straddling Rusty. He leaned forward to growl a single word into Rusty's ear: "Stay."

Rusty obeyed, immobile and trembling as the man's footsteps echoed away into the foyer. The front door squeaked opened and slammed closed.

The sudden silence of the empty house was almost as jarring as the unexpected assault. What to do? Make a break for it?

Not likely with bound limbs.

He tried to remember where he'd put his phone. The kitchen perhaps? Even if he got on his feet and hopped into the kitchen before the man returned, what could he possibly hope to do? How could he unlock his phone with his hands bound behind his back, much less call for help?

Perhaps this was nothing more than a run-of-the-mill robbery and the man would simply take what he wanted and hit the road, leaving Rusty tied-up for the neighbors to find him later?

He desperately wanted to believe that, but the fury, the purposefulness of the man's movements, had told a different story.

Before Rusty could settle on a plan of action, time ran out. The front door squeaked open and slammed closed once more as approaching footsteps grew ever louder.

Rusty turned to find a pair of dirty work boots inches from his nose. A bright red metal toolbox slammed onto the floor, tools jangling inside.

Clasps were flipped and the lid was lifted. The man retrieved a small ball-peen hammer and an odd-looking spike, bluntly tapered at one end, flat on the other.

The man set the hammer down and sat atop Rusty once again, pinning him to the floor. Calloused fingers pressed firmly into Rusty's spine, starting at the back of the neck and working their way down, vertebrae by vertebrae, as if carefully counting.

The man's probing fingers came to a stop several inches below Rusty's neck, holding their position until replaced by cold steel.

Rusty struggled to free himself as the man reached for the hammer, but to no avail. Shadows scurried along the wall as the man brought the hammer up and swung it back down, striking the spike with a sharp *ting*.

In that instant, Rusty's body burned as if he'd been stabbed with a billion needles and set aflame. A scream burst from his lungs, but the tape over his mouth redirected the exhalation through his nostrils where it exited with nothing more than a snort.

His agony swelled to a crescendo of searing pain before ebbing away into a vague sense of nothingness, departing as quickly as it had arrived.

The man kicked a boot beneath Rusty's ribcage, flipping him over to stare at the ceiling.

Rusty tried to roll over, to crawl away, but his body had hardened into cement. He was lying atop taped wrists and hands, but he no longer felt them beneath him. He had the sensation that his body was melting into the floor.

Hysteria surged, triggering a wave of nausea that threatened to sweep him away. He was being suffocated by the duct tape, used-up air welling up inside him.

Rusty looked towards the man, his head the only part of his body still obeying orders. He wanted to beg for mercy, but his lips were sealed.

The intruder fiddled with something just out of view, ignoring him. Rusty closed his eyes to calm himself, get control of his breathing, slow his pounding heart. He told himself everything would be okay, that he was going to make it out of this alive.

Hands tugged at his hair, lifting his head from the floor. A plastic brace was slipped around his neck and locked into place with a loud "click".

The room spun as vertigo threatened to swallow him whole. The man folded the tarp over Rusty's body, rolling him over and over until he was fully swaddled in plastic sheeting.

He lay trembling, eyes closed, bracing for the next terrible thing. Many seconds passed in silence before Rusty opened his eyes. When he did, the man's face was millimeters from his own.

"We're going to play a game, you and me, gonna make it last as long as we can. You don't know me, but you'll soon discover I win every time."

The man stood and moved silently through the house, turning off the lights one by one until nothing but darkness remained.

"I owe you no explanation, Mr. Husk, so I won't be giving you one," said the voice from the void.

A moment later, Rusty felt himself rising into the air, as if he were flying. It was a strange sensation, as though his entire body had sloughed away, leaving behind nothing more than a solitary head floating through space.

Flashing orange and purple lights appeared as he drifted through the front door, past the empty rocking chair, down the front steps and through his front yard, over decorative gravestones with grasping hands before taking a sharp left into the dark driveway beside his house.

A battered pickup sat waiting. The man threw Rusty into the back, his body landing with a clang on the metal bed. Footsteps crunched away. A door squeaked open and closed. A rumbling diesel engine growled to life.

They drove beneath traffic lights, past billboards, picking up speed as they moved onto the highway. Stars blinked in the dark sky. A frigid breeze lashed his cheeks. Vibrations rattled up from the road straight into his skull, creating a tingle that descended into his throat but went no further.

After what seemed like hours, the truck slowed and went through a succession of turns. A fine dust flowed into Rusty's eyes, into his lungs, choking him as wheels crunched upon gravel. They were headed away from town, into the country, a fact made obvious by diminishing streetlights and bumpier roads.

Rusty sensed something beside him, but was unable to turn his head to see what it was. The truck took a sharp turn, hitting a hole in the road, bouncing Rusty, knocking him onto his side.

The sand in his eyes triggered a flow of involuntary tears, eventually clearing his vision. The object beside him jostled ever closer, until it was close enough for him to see what it was.

It was Bertha. He hadn't seen her without the pumpkin head since he'd sealed her up tight and dressed her in overalls and a flannel shirt, a full month ago. Her decomposing face was smashed against the transparent vacuum-packed plastic, her gooey sunken eyes open wide. Those vacant orbs stared at him, the mouth beneath them splayed in an eternal scream.

He wanted to push her away but discovered once again that he was helpless, unable to deter her relentless advance. Each bump in the road drew that vengeful countenance closer and closer, until at last her nose pressed into his cheek, those ghastly eyes glaring straight into his own. He attempted to knock her back with his forehead, but the brace around his neck was his master, unyielding.

Unable to do much else, he closed his eyes and tried to escape inside his mind, seeking peace but finding only nightmares.

Eventually, the truck slowed and rolled to a stop. The tailgate banged down. Rusty watched with relief as Bertha's hideous face slid away into the night. Finally, that ordeal was over.

But he was certain another had just begun.

Rusty lived in the big steel shed, in the far corner, away from the door. His body was bound, upright, to an old wheelchair that had been freed from of a pile of rusty old medical equipment, apparently left over from a family member who'd once required extensive care.

Rusty counted time for as long as he could, but eventually lost track as the relentless transition of darkness into light and light back into darkness blended into a single amorphous and never-ending day.

The man—the *Farmer* as Rusty had come to know him—had retrieved the Halloween decorations from Rusty's house, his tombstones and fog machines and glow-in-the-dark ghosts, and stacked them in the steel shed alongside him.

Besides those decorations, his only company was a picture of the Farmer and Bertha. The photograph of the couple was clearly taken in happier times, but it now hung on the wall at eye-level directly in front of him. The brutal grip of the neck brace refused to let him look away from it, not even for an instant.

At first, the sight of his possessions had made him hopeful. Surely his neighbors, especially Luther, would've spotted this man pilfering his property, would've realized he'd gone missing and called the police. But the cops never came and after a while that singular hope fell as lifeless as the decorations themselves.

The insects of the barn soon understood that Rusty's presence represented no threat. Spiders took up residence in the crevasses of his body, where they spun webs and laid eggs, grew old and died as their younglings spun fresh webs across his eyes and laid their eggs inside his ears.

Each morning before sunrise, the Farmer carried a leather bag and a cup of water into the shed, never speaking a word, never allowing Rusty's eyes to make contact with his own. The Farmer would insert a straw into Rusty's mouth, giving him a single long sip of water. He'd fiddle with feeding tubes, replace the IV drip bag and swap out the gatherings from a catheter, after which he'd not be seen again until the next day. Rusty was more livestock than human, nothing more than another farmyard chore.

When the Farmer had first removed the tape from his mouth, Rusty had screamed and cried and threatened and begged. His reward had been the prompt replacement of the duct tape, forcing him to snort each and every breath through stuffy nostrils for another week.

By the time the tape was removed once again, he'd learned his lesson. Rusty never uttered another word in the Farmer's presence, though he sometimes spoke softly to himself when certain he was alone.

After the chill of winter and dampness of spring had passed, the Farmer would leave the door open during the day, allowing summer breezes to flow through the steel shed so Rusty wouldn't bake alive.

Occasionally, he'd spot the Farmer, crisscrossing the fields atop some large piece of farming equipment or other, but never did he see or hear another soul. His hope of ever being rescued diminished with each passing day.

Delirium overtook him as summer burned on. During these episodes, he ceded all grasp of time and space, of night and day, drifting in and out of consciousness, searing bouts of phantom pain his solitary tether to reality. When that agony struck, the nerve endings of his paralyzed body re-materialized, piercing and tearing him in places he would never again touch. He was powerless to escape the pain, to seek comfort, left to drench his foul flesh with tears until the torment receded and the phantasms of derangement returned to drag him away.

His fevers decreased in frequency as autumn arrived, its

coolness bringing the realization that almost a year had passed since his arrival. The harvest air, heavy with the scent of decaying cornstalks, reminded him of his Halloween scarecrows.

Rusty couldn't resist reminiscing on those former forbidden pleasures, his beloved scarecrows from Halloweens past. Obtaining a scarecrow had been an annual pilgrimage for him, eagerly awaited. He'd carefully plotted his trips, travelling far, taking his time, covering his tracks.

His final scarecrow, Bertha, had been procured from a gas station in a squalid part of a decrepit rural town. Even though she had only been one of many, he remembered that night so clearly.

He parked in the shadows behind a grimy convenience store, positioning his rental so it was hidden from the street. He stepped from the car onto ground littered with wads of burnt foil and broken syringes that sparkled like jewels in the moonlight— evidence of drug abuse and reassurance that his choice was sound.

He peeked into the women's restroom behind the station and found several filthy stalls, all empty, as he'd hoped. After checking that no one was watching, he slipped inside.

He believed a single man could make a difference in the world. He was doing something. He was making a difference.

Although many Halloweens like this had come before, nervous excitement surged through him as he sat on the seat in the far stall. Waiting for his scarecrow to arrive was the hardest part, even if the anticipation was sweet. He hadn't tried a gas station bathroom before, wasn't certain it would work, but could easily feign confusion if discovered.

At last the restroom door opened. A pair of petite shoes appeared below the divider of the neighboring stall.

The moment had arrived.

He stepped out of the stall and tiptoed to the restroom door.

A single beat-up car sat outside. With a convenience store around front, the woman might not be alone.

Rusty walked over to the occupied stall and kicked in the door, grabbing the woman from the toilet and pulling a thick black garbage bag over her head.

He retrieved duct tape from his pocket and deftly bound it around her head—one, two, three times—precisely positioned to seal her mouth and nose, then tightly around her neck—one, two, three times—choking off her cries for help. He secured her wrists behind her. Each move was precise, skillful, practiced.

He dragged the woman out to his car and stuffed her into the trunk, closing the lid, leaving her to asphyxiate.

As he pulled away from the station, he checked his watch: ninety seconds had passed between the woman's arrival and his exodus. Not bad at all.

He traveled down darkened back streets on a winding and unpredictable course toward home, away from surveillance cameras and potential witnesses, pleased to know that he was serving the public good, as would the new scarecrow in his trunk.

Rusty had helped the community by removing another drug-addled leech from the streets and welfare rolls—this one was named Bertha, according to the driver's license he'd found in her purse.

Now she would finally contribute to society, as had all his other Halloween scarecrows before her, by decorating his porch for the delight of law-abiding neighbors.

Behind the dusty webs that draped over his face, a smile came to Rusty's cracked lips as he reveled in past pleasures, dreaming his dreams while tied to a wheelchair in the back of the shed.

One morning that same autumn, the daily routine changed. The Farmer slid the shed door all the way open, startling Rusty awake as metal screeched upon metal. The battered pickup waited outside, tailgate down.

The Farmer stacked Rusty's old Halloween decorations neatly into the truck and then came to collect Rusty himself, removing his IV and catheter tubes, packing them back into his leather bag. The Farmer sealed Rusty's mouth, placed a burlap sack over his head and stowed him neatly alongside the rest of the cargo in the back of the truck.

Rusty lay there until sundown, inhaling the stench of his decaying teeth, left to wonder what was going on. Was he being disposed of, put out of his unending misery? He hoped so. He'd had more than enough. Death would be a blessed release.

Shortly after sundown, the truck rumbled to life. Through the dead of night they traveled, over potted roads and highways until the truck finally rolled to a stop.

The tailgate thunked down and he felt himself flying again, Rusty the disembodied head, floating up out of the truck and into the darkness.

Blind inside the burlap bag, he listened intently to the world around him. It had been so long since he'd heard anything more than the patter of rain on the roof of the shed or the chugging of tractors through the cornfields. It all seemed so foreign to him: keys turning in a lock, a door opening, footsteps on a wooden floor, plastic sheeting crinkling against his face—the sounds painted pictures in rapid succession inside his mind.

Artificial light bloomed somewhere above. The Farmer pulled the burlap sack from his head and walked away.

Taking in his surroundings, Rusty wondered if he had died. He was inside of a house.

His house.

His heart leapt for joy, but landed with a thud as the Farmer returned with a bale of hay at the end of one muscled arm, folded denim overalls and flannel shirt clutched in the other.

As the Farmer knelt down to dress him, Rusty's eyes came to rest on the kitchen counter.

A freshly carved jack-o'-lantern stared back.

"I was so sad to hear about Rusty. Hard to believe it's been a year already."

The man's gravelly voice was instantly recognizable: Luther, his old next-door neighbor. Excitement coursed through Rusty. He'd been waiting all evening to see if Luther would still make his annual Halloween visit.

"Massive stroke last Halloween, dialed me as he was collapsing, I suppose," the Farmer said, his voice strangely soft and caring. "Didn't even get the chance to say why he was calling. I drove over to check on him later that night since he wouldn't answer my calls."

Luther clucked as he listened. Rusty couldn't see the man's face from behind the pumpkin's triangle eyes, only the front of his shirt. Its color shifted from purple to orange and back again in the flashing Halloween lights.

"It was too late by the time I found him, the damage was already done," the Farmer continued. "Uncle Rusty never regained consciousness, passed away last summer in the hospice, God rest his soul."

Rusty didn't have much time. The conversation between the two men appeared to be wrapping up fast. He had to get Luther's attention, somehow get his neighbor to see him inside the scarecrow, see that he was still alive. Then Luther could slip away and call for help. If he was rescued, maybe there was still a way to reverse his paralysis, get him up and moving again.

"Would've been nice to say goodbye," Luther said. "I know the community would've appreciated a proper funeral in return for all the fine things he did for us."

"I wish I could have made that happen, but consider this Halloween display to be a goodbye from Rusty, his final gift to the neighborhood."

"He loved Halloween, that's for sure, especially his scarecrows. You've done a fine job with this one here, I might add, a proper tribute all right. The IV bag's a nice touch." Luther rapped the pumpkin head in approval, squatting to examine it more closely.

As his neighbor peered into the jack-o'-lantern, Rusty found himself looking directly into Luther's squinty eyes. Rusty sucked in a big breath. It was his one shot for salvation.

"Damn, there are eyeballs moving around in there!" Luther said.

Rusty took that as his cue, letting loose the loudest moan he could muster. Even with lips sealed by duct tape, he could still make noise.

Luther jumped back, clutching his chest.

"Goddamn. Now that's *too* fucking scary," he shouted. "Pardon my French, but that thing should have a warning sign on it. You almost gave me a heart attack."

The Farmer laughed heartily, patting Luther on the shoulder.

"How *do* you make these scarecrows look so real, like they could jump right up and grab you?"

"Sorry, Luther, but that's a family secret."

"Well it was worth a shot," the old man said. "Rusty was lucky to have such a fine nephew to put his affairs in order. Have a happy Halloween, son. I'd better get out of here so you can tend to these kids . . . and before this blasted scarecrow scares me again."

With those words Luther departed, almost taking Rusty's hope along with him. But he'd gotten a response. Luther *had* heard him.

As Rusty sat on his own front porch for what he figured might be the last time—dressed in a flannel shirt and overalls stuffed with hay, head inside a pumpkin, face coated in black greasepaint—he watched as daring trick or treaters gathered their courage to make their way through the flashing lights and billowing fog to confront him, the horrifying scarecrow.

Relegated to being a passive observer, he was helpless, unable to intervene as the same kids he'd watch grow up over the years received sweets from a man he didn't even know. A man who had easily tricked his neighbors into believing he was family and taken over his house, over his life.

The Farmer grew bolder as the evening wore on. Amused by the elderly neighbor's frightened response to Rusty's cry for help, the Farmer encouraged the children to peek inside the pumpkin for a surprise.

"It's blinking!" one boy shrieked as he ran away, laughing, to tell the others about the horror he'd found the courage to face.

As child after child peered into the pumpkin, Rusty tried to show them he was alive using only his eyes, afraid they'd be frightened away if he made noise. When the children leaned forward he squinted his eyes, popping them wide open once they were looking, blinking furiously to show them he was real.

But his efforts only made the children scream louder as they took flight.

Halloween night came to an end. Once the candy ran out and the trick or treaters stopped coming, the Farmer turned off the porch light, locked the front door, packed Rusty and the rest of the decorations neatly into the back of his truck and set off on the long journey back to hell.

RUSTY HUSK

That night back at the farm, Rusty found himself granted a reprieve from the hellish steel shed, from the unrelenting regimen of spiders and darkness, of days spent inhaling his own dank filth and decay.

The Farmer set Rusty the Scarecrow in a rocking chair on the creaky porch of his own modest home, placing the hollowed-out pumpkin back over his head.

There Rusty remained all night, gazing towards where the moonlit driveway disappeared among fields of harvested corn.

The next morning, the first rays of dawn fell upon an empty rocking chair. Farther off in the fields, a rapidly moving silhouette sliced into the sky.

Elongated shadows scurried alongside the Farmer as he strode amidst brown stalks and scattered husks, Rusty the scarecrow tossed over one shoulder. Turkey vultures circled overhead, hissing as they followed.

The Farmer stopped when he arrived at a tall pole in the middle of the cornfield, where, at long last, he granted Rusty Husk the right to die.

ADAM'S BED

Josh Malerman

1

HALLOWEEN. ALSO ADAM'S birthday. Five years old.

Dad, Ronnie, would rather have spent the day on the boat. But, for the love of Christ, he had a son. For five years now he'd had a son. It was tough. Sometimes. Being a dad. He loved the kid. Yes. Bragged about him endlessly. Bothered his friends with pictures, videos, and quotes. Yet, the Florida sun called, and the lake that lapped at Ronnie's lawn was like an old college buddy who hadn't given up the ghost, who constantly said, *Come on, Ronnie. Let's have fun.*

Still, Ronnie liked nice things. Especially things that made him look good. His Florida lake house was one. His cars another. His full head of red hair, his tan skin, and his athletic frame, too. And Adam. Yes. Despite the baggage, Ronnie couldn't shut up about his boy. And he wouldn't stop comparing him, either. What age was Tony when he started walking? Adam started before then. Jeremy drew that? Look at Adam's drawing. It's better. Good kid. *Great* kid. A little flighty, okay. Cries for Mommy on the days I have him, okay.

Afraid of the dark in his bedroom at night.

But aren't they all?

Ronnie was rich. Rich enough where the kitchen wall

overlooking the lawn and lake was entirely glass. Rich enough that he could spend days on the lake, flirting with the women who boated, drinking 'til he blacked out, with no fear of work in the morning. There were people who were richer, but Ronnie was the richest of his friends. That meant something. To him it did. It was a great feeling, actually. Fucking fantastic. Most the time Ronnie felt fantastic. There wasn't a holiday or reunion Ronnie didn't look forward to. Why wouldn't he? Every time everyone got together, Ronnie felt the glory, sporting, harmless, by way of his admiring friends. It felt good to be successful. Ronnie felt good.

Halloween was one such holiday. So was Adam's birthday. Both on the same day. Every year. And while Ronnie wanted to spend it drunk on the lake, a little love from his peers never hurt.

"Over there," Ronnie said, in shorts and sandals, standing on his deck, directing Ashley and her crew as to where to set up the tables, the props, the decorations. A lot went into being a good dad, especially if you wanted everyone to notice.

Down in Florida, Halloween didn't look much like it did in the movies. No colored leaves and crisp air. No sweatshirts over the costumes. No cloud of breath accompanying the words *trick or treat*. It was eighty degrees and sunny. And the lake in autumn kissed the lawn like it did at the height of summer.

"Is Claire coming, Ronnie?"

Ashley was asking. Ashley who had worked as Ronnie's personal assistant for three years. Who knew Claire wasn't coming, but asked it every time.

"Naw."

"That's too bad."

She stepped by him then, from the deck to the dark green grass, directing her crew as she went.

Claire.

Ronnie brought his drink to his mouth and smiled. His ex-wife was something else. Constantly haranguing him about being a better father, but never asking for Adam on his birthday.

"It's because she loves Halloween," Ronnie said to nobody. A muscled man in a tight black shirt paused while hanging fake cobwebs in a tree, looked over his shoulder towards Ronnie on the deck. "She likes dressing up like a skank," Ronnie said, cheering the crewmember, "while I provide the memories of a kid's lifetime."

"You got a costume of your own, Mister Stern?"

This from another guy in a black shirt.

"Well, I'm not dressing up like a nurse, I can tell you that much." Smiles from the crew. "But yeah. I'm game."

He pulled from his pocket a pair of Groucho Marx glasses, nose and mustache and brows attached. Placing the plastic on his face, securing it around his ears, he extended both arms, silently saying, *See?*

The crew continued working. A speedboat passed fast across the lake. The echo of women laughing reached the deck.

Claire, he thought. *I could be out there right now, too.*

Ronnie would love it if Claire hosted one of these Halloween birthdays. Just once. That way he could stop in, make an appearance, play Dad for a couple hours, show off to some of her friends. He'd have time to get back home, here, play on the lake, make some magic happen. Halloween was the perfect day to pull up next to Lana Ann and her crew of half naked bombshells, ogle their costumes, offer them a joint, offer them a party.

You know who didn't wanna party? The parents of two-dozen five-year-olds.

Maybe Claire knew that.

"Hey, pal," Ronnie called, gesturing to a man hanging a witch piñata from a low branch. "Let's keep the center aisle open. A clear path to the dock."

Ronnie didn't like the witch. Didn't like how out of proportion the big nose was. Made him think of Adam's bedroom.

Why?

"You got it," the crewmember said.

You got it. Damn right Ronnie had it. Screw Claire. And you know what? Some of Adam's friends had fine moms. *Beautiful* moms. Maybe today Ronnie could make them laugh a little, get a second little party going. And from there? Who knew? A little rum, a little coke, and maybe Tiffany Gold would end up staying the night. Maybe. Weirder things had happened. Especially for Ronnie Stern. Women and fun popped out of the shadows all the time. One of the biggest mistakes a man can make is thinking nothing extraordinary will happen, not here, not today. Hell, one time Ronnie met a woman in *court*. Figured the officer wasn't going to show. He did show. But so did a needy little thing named Ursula, fresh off the boat. And Ursula had never been on *his* boat and thank-fucking-Zeus for that ticket. They went at it for three days. Practically roommates. Seventy-two hours of highs and lows that saw Ronnie naked on the dock at midnight, posing for pictures as the woman took them. That was a good one. A great one. The shadows, man. Woman and fun. Hell, Ronnie had more luck in unlikely situations than he did when he went out looking for it.

So, screw it.

Halloween. Also Adam's birthday. Plenty of shadows from which to pluck some fun.

He'd invited all Adam's little friends and their parents, too. He even told the parents to bring whoever they wanted, because you never knew what might show. *Wear the most scandalous costume you got!* He'd said, but he knew nobody would. He'd ordered a huge cake, a mammoth sub, balloons, orange paper plates, black forks and knives. Yard games and the grill, cobwebs and plastic spiders. Clowns, too. Clowns were a good idea. Make

Tiffany Gold laugh until her laughter caught the attention of the women on the lake. Like a lure.

How much longer is this kid party going on, Ronnie?

Not so long. Stick around.

Why should we?

We'll do some blow. Smoke some grass. Boat our butts off after the kids leave. Steal each other's faces out on the water. Got any acid, Carrie? I'll do it. Let me just get Adam to bed. Of course he has a bed here. Has a whole bedroom. A kickass bedroom. Destroys the one he has at Claire's.

Ronnie brought his arms up to his chest and looked to the sky. He'd felt a chill so defined it was as if, in hindsight, he'd been able to see it physically cross the lake, come up his lawn, greet him on the deck.

Adam's bedroom. Why did Adam's bedroom always freak him out? Was it because it was empty most of the time?

"Ronnie?"

He didn't remember finishing his drink but there he was, slurping the watered down remains. Ashley stood on the lawn at the foot of the deck steps, holding a Frankenstein banner.

"Hang it on the oak," Ronnie said.

He watched Ashley and her crew set up the tables, the cake stand, the chairs, the volleyball net, the fake coffin, the green slime, and the rest.

A party unfolding like a XXXXX before him.

"Where's the birthday boy now?" Ashley asked, making sure each plate had a napkin.

"Out front. On the phone with his mombie."

"Mombie?"

"Zombie mombie."

Ashley laughed. "You're terrible, Ronnie."

"Thank you, Ashley."

He entered through the back glass door and, for a moment,

had the house to himself. But he didn't like having the house to himself. Liked having women and fun in his house. Did all he could, always, to not have the house to himself.

He crossed through the kitchen, took the stone corridor to the stairs, climbed them, and paused at his bedroom door. He looked over his shoulder, down the upstairs carpeted hall to Adam's bedroom.

The door was closed. Was Adam in there after all? Ronnie thought he was out front in the driveway or sitting on the hammock in the front yard, talking to Claire.

But was he? Whether he could see into the room or not, it felt like someone was in there.

Ronnie took a step toward it. Stopped.

"Screw it," he said. Then, louder, "Adam! Get ready, buddy!"

He waited for a response, got none, and entered his own bedroom with a mind to take a shower, a loud one, as he closed the door behind him.

2

Seventy-five people, Ronnie thought. *Wish Claire could see this.*

Oh, fuck Claire. Adam was having the time of his life. Dressed up like a little Ronnie in a red wig and a Hawaiian shirt (Adam had insisted), the kid was racing all over the yard with his friends, playing games that didn't make any sense to Ronnie at all. Who cared? Ronnie was drinking, talking, hosting. He was also wearing those Groucho Marx glasses and using the grill spatula as a cigar. Just enough to play along, but not so much that he'd cover up his shorts or bare feet, giving anybody the impression he wasn't up for some fun.

Speaking of fun, the clowns weren't as big a hit as he'd hoped. The kids weren't interested at all. Maybe it was because they weren't scary clowns. Maybe it was because they were obviously middle-aged men in makeup. Who knew? Ronnie caught one of them smoking a cigarette on the side of the house. Reminded the guy he was getting paid to entertain kids. The guy was obviously hung over. Bad shape. They all seemed a little hit. But what did Ronnie care? As long as they kept making balloon animals and pretending to fall down and hurt themselves, he couldn't really fault them. Not Ronnie. Not with Paula Thomas walking around the yard in a pair of jean shorts small enough to be a blindfold. Part of her cowgirl costume. Forget Tiffany Gold. Paula was outrageous. Ronnie had to shake his head a couple times after looking at her, wipe the sight from his eyes.

"You buy that place up north yet, Ronnie?"

Dan. Fucking Dan Mickey. Dan liked to talk business no matter where they were and no matter what was going on around them. Guy would talk stocks at a strip bar. One time, back when Ronnie and Claire were still married, they went out to a movie with Dan and Beth. Back when Dan and Beth were still married, too. Halfway through the movie Dan leaned across the wives and asked Ronnie if he'd bought the Porsche they'd talked about last time they saw each other. Ronnie told him he had. Dan asked for how much. Ronnie told him how much. Dan asked if that was a good price. Ronnie told him he was watching a fucking movie here. No wonder Beth left the prick.

"No, I didn't." Ronnie sipped a Corona. Dan Mickey wore a checkered tie. As if that counted as showing his Halloween spirit.

"Why not?"

"Didn't sing to me."

Dan laughed. "You're into singing now?"

Two clowns ran into each other in the yard. Didn't look planned. Looked like they actually ran into each other.

"Careful," Ronnie called. "I'm not paying for the emergency room."

"Happy Halloween," Dan said.

Ronnie flipped a burger on the grill. When he turned around again he saw a couple more men on the deck beside Dan. They were already talking money. Even at a birthday party on Halloween, all business these guys.

They sipped beers and Ronnie flipped burgers and watched the kids play. Adam was racing through the yard, the party streamers in his hand drawing tracers in the air behind him like some wild acid trip. The clowns tried to play with him, egged him on. But Ronnie could tell Adam didn't give a hoot about the clowns.

"You believe these fucking guys?" Ronnie said to the others.

"To think," Mark Brewster said, "that this is how they make a living."

"Well," Ronnie said, "it beats making a dying."

The men laughed but Ronnie was thinking of Adam's bedroom again. As if their laughter came from the second floor window of his own house.

A kid threw a rock toward a crowd of others and Ronnie raised a hand to say something but the kid's mom, dressed as a playing card, came quickly and grabbed him by the wrist.

"You do *not* do that," she said.

But you do, Ronnie thought. *You pull fun from the shadows.*

Music played through the speakers mounted on the deck. Seventy-five people made a lot of noise. Ronnie looked out to the lake. A handful of boats out there. Orange Halloween streamers on one. He checked his watch. How long did parties last? A few hours? Tops? He thought about Claire. Wished Adam was spending the night at her house.

"Want a poodle, Mister Stern?"

Ronnie looked to the foot of the deck and saw one of the hungover clowns holding up a flaccid balloon. Through the smoke of the grill and the poor application of face-paint, the guy looked like a mess.

"Do I want a poodle?" Ronnie asked. The men laughed. Paula

Thomas walked to the deck steps. "You like poodles?" Ronnie asked her. Her legs like gold pouring out of her shorts.

"Not really," she said.

"Not really," Ronnie echoed. "Neither do I." Then, to the clown, "Sure, make me one."

Adam raced up to the deck, flew between the clown and Paula, raced to his dad's legs and tugged on his shorts.

"Daddy, Daddy!"

"Hey hey, What's up, spaz?"

"Can we go swimming?"

"Of course you can go swimming. Let's eat first though."

"Then you gotta wait thirty minutes," Dan said.

Ronnie rolled his eyes. "That's bullshit. And always has been. We'll go swimming after we eat, Adam."

Ronnie flipped a burger. Tiffany Gold joined Paula by the foot of the deck. Ronnie liked this. Liked the two of them together.

The clown worked on the poodle.

"That dog giving you a hard time?" Ronnie asked.

He imagined all the clowns drunk at a bar the night before, throwing darts, doing shots, moaning about the party they had to work the next afternoon.

"No, sir," the clown said. He raised the finished red poodle.

The women clapped.

"Do another one," Dan said. "Do an eagle."

Ronnie flipped a burger. Placed a hand on Adam's head.

The clown pulled out another balloon.

Ronnie looked up to the lake, thought about Marla Meyer and Lana Ann. *Fine* women who would no doubt be on out the water today. The music was loud through the deck speakers. Maybe they'd hear it? Maybe they'd come?

"I don't wanna bird!" Adam said. "I wanna poodle!"

"He already did a poodle, buddy," Ronnie said.

He sipped his beer.

He looked to the shore where the boat born waves crested the grass. A man stumbled there, stumbled toward the party and the house, as if he'd just pulled himself from the water.

"Who the fuck is that?" he asked.

The man had one hand on his belly, the other raised, like he was reaching for the party, the deck, the house. Ronnie couldn't make sense of his costume. Was he wearing long johns? Looked like it. Brown? Green? He couldn't tell. Jesus, the guy looked out of place.

"Fucking clowns," Ronnie said.

But this one was *really* something else.

He limped through a slat of sunlight, just shy of the kids playing, parents gathered in wicker chairs on the lawn. Pieces of green paper were visibly taped to his brown long johns. Ronnie could see that now. Were there clumps of hair, too? Looked like he'd been sleeping with a cat.

And a mask. A green rubber face.

Wolf snout? Ronnie thought. *Teeth? What is this?*

It was the most haphazard costume Ronnie had ever seen. Not lazy like Dan Mickey. Not poor like he himself had once been, when he cut holes in a bed sheet to join the middle school parade.

It looked more like the handiwork of someone who never considered what others might think of him at all. A crazy man's costume.

"Jesus," Ronnie said.

"A bird!" the clown declared. Tiffany reached out to touch it.

The man in green and brown, the man in the mask kept limping up the lawn.

Ronnie felt a chill. Despite the heat of the grill and the heat of the day, despite the fact that his son was having the time of his life on his birthday, on Halloween, Ronnie suddenly felt downright cold. The man had reached the kids, through the party

72

like a vision of a hobo, peeled from his rightful place down by the docks and placed here at Adam's party.

He was closer now. The snout was not a snout. Rather, a nose. A hag's nose. A troll's nose. Big as Adam's head.

Ronnie pointed at him with the spatula.

"Seriously. Who is that?"

Smoke rose in a cloud from the grill.

"Adam!" the man called from behind the mask. "Adam!"

Adam, Ronnie thought. *He's calling Adam by name.*

Adam turned to look.

The man waved his raised hand.

"Daddy," Adam said.

Ronnie set the spatula down. "Is this guy with you?" he asked the clown.

"Us? No."

"Adam!" the man cried. He was halfway to the deck. He'd split the party in two. Every child watched him stumble. Every parent pulled their kid closer.

Ronnie saw more of the costume now. The thick green construction paper made to look like hair. Or scales. Wrinkles in a rubber face. Eyes completely obscured by the folds of green skin.

"Adam!" the man waved.

"Hey," Ronnie called, still pointing the spatula. "Who the hell–"

But the man interrupted him.

"Adam! Adam! I'm the monster under your bed!"

"*Ashley*," Ronnie said. "Get this fucking guy out of here *now*."

Two members of Ashley's crew were upon him immediately. Two men in black gripped a shoulder each and dragged the stranger off the lawn. The man did not struggle. Only turned his disproportionate and wrinkled mask toward Ronnie and Adam as he was eclipsed by the side of the house.

Ronnie looked up to the second floor window. Adam's bedroom.

I'm the monster under your bed!

He knelt by Adam's side.

"Hey, buddy. Don't worry. Bad clown. Shitty costume. Okay?"

But Adam didn't look convinced. Adam didn't look anything at all. He stared blank to where the man had last been, by the bushes framing the path along the side of the house.

"Don't worry, buddy. It's your birthday party. It's Halloween. Some freak."

Adam raised a thumb to his mouth.

"Oh Christ," Dan Mickey said. "Your boy is . . . peeing, Ronnie."

Ronnie looked to the deck then leapt out of the way of the spreading urine.

"Adam? What the fuck's going on?"

"Oh my God," Paula said. She went to him. "He's not okay."

Ronnie looked to Dan. "You didn't hire that guy, Mickey? None of you did?"

"Hire him?" Dan said. "Jesus, I don't even understand what he was supposed to be."

"Supposed to be?"

Now Paula and Tiffany both led Adam inside. Other kids were gathering by the deck to look at the piss there.

Ronnie looked back out to the lake. Speedboats. Men howling. Women screaming.

Adam!

I'm the monster under your bed!

Again, Ronnie looked to the second floor window. He should be mad and mad alone. But he wasn't.

He was scared, too.

You've heard things in the house, buddy, he thought. *And either you admit it now and face it or you go mad denying it.*

But what did this mean? What had he heard?

"The police are here," Ashley said, appearing suddenly by Ronnie's side.

Ronnie nodded. He followed her through the house. At the bathroom by the kitchen he saw Paula and Tiffany comforting Adam.

"You okay, buddy?" Ronnie asked.

Adam looked up at him. Didn't look like he recognized him. Not at first. Then he nodded. A good solid shake of the head.

Ronnie smiled. "That's my boy. I'm gonna go talk to the police outside. Make sure that crazy man never comes by here again." Then, "Cool?"

"Cool."

Little red wig. Hawaiian shirt. Wet shorts.

Ronnie felt tears in the distance. Then he was out the front door, walking toward two squad cars shining under the high Halloween sun.

"Mister Stern?" An officer asked. There were four of them.

"Yes."

"You had an uninvited guest?"

"I did. Yes."

"What did he look like?"

"Don't know. He was wearing a mask. Looked like a . . . like a . . . "

He looked to Ashley for help.

"Like a witch," she said.

"A witch?" Ronnie asked. He shook his head no. "Maybe."

"He didn't take off the mask?"

"No." Ronnie looked around the neighborhood. He didn't want two squad cars in his driveway. Didn't want this scene. "Look, it was no big deal. Maybe check the doors? Check the windows? Make sure he didn't try to break in?"

"You think he might've?"

"I don't think so. I don't know. Just check. If you don't find anything . . . okay." Then, "And make sure he never comes back here again."

The cops exchanged looks.

"What?" Ronnie asked.

"Well your security let him go at the head of the drive. They said he limped away, up the street."

"Let him go?" Then Ronnie nodded. What else should they have done? "Well go find him. And warn him. I don't know. Scare the shit out of him for me."

"Did he say anything?"

Ronnie hesitated. Then, "Yes, he did."

"What was it?"

Ronnie looked to the side of the house, could see the very edge of the party in the backyard.

"He called out my son's name. Said, 'Adam, I'm the monster under your bed.'"

3

The party wasn't worth saving. People kept bringing up the stranger even when Ronnie asked them not to.

"You're gonna freak Adam out. Come on."

It was the last thing Ronnie needed Claire to hear. And he was sure she was going to hear about it.

What's this about a prowler calling out to our son at his party?

It was nothing.

Nothing? How'd he know his fucking name, Ronnie?

There was a sign as big as my dick hanging on the deck, Claire! Happy Birthday Adam!

Adam had made his way back out to the party. But even his return couldn't bring it back to life. Soon, Ashley and her crew picked up the empty plates and Halloween decorations. Most of the people left. Adam and two friends played with Adam's new presents on the deck. One was a Captain America mask. Adam took a few seconds before trying it on. Many feet from them, Ashley was on hands and knees, scrubbing urine.

Ronnie watched all this through the glass wall, seated at the kitchen island with Paula, Tiffany and a very drunk Ben Ornstein.

"That was fucked up," Ben said for the fourth time. He poured another vodka tonic. He'd spilled his last one on his flowered shirt.

"Yeah, okay," Ronnie said. "Enough. It's exactly what he wanted, for us to be talking about him all day."

"Where'd he come from?" Paula asked.

Ronnie shrugged. "Who the fuck knows? The lake?"

They looked out the wall of windows, out to Ronnie's dock.

"He was ill," Tiffany said, firing up a joint.

"Ill?' Ronnie asked.

"Yeah . . . mental."

She took a deep drag and handed the joint to Ronnie.

Ronnie watched Adam on the deck as he took a hit and passed it to Ben.

The ceiling creaked then, the unmistakable sound of weight upon a second floor.

They all looked up. But only Ronnie felt a chill.

You've heard this sound before, buddy. When Adam's not here. When you've got the house to yourself and all you wanna do is get outside. When all you wanna do is get stoned and drunk on the lake. When all you wanna do is–

The girls started giggling. Then Ben did, too.

"What?" Ronnie asked.

"You look scared as a snake in a belt factory," Ben said.

Ronnie got up and looked outside. Scanned the yard, the dock, the water beneath the dock, his son.

"Watch them a minute," he said to Paula.

"The kids?"

But Ronnie was already stepping through a thick cloud of smoke as he left the kitchen and took the long stone hall to the foot of the stairs.

"Ashley? You up there cleaning?"

But Ashley was outside. He knew that. He'd seen her there.

Ronnie looked once to the kitchen, saw Ben's elbows on the island edge. Then Ronnie bounded up the stairs.

"Someone up here?"

He checked the master bedroom first. The bathrooms. The guest room. The closets.

He saved Adam's room for last.

"Anybody up here?"

He opened Adam's door and entered. In the open closet he spotted older toys from Halloween birthdays past.

He was stoned. Really stoned. A rare nostalgia crept over him. Adam as a baby. Adam's first birthday. Now Adam on the weekends.

He turned around. Looked to Adam's bed.

Adam was a good kid. A great kid. Made his bed all on his own whenever he slept over. Kept the room clean. Ronnie loved him.

On top of the dresser he saw the pajamas Adam would wear to bed tonight. Blue and white striped cotton.

He looked to Adam's bed again.

Adam!

The red comforter was tucked tight under the mattress ends. Nothing hung over the edge, nothing hung to the floor.

Ronnie knelt. Looked under the bed.

He could see clean through to the wall. Nothing there.

Getting up, he felt a rush of grey to his head. Stoned. He left Adam's room, checked the bathroom, and hurried to the stairs. Halfway down he heard the stoned women. They'd gotten

78

higher. Was Ben conked out on the table? Ronnie bet he was. At the bottom of the steps he ran his fingers over his arms and looked back up once more.

Houses creaked. Who cared? He had two fine women giggling gibberish at the kitchen table.

He went to them.

"You girls wanna go on the water?"

Ben was asleep, his forehead on the island.

"Where'd you go?" Paula asked.

"Upstairs."

"Why?"

They were both laughing. It bothered Ronnie for a second. Were they laughing at him?

"I was checking on spooky sounds, remember?"

"Oh yeah!" It was like Ronnie had told them a very big secret. Ronnie didn't like that. Didn't want to think that checking his second floor was a big thing.

He crossed the kitchen and opened the deck door.

"Ashley?" he called.

Ashley was still on her knees, removing the yellow rubber gloves now.

"Yes?"

"You mind watching the kids while we go for a spin?"

"Of course."

Adam leapt up, tore of his Captain America mask.

"I wanna come!"

Ronnie smiled to humor him. He was about to say, *Not this time kiddo.* But he thought of the toys in Adam's closet. Felt some of the nostalgia he'd felt upstairs.

"Of course you can come." Then, "It's Halloween, for crying out loud. And you know what else it is?"

Adam smiled but it looked like it took some effort. The way adults smile when they're exhausted.

71

"Can my friends come, too?"

"Bring 'em," Paula said. "We'll go tubing."

They headed down the grassy slope toward the dock. The same slope the stranger had stumbled up less than an hour and a half ago.

"Jesus," Ronnie said.

"What is it?" Paula asked.

Ronnie turned to answer her but the sun was hitting her chest just right. Two sandy hills under a perfectly blue sky. It was exactly what he needed to see to wipe the unsettling feeling away.

"You're gorgeous," he said.

4

Fuck it felt good to be high on the water.

"Faster!" Paula howled. Ronnie was surprised. Hadn't pegged her as Queen Fun, party girl, louder than the engine he revved. He was glad for it.

"You got it," Ronnie said.

Adam's friend Bobby was at the end of the long white rope, hanging tight to the tube, fear in his eyes. The kids wanted to go tubing? Okay. Ronnie would take them tubing. His way. Party spin. Good Dad. Great Dad. Scare the shit out Bobby and he'll remember this day forever. And you shoulda seen Paula Thomas tying the rope to the back of the boat. Ronnie watched the whole thing, hardly heard it when Bobby asked where he was supposed to grip the tube. Adam showed him.

"Go Bobby!"

Adam and his friend Nate were crowded at the back of the boat, their little faces just jutting out of their orange life jackets. The ladies were up front, hanging onto the cushions, the bow of the speedboat up in the air. The faster Ronnie went, the higher that bow went, and it started to feel like he was directing a movie; panning the camera up, a better angle on Paula and Tiffany both.

"Bobby!" Nate called out.

Bobby on the tube looked like he was going through something. Like he would never be the same again. Ahead, the women were laughing. They'd circled the lake and Ronnie saw his house again. Couldn't even tell there was a party today. Ashley and her crew were great. If not for the HAPPY BIRTHDAY ADAM sign still hanging, you'd think nobody was home.

Except somebody was.

Somebody was on the deck, looking out at the lake.

"Hey," Ronnie said, slowing the boat down.

A second person came out the glass door and Ronnie recognized it as Ashley. So the first guy must've been part of her crew.

But for a second there . . .

Jesus, Ronnie felt piqued. He thought of the ceiling creaking. Thought of the feeling he had upstairs, any time Adam's bedroom door was closed. Thought of the fact that, come tomorrow, he'd have the house to himself all over again.

He revved the boat and Paula fell back into the bench, spilling half her beer on her belly and crotch. This made her laugh even harder and Tiffany reached from one bench to the other and helped her wipe the beer off her body.

Ronnie smiled.

Women and fun. Exactly what he needed. You just never knew when they'd pop up. Never knew which shadows they were hiding in, just waiting to leap out at you.

In the rearview mirror Ronnie saw Bobby duck his head into the tube. He was hanging on one handed. When he came up again he was wearing a mask.

A green one.

Wrinkled flesh over the eyes. A nose that reached its lips.

"HEY!" Ronnie yelled, turning the boat fast.

Bobby was tossed from the tube.

"Ronnie!" Paula said.

But Ronnie was turning the boat around faster than he should. Approaching Bobby faster than he should, too.

But when the boy was in sight, Ronnie saw he was wearing a Hulk mask. Nothing more.

"You sure you're okay to drive this thing?"

It was Tiffany, close to his ear. Her breath cooler than the warm Halloween air.

"Yeah. I'm good."

"That was *awesome*," Nate said.

"Awesome!" Adam repeated. It sounded good, hearing Adam's voice back to the way it should sound.

Ronnie went to the back of the boat and drew the rope in. Bobby swam to the ladder.

"You looked like you saw the devil out there, Bobby," he said, helping the kid back onboard.

Bobby looked at him funny. "You did, Mister Stern."

Ronnie stood up straight. "I did what?"

"You looked like you saw something."

Then Adam and Nate were pulled Bobby into the boat. Ronnie looked out to the water. As he crossed the boat, heading for the wheel, he overheard Adam say the word *bed*.

"What's that?" Ronnie asked, stopping.

"Nothing." But Adam looked like he was keeping a secret.

"No. You said something. What was it?"

"I didn't say anything, Daddy. Bobby did."

Ronnie looked to Bobby. To Nate.

"Adam," he said. "There's nothing under your bed. I just checked. You don't even have any *lint* under there, buddy."

Tiffany laughed

"You just checked!" she repeated.

"You hear me?" Ronnie said.

Paula got up and hunched her shoulders, arched her eyebrows, made her hands into pretend claws.

"*I'm the monster!*" she said. "*Under your bed!*"

The kids screamed.

"Jesus, Paula," Ronnie said. "You're gonna scare the shit out of them."

But the way they were all looking at him, he could tell the person who looked most afraid was himself.

5

The kids were in the basement on the couches. Ben was long gone. Ronnie had the two women upstairs, sitting at the bar, *his* bar, down the stone hall, past the stairs. They passed a joint.

Night had come.

"Don't trick or treaters come by?" Tiffany asked.

Ronnie shook his head. Standing behind the bar, he mixed three drinks. "No. Our drive leads right to the main road. Who's gonna walk that with their kid?"

"Let's scare them," Paula said. She pointed to the floor.

"Jesus," Ronnie said. "What is it with you and scaring little kids?"

"It's fun," she said. Then she took her top off.

Women and fun. Out of the shadows. Who knew?

Ronnie leaned on the bar, smiled at them both.

"So," he said. "What happens next?"

But the doorbell interrupted whatever might've happened next.

Ronnie walked the hall to the front door. He opened it and stared blankly at a woman who looked like an IRS agent next to the two he'd just walked away from.

"Hi. Are Bobby and Nate ready?"

Ronnie almost said, *I didn't know who they belonged to.*

"Sure. Give me a second."

He left her there, went downstairs, and rushed the kids out of the basement.

The lady thanked Ronnie for the party. For watching the kids. For everything. Ronnie nodded. Waved goodbye. Closed the door.

Relief washed over him like a bigger, unseen drink. The party was over. Adam would go to bed. He could lose himself in these women.

"And you," he said, kneeling down to Adam's height in the dark foyer. "Did you have fun today?"

Adam nodded. Then, "Is it time for bed?"

Such a good kid. You didn't have to tell him. He told you.

"Yep city, Adam. Come on, I'll tuck you in."

At the foot of the stairs, Ronnie heard the women giggling and wondered what he was missing. He looked up the stairs.

Adam climbed first and Ronnie followed. Adam, obviously tired in the way only kids are, went straight to his bed. Ronnie didn't bring up brushing his teeth. Had him in his pajamas and tucked under the red comforter in minutes.

He kissed Adam's forehead.

"Had a great time today, buddy. Thank you."

"Thank you, Daddy."

Ronnie looked once around the room.

"Hey, Adam."

"Yeah?"

"You okay?"

"Yeah."

"You're not . . . "

He wanted to ask Adam if he was freaked out. Wanted to ask him if that man in the fucked up dollar store green troll mask freaked him out. Did he need Daddy to sleep with him tonight?

"What, Daddy?"

"I was just gonna ask if you wanted pancakes in the morning."

"Yes!"

"Good. Me, too. I love you, kiddo. I'll be downstairs if you need me. Knock first."

"Okay."

Ronnie got up and paused at the doorway, a finger on the light switch. He watched Adam close his eyes. Such a good kid. Looked so tiny under all that red.

Adam!

Ronnie looked to the floor beneath the bed.

He was stoned. Imaginative. That's all. Heard Adam's breathing and tried not to think it could be someone else. Down there under the bed.

Before leaving, Ronnie knelt to the floor. Put his ear to the wood. Looked all the way under the bed.

Nothing.

He got up and, thinking of the women downstairs, turned off the lights and went to them.

6

"Oh, come on," Ronnie said. "You're *leaving?*"

Paula shrugged. She looked dour. They'd both lost a little something since he last saw them. Ronnie knew the feeling well. When the drinks and the drugs wore off, when the sweet spot of the night was behind you.

"Fuck!"

"Hey," Tiffany said, no longer the party girl. "Don't get mean."

"Hey, I'm not. I just thought we were going somewhere."

"Where?" Paula asked.

85

Ronnie tried to buy some time.

"How are you guys getting home? How about that?"

"Called a cab," Paula said. Then she burped.

"Jesus."

"Hey," Tiffany again.

"All right. Whatever. Go home. I hope you had fun. Happy Halloween."

He wished he hadn't said it. Reminded him of masks.

Tiffany's phone lit up.

"Cab's here."

Ronnie felt a sudden stab of something deeper than loneliness. He didn't want these women to leave. Ridiculously he considered going back out on the lake. Anything to get out of the house.

But he walked them to the door and saw them off. Made jokes. Laughed at theirs. Said goodbye.

Then they were gone. And the house felt much colder for it.

Except he wasn't alone. Adam was asleep upstairs.

Ronnie locked the front door and returned to the bar. He fixed himself a rum and coke and drank it. Mostly in the dark. He thought about calling someone. Who? He'd suggest skinny-dipping. Night swimming. Women liked that kind of thing.

"Dammit."

Ronnie set his phone face down on the bar. He was stoned. Drunk. Very. He fixed a second drink and carried it with him through the house. Through the kitchen. Out the deck door. Onto the deck. He stood in the dark and listened to the frogs and crickets. Mating calls.

Life could be hard sometimes.

"I feel you guys," he said, raising his glass to nature.

He looked down to the slope and thought about the guy who wasn't with the clowns.

He considered calling the police, see if they had an update.

Did they find the guy? Did they talk to him? He reached into his pocket but his phone was still on the bar.

Fuck it.

He carried his drink inside. He liked the feel of the cool floor against his bare feet. That was something, anyway. Not a threesome with two bombshells in daisy dukes, but something.

He sipped as he took the stairs, upstairs, on his way to his bedroom. The carpet felt good under his feet, too. Good. Good was good.

At his door, he paused, looked over his shoulder, down the long hall to Adam's bedroom.

The yard light, shining through Adam's window showed him an approximation of his son.

Showed him the foot of the bed.

Ronnie turned to enter his own bedroom but stopped.

He looked back down the hall.

"Come on," he said, the way people do when they don't realize they're speaking, when they need to say something to stave off fear. Real fear.

Something was under Adam's bed.

A blanket? Had Adam shoved a blanket down there? Maybe he was scared. Wanted to fill the space. That way nothing could . . .

Ronnie started shaking. He didn't want to believe it, but the ice was rattling in his drink so it meant it was true. Meant he was scared.

Was something beneath Adam's bed?

He reached for his phone again.

Dammit!

Still on the bar.

He took the hall slow, stopping every two steps to squint, to look harder.

Something moved. Under Adam's bed.

Ronnie stopped.

Fuck, you're breathing loud.

He thought something moved. But did it? Just a bit? Enough to show a flash of color?

A spot of green?

Halfway to Adam's room, Ronnie hurried downstairs, then down the hall, into the bar. He grabbed his phone and rushed through the contacts.

Claire.

"Hello?"

"Claire, Claire!"

"Why are you whisper shouting?"

"Something's beneath Adam's bed."

"What?"

"Something. Is. Beneath. Adam's. Bed."

"What the fuck is wrong with you, Ronnie? Are you on drugs? Are you out of your fucking mind?"

"I don't know what to do."

"Turn the fucking lights on! What's under his bed? A spider? What the *fuck* is wrong with you? Is he alone?!"

"I'm here. He's not alone."

"Are you in his bedroom? Look under the fucking bed! Did you call the police? Get on your knees and—"

Ronnie hung up. He called the police.

"Police?"

"Hello hi, this is Ronnie Stern."

"Sir, can you speak up?"

Ronnie was standing at the foot of the stairs. When did he walk there?

"This is RONNIE STERN. You guys came by my house today."

"Mister Stern? Is there another problem?"

"There's something beneath my son's bed."

A pause.

"Can you say that again?"

"THERE'S SOMETHING BENEATH MY SON'S BED."

"Can you elaborate? What's beneath his bed?"

Claire called. Ronnie didn't switch over to answer her.

He looked to the top of the stairs, to last trickle of light coming from Adam's bedroom window.

"Send someone," he said.

He hung up.

He took a huge gulp from his drink, set the glass on the floor.

He climbed the stairs.

Two steps from the top he got on his knees and put his ear to the hall carpet. He tried but couldn't quite see into Adam's room.

There might be a prowler beneath your son's bed, Ronnie thought. *GET UP AND FIND OUT.*

He got up.

Then, trembling, he ran to Adam's room.

He turned on the light, saw Adam already wide eyed, clutching his red comforter to his chin.

"Daddy," Adam said. "There's someone under my bed."

Ronnie looked to the floor.

That's an arm, that's a real arm. That's green hair at the elbow. Those are fingers gripping the bed frame. That's a face, THAT'S A FACE, Ronnie, not a mask, no mask, looking at you, has eyes, looking at you, Ronnie, looking right at you.

"Jump!" Ronnie yelled. He saw the eyes under the bed, deep in a troll's wrinkled face, roll up toward Adam. *"Now!"*

Adam jumped. Landed hard on the wood floor. Went to his dad.

Ronnie gripped him and ran.

Not a mask, no mask, not a man.

Adam clung to him, whining, crying, yelling in his ear.

Down the stairs, down the hall.

Ronnie kicked the front door, realized he'd just locked it. He unlocked it, shaking.

Police lights outside, red and blue. Not green.

"Help!" Ronnie called.

The officers were out of their cars, guns drawn, surprise in their eyes but not like the shock in Ronnie's.

"He's in there."

Ronnie turned to point but it was already there, standing in the doorway, lifting its hand to wave.

"Adam!" it called.

For a moment, even the officers didn't move. Then they were upon him and the stranger dropped like drapes to the threshold.

"Jesus *CHRIST!*" Ronnie yelled. He gripped a hard hand over Adam's eyes.

The officers cuffed the man, telling him what he could and couldn't do. But they didn't remove his mask. Not yet. And Ronnie stared into the green folds that covered his eyes.

"You're not gonna be able to take off his mask!" Ronnie said. "It won't come off!"

An officer went to Ronnie. Put a hand on his shoulder.

"It's okay, Mister Stern. We got him."

"But the—"

The other officer removed the mask. In the cruiser lights Ronnie saw an unshaven man looking back at him.

Not a mask, no mask, no.

"Same man from earlier today?" the officer beside him asked.

Ronnie only stared. What he'd seen upstairs. This man was not what he'd seen under Adam's bed.

"Mister Stern?"

Ronnie lowered Adam to the driveway. He walked to the front door.

Just a man. Thin. Brown long johns. Green construction paper.

"Let me see that mask," Ronnie said.

The officer held it up.

No, Ronnie thought. *No.*

"Just another Halloween nut," the officer said. "Glad you two are safe." Then, "All that matters."

But it wasn't all that mattered. Not to Ronnie.

The two cops got the man standing and walked him quick to the cruiser.

Then, more bright lights. Another car in the driveway.

Claire. Oh, Claire.

"Adam?! *ADAM?!*"

She was running up the drive.

Ronnie met her at Adam.

"We're spending the night at your house," Ronnie said. "No argument."

"What's going on? What happened?"

Then Claire was on her knees, hugging Adam. One officer had the man in the car as the other explained it to her. Ronnie stared at the man's face through the glass.

No mask, he thought. *No man.*

"You're just gonna . . . take him away?" he asked.

The officer looked confused. "What would you have us do?"

Get rid of it, Ronnie thought. *Erase it from this world.*

Later, after Ronnie had told the story ten times, told her about the man in the yard, about hiring the clowns, about the party, the boating, about putting Adam to bed, about seeing it, down the hall, about calling, about seeing it then for real, not a mask, real eyes, peering, wise eyes, *old* eyes wedged into deep green folds, Ronnie laid down on Claire's couch and looked to Adam, sleeping on the floor under a blanket.

Claire didn't speak. Bless her. If she spoke, if she said Ronnie had done something wrong, Ronnie might've gone mad, might've leapt from the couch and ran out of her house, onto the street, tumbling, mumbling *no mask no mask no man* as he fell then got up and ran again, still chanting *no mask no mask no man.*

Instead, he lay as still as he could, looking into Claire's eyes, and raised a finger to his lips, silently telling her to listen, do you hear that? Do you hear something breathing inside this room? Behind this couch?

Under it?

Can you, Claire? Can you hear it? Maybe it's not breathing I hear. Maybe it doesn't breathe. But it lives all the same.

Can you hear it living in this room, Claire?

Living under the couch I lay on?

Living under Adam's bed?

KEEPING UP APPEARANCES

Jason Parent

THE OLD LADY screamed as Lisa tore the pearls from her neck. White globes bounced like marbles off the hardwood floor.

Samson ended the old woman's noise with the butt of his Glock, and she crumpled to the floor.

Carlos watched her go down, wincing as if the blow had landed against his own forehead. Although his trusty sawed-off shotgun was tucked under his arm, he didn't like using more violence than was necessary. The old bag's caterwauling had needed to stop, but he might have chosen duct tape in lieu of Samson's brute force.

Before Lisa had touched her, the lady of the house had composed herself with dignity, which was more than could be said for her limp-dick, Daddy Warbucks-looking fruitcake of a husband, who was pissing himself and whimpering in the corner. Carlos stared at the pathetic excuse for a man, watching as urine pooled on the floor around him.

I should have stayed in school. Carlos sighed, his hot breath whistling against the inside of his Donald Duck mask. And what better night for masks than Halloween? He wanted to take it off. The plastic edges were scratching against his skin.

But he had made the rule, and it had been a good one: the

masks stayed on at all times. If no one saw their faces, no one had to die. No one had died since he'd begun running his own crew — Carlos, Samson, Breck, and Lisa. They were two years death-free, which was a lot more than he could say for the other crews he'd run with. *Maybe I should tack up a poster like they got at job sites. This crew has been murder-free for seven hundred days.*

Carlos glanced at the old couple, one sniveling and one unconscious, and wondered, not for the first time, if he would have been better off commercial fishing like his brother. He shrugged. "Tie them up."

"Yes, sir," Breck said, snickering as he danced around Carlos and over toward the unconscious woman.

Carlos grimaced. His young associate, and sometimes loose cannon, looked a bit too apropos in his costume, which consisted of an untied straightjacket and a bite mask that reminded Carlos of Hannibal Lecter.

Breck waggled a Bowie knife the size of Excalibur as he passed. He called the blade his "all-purpose tool," but as far as Carlos could tell, it only had two purposes: slicing and stabbing. After the last time the crazy asshole had brought the knife, Carlos had been tempted to veto weapons altogether, but his eagerness to leave his shotgun at home ranged somewhere between *not going to happen* and *fucking hell no.*

His grip tightened around its stock. The shotgun was as much for colleague control as it was for crowd control. That sparkle in Breck's eye and the jig in his step confirmed the need for double-barrel deterrence.

"I'll do the lady." Breck tittered with excitement. He pulled a zip tie from his pocket, gyrating his hips as he straddled the old woman.

"If by 'do' her," Carlos said, "you mean 'tie her up,' then be my guest. Just make sure you do it tight . . . and *not* to a table leg. Let's not repeat the shitshow we put on at the last house."

Breck laughed and tugged at the woman's arm. He lifted her

14

to a sitting position. Unable to pull her up any farther, he dropped her arm and let her collapse back against the floor. "Well, I give up." He wiped his brow, slapped his thighs, then danced over to the man cowering in the kitchen corner, waving his knife as if he were composing a symphony with it. When his foot splashed down in a puddle, he turned his nose up in disgust.

The man in the corner buried his face in his hands and wailed.

"S?" Carlos called, careful not to use his partner's real name. "Would you kindly silence our other host?"

Samson, who was built like a rhino, raised his pistol.

"Nicely," Carlos added.

A man of few words, Samson grunted. He lowered his weapon, his face impossible to read beneath his clown mask. Carlos found the mask's toothy smile ironic since there was no humor in Samson. The man had the personality of a walking refrigerator. But he was a capable partner, one Carlos could count on. Samson grabbed a roll of duct tape off the kitchen table and spiraled it around the homeowner's head, covering his mouth.

And he's got more sense than the other two. Carlos glanced at his girlfriend. Lisa scooped up the pearls that had broken off the chain. Pink pigtails flopped like rabbit ears over her furry mask and its wicked grin full of sharp, bloodstained fangs.

Carlos shook his head. Lisa was a decade younger than him. She still lived for excitement—sex anywhere, party anytime— making his life more worth living and his lifestyle more likely to get him killed. She'd never done any real time and didn't know what it was like to be locked away.

Carlos, on the other hand, liked to play it safe—as safe as crime could be anyway. He took only those jobs that seemed like sure things, and those he planned generally involved an absence of people, security measures, and threats to his life or freedom. His work was neither glitzy nor glamorous, but he got by, rarely hurting anyone in the process.

But instead of mellowing out, Breck had become too wild, and Samson didn't know his own strength. Lisa was Carlos's biggest concern, though. When, half in jest, he'd suggested they use the cover of Halloween to go door-to-door and rob the rich in their secluded mansions, she'd jumped all over the idea. She hadn't stopped talking about it until Halloween night had arrived and the talking became doing.

What a sight she was. Her nipples tented the fabric of her T-shirt, which was spattered with blood from the owner of the second house they'd hit, a man who'd thought himself a hero. Her body was so fine and tight and young, while Carlos's own was beginning to sag in all the wrong places. He thought he loved her, the kind of love that was equal parts wet dream and nightmare but addictive as all fucking hell.

And that made him wonder how the night was going to end.

They tied up the old couple and removed the man's duct tape just long enough for him to spill where he kept his most prized possessions, a task that took all of eight seconds. Then they tossed the place, nabbing anything that caught their fancies.

When they finished loading up their van with trash bags full of loot, Carlos tossed his mask onto his lap and turned the key in the ignition. He smiled at Breck and Samson, who were crammed in the back with the trash bags. They'd pulled it off, come away with a nice haul, and were safely on their way ho—

"Can we do one more?" Lisa asked from the passenger seat.

"I don't know, babe," Carlos said. "Third time's the charm, right? We did good. Best not get too greedy."

Breck poked his head between the front seats. "But this street's a freaking gold mine. Big houses with giant yards. No one can see dick going on at their neighbors'. People opening their doors for four grown-ups in masks without even thinking it might be a bad idea. I say we make the most of what we've been given. I say we hit up the whole damn street, cash and jewelry only, here on out."

Carlos frowned. "Samson, what do you think?"

Samson grunted and shrugged.

Outvoted. Carlos slouched in his seat, resting the back of his head against it as he stared at the ceiling for a moment, searching for a good reason to veto them. Thinking of none, he slumped over the steering wheel, put the van in drive, and climbed the hill to the next house.

Lisa jumped in her seat and turned to look out the window. "Whoa! I'd sell my soul to live there."

Carlos peered over her shoulder. He couldn't make out much of the house. It sat at a distance, atop a sprawling estate that was accessed by a long, winding driveway. But he could tell it was big—big enough to make all those celebrities feel small back in their Beverly Hills mansions. A wrought-iron fence—its nine-foot posts resembling lances that stabbed at the night—bordered the property as far as he could see. Through the bars, he saw fancy gardens, statued fountains, geometrically patterned hedges, and still ponds that he bet were well stocked with koi. But the ponds were overrun with leaves, and the hedges and gardens had grown into tangles and thickets.

"Now we know who was responsible for the water shortages this summer." Carlos pointed at the untrimmed hedges. "Looks like the gardener finally gave up, though."

"Who lives here?" Breck asked. "Edward Fucking Scissorhands?"

"Look!" Lisa pressed her face against the window, her mask squeaking as it slid along the glass. "The gate's open."

Breck slid between them. "No way!"

"Guys." Carlos threw up his hands. "A house like this has got to have security, staff—"

"That's what you said about the last one and the one before that," Breck said. "Oh no. We gotta go in there."

Lisa tilted up her mask. Pink hairspray ran in sweaty rivulets down her face. Her big, round eyes, so beautiful and innocent in appearance, stared at him from underneath batting lashes, and he knew he could not deny them.

He sighed and sat up straight. "Fine. But we do this my way. Any sign of danger, we hightail it the hell out of there. Agreed?"

Nods and grunts answered him.

"Okay. Get your masks on." Carlos pulled through the open gate and stopped at an unmanned security box. "That's funny."

"What is?" Lisa asked.

"The security booth. There's no one in it."

Breck laughed. "As my mother used to say, 'Don't look a gift horse in the mouth.'"

Carlos didn't respond. The unmanned booth filled him with unease.

He continued up the drive and circled around to the front steps. No lights came from the house or anywhere else on the estate, yet everything glowed under the bluish light of the waxing moon. No spiders, skeletons, or witches decorated the yard or home. No pumpkins or candy or costumed brats begging for treats could be seen. Carlos could find no reason at all to believe the homeowners were receptive to company. If anyone was at home, they were not expecting any trick or treaters. The few kids they'd seen in the neighborhood probably thought the house's long driveway wasn't worth the effort.

Breck laughed. "Where's their Halloween spirit? Maybe no one's home, and we'll have the place to ourselves."

"I don't like this." Carlos checked the rearview, and his stomach gurgled with the feeling he'd just driven into an ambush. He gripped the wheel a little tighter and checked each window for anything hidden behind pretense, but he wasn't sure exactly what he was looking for.

Breck tapped him in the back of the head. "Man the fuck up already."

The strike was hard enough to stir Carlos's anger but also enough to jump-start his rational thinking. The house wasn't decorated because either its occupants didn't celebrate the holiday, or more likely, given the deserted look of the place, they weren't home to celebrate. He couldn't have asked for better circumstances.

His teeth clenched, and his heart chugged along a little faster. "Samson, check for alarms and cameras while I take the kiddies trick or treating. Everybody out. Quietly."

They got out of the van. Stealthy despite his size, Samson started his circle around the house, peering in each window he passed. Lisa headed toward the front door, a pillowcase under her arm that doubled as a supply cache and candy collector.

As his girlfriend climbed the steps, Carlos grabbed Breck by the arm before he could race her to the doorbell. "Let Lisa go first. Even with that mask on, you can't pass for anything less than a teenager with a receding hairline."

"I know, I know," Breck whined. He shook his arm free and started toward the door. "I'll hang back a bit." Then in a lower tone, he said, "Never lets me have any fun." The giant knife swung at his side.

As Lisa's foot landed on the first of the cathedral-style stone steps, a loud *clunk* and dazzling light froze everyone in their places. Carlos blinked until his eyes adjusted. A spotlight under a second-floor landing illuminated the steps and the drive.

No one moved. No one made a sound. Carlos thought he saw a flicker of orange pass by one of the dark windows to the left of the door, but it disappeared as quickly as it had come, leaving him wondering if it had just been some residual effect of the spotlight's flash.

"Sensor light," Lisa whispered. "I don't hear anyone inside."

Carlos couldn't shake the feeling that something was off, but he couldn't put his finger on it. By all appearances, they'd stumbled upon the Holy Grail of break-ins. That was, if the residents truly weren't home. "Maybe we should just leave it," he said.

"God!" Breck waved his arms with melodramatic exasperation. "You sound like such a pussy."

"I can't see anything inside," Samson said, appearing so suddenly beside Carlos that Carlos's heart jumped. "It's like the windows are tinted or something," he continued, shrugging. "Everything's black. Weird."

"Security?" Carlos asked.

"None I can see."

"No one this rich would leave his house unprotected."

Breck jumped in. "It's not like we're in downtown Detroit here." He spun around, arms out. "This place is old, like at least a century old, before they had things like alarm systems and cameras. I bet the dumb shits didn't put any in because it might ruin the ambiance . . . or whatever."

"Guys," Lisa whined. "Am I ringing the doorbell or not?"

Carlos and Breck simultaneously gave different answers.

Lisa huffed and turned back to the door. She studied it for a moment. "Guys, there's no doorbell."

"Use the knocker thing," Breck said.

A brass knocker in the shape of a gargoyle's head, with cruel eyes and gnashing teeth, sat in the center of the door just over Lisa's pigtails. A thick ring hung from its nostrils. Lisa grabbed it and swung it against the wood.

A dull thud echoed through the still air, then nothing. They waited in silence.

"Should I knock again?" she asked.

"Samson," Carlos said. "Get the crowbar."

Before Samson could take a step toward the van, the door creaked open. A little girl in a wrinkled white nightgown stood behind it, her skin as pale as her clothing. Her feet were bare. She looked to be seven or eight. She rubbed her eyes as if the moonlight were too much for them. Her skin shifted with each rub, loose upon her bones as if she'd recently lost a lot of weight.

"Trick or treat!" Lisa shouted, thrusting her pillowcase out in front of her.

The little girl stared blankly then blinked. Slowly, a grin wormed its way over her lips then full-on excitement as she jumped and clapped. "Oh! Trick or treat! Halloween!" As she looked left then right, her excitement drained. She pouted and cast her eyes downward. "But I don't have any candy."

"That's okay, dear," Lisa said. "Are your parents home?"

"They should be, unless they've gone out for Halloween. They usually bring home candy for us. Sometimes they keep it all for themselves, though."

"Us?" Lisa asked. "Anyone else home?"

"Just me and my brother. He's sick and very little, so I stay home with him." The girl stared at Lisa's pillowcase then at Lisa. "You have candy. Will you give us some?"

Lisa smiled. "Sure."

"Yay!" The little girl curtsied. "I'm Sophie. What's your name?"

"I'm Li—" Lisa cinched her pillowcase shut as the little girl's eyes drifted toward it. "Can we come in?"

"Okay." Sophie ran off into the darkness of the house, leaving the door open behind her.

Breck shrugged. "That was easy."

He started inside, but Carlos again held him back. "No one

gets hurt," he warned. "Particularly not the kids." He pointed at the knife. "So put that thing away."

Breck scowled but obeyed. "Yes, sir."

"Flashlights," Carlos said. "And be ready. The parents may be home."

They entered the house with flashlights drawn and weapons at the ready, as if they were a band of trained soldiers and not a gang of armed criminals. Their beams illuminated old portraits, cobwebbed mantels, and furniture that looked as though it hadn't been dusted in ages. With every other step, what sounded like tiny bones crunched beneath Carlos's boot. When he aimed his beam at the floor, the light repelled skittering black insects that vanished under furniture or into cracks in the floorboards.

The filth reminded him of his home back in the projects. If the outside of the house had looked recently neglected, the inside looked outright forgotten. The place looked unlived in, which didn't seem right if people lived there—at least four of them, according to the girl. *Squatters?* He paused. *Something else?*

He was about to voice his concern when Breck spoke. "I'm no expert, but this shit looks old. And expensive. I bet we could sell it to Ritchie."

Ritchie was Carlos's antique dealer, and he had no qualms with brokering stolen goods. As much as Carlos hated to admit it, Breck was right. Despite the lack of care its owners had shown it, the place was a gold mine. It reeked of wealth and antiquity. "We don't have room in the van for—"

A candelabra-shaped chandelier hummed above as the bulbs it held flickered. At once, they flashed brightly. An explosion of glass followed, plunging them back into darkness.

Carlos's finger jittered on the trigger of his shotgun. He raised the stock under his shoulder.

"My, my," a man called from the next room. He chuckled. "We must really get that fixed, darling. Our guests must think us paupers. Such modern delicacies, necessities of a modern world."

"Keeping up appearances, my love, means keeping up with the times, I'm afraid," a woman answered, tittering as a small flame danced across the pitch-black of the adjacent room.

"So wise you are, my dear," the man answered. "So wise."

One after another, candles illuminated the darker reaches of the next room. In it, Carlos saw a long table made of fine wood, mahogany if he had to guess. Its legs were ornately carved dragons. China so fine that it shimmered in spite of its disuse decorated the mahogany surface. Masterfully crafted chairs circled the table. Something scurried under the edge of a plate.

"Do come in. Come in," the man said, a candle lighting up in his hands as if by magic. "It's been so long since we've had guests. Welcome!"

Carlos didn't move. Samson looked to him for guidance. No one made a sound.

The man stepped closer. He wore a penguin suit, complete with long tails, a frilly shirt, white gloves, and a bow tie. The suit hung from his frame, two sizes too big. He floated over to Lisa, causing her to take a step back. "Forgive me. Where are my manners?"

Carlos's eyes adjusted to the candlelight, which illuminated the room with a dull orange glow. He felt as if he were inside a jack-o'-lantern. Other than the old clothes and the fact that he didn't seem alarmed that four home invaders were standing in his dining room, the man appeared somewhat normal and defenseless. If something was off about him, Carlos couldn't figure out what it was.

Still, goosebumps rose on Carlos's forearms. What felt like a millipede's thousand legs tickled the back of his neck.

"I'm Oliver," the man said, his face even paler than the little girl's. His skin sagged, and white bumps speckled the purple rashes which circled his eyes. In the flickering light, the bumps appeared to be moving.

Oliver waved a hand to his side, and a woman seemed to teleport there. "And this is my wife, Veronica."

Veronica wore a black sequin gown with a tapered fringe that hung to her shins. She'd paired the gown with matching sleeve gloves and a headband which sparkled with diamonds. Lisa stared at them with eyes that sparkled nearly as brightly.

At first glance, Carlos thought Veronica was beautiful—if he didn't look too closely. But when he did, the closer examination revealed similar ailments to those afflicting her husband and child.

Leprosy? Carlos guessed. *We shouldn't be here.*

Together, the husband and wife looked like a couple headed to a 1920's gala. Carlos assumed they were dressed up for a Halloween party. If that was the case, were they leaving the children home alone without a babysitter? No matter how he added it all up, nothing made any sense.

Oliver's eyes met Carlos's stare. "We were heading out for some Halloween mischief, but it appears the party has come to us this year instead, doesn't it, dear?"

Veronica hooked her arm around her husband's. "It does, my love. It does indeed. Aren't they delightful?"

Oliver smacked his lips together. "Delightful, mmm, yes."

Lisa yelped, her hand recoiling. "So cold!"

Carlos hadn't even noticed that Sophie was in the room, much less that she had reached for Lisa's hand. The girl was like a phantom, moving unseen and unheard.

"Ah, I see you've met our precious daughter, Sophie." Oliver puffed out his chest, beaming with pride. "That just leaves our boy, Junior." He swung his arm back.

A toddler sat in a high chair at the far end of the table. A tattered and filthy rag circled his head, covering his eyes. Carlos hadn't noticed the boy before that moment. The child seemed to have materialized out of thin air, possessing an ethereal quality which matched his sister's. Fork in hand, the boy pounded on the table.

"Enough of this," Breck said, unsheathing his knife. He stepped up to Oliver and pressed its point under his neck. The man's skin folded over it like laundry hung out to dry. "Since we're making introductions, let me introduce you to my pointy friend here. Knife meet Oliver. Oliver"—he pressed the point into the man's skin—"meet Knife."

"Delightful!" Oliver's smile broadened. "Aren't they delightful, love?"

"They certainly are, dear," Veronica answered.

Lisa held out her hand. "The headband, *por favor*."

"Oh, this thing?" The woman pulled the headband off. Like strings of glue, the skin beneath it stretched and snapped. Patches of hair hung in matted blotches around the band. A horizontal line of raw red tissue ran across Veronica's forehead.

She handed the band to Lisa. "Go ahead. Try it on." She laughed. "You know, there was a time when I wouldn't have let the likes of you anywhere near my jewels. But our wealth hardly seems as important now as it once did. Still, it has its uses."

"Keeps the electricity running," Oliver said. Then as if realizing his gaff, he laughed. "Oh ho! Guess we forgot to pay that bill, honey."

Lisa backed away, her nose twitching in disgust. It took another second for the rank odor, like that of rotten pork, to reach Carlos's nostrils.

Removing the knife from Oliver's neck, Breck grabbed the headband and tossed it into his pillowcase. "That's a good start. Now, what else you got?"

"I propose a trade." Oliver swiped a palm through the air, his movement so quick and effortless it was hardly noticeable.

Silence.

Then screaming. Breck fell to his knees, his hand covering his right eye. Blood oozed under his palm, running onto his bite mask.

Fast as lightning, little Sophie snatched something from the floor and shoved it into her mouth. Junior began to cry.

"Sophie!" Veronica scolded. "It was our selfishness that got us into this predicament to begin with. You know Junior needs those more than you. Now he'll only have three matching sets to choose from."

"Sorry," Sophie mumbled, her mouth full.

Carlos took in the scene. Breck on the floor, sobbing and convulsing. Sophie licking her lips. The blind kid, cloth gone and empty sockets revealed, wailing and pushing his chair away from the table. Sweating, he pulled his mask off and tossed it onto the floor. The pieces of the puzzle were coming together slowly, yet he had no idea what picture they were forming. He was too horrified to move, too shocked to scream.

Samson recovered first. He raised his gun and put two bullets into Oliver's chest.

The blast sent Oliver staggering back against the wall. He slid down it, ending in a sitting position on the floor.

Veronica pressed her hands against her cheeks, her mouth dropping in awe. "Wonderful!"

"What?" Lisa asked, stepping aimlessly backward, her lips quivering.

"Aren't they marvelous, dear?" Oliver stood and dusted himself off. "One for each of us."

Junior crawled over to Breck, jabbed his stubby thumb and forefinger into the man's remaining eye, and plucked it out cleanly.

Sophie snatched the eyeball from his hand.

"Sophie!" Veronica scolded. "You give that back to your brother right now!"

The ghastly little girl pouted. "But I like the eyes!" Nevertheless, she did as she was told.

Junior took the eye and fitted it into his own empty socket. Carlos gagged as the eye blinked. He tucked his shotgun against his shoulder, not knowing where to aim it.

Sophie knocked her brother aside and lunged at Breck, her mouth opened wide to expose row after row of sharp, needlelike teeth. She sank them into Breck's collar. The man's agony echoed throughout the room.

Samson sprang into action, firing rounds into Sophie's head. Pulpy gore spattered the floor. Veronica leapt toward Samson, but Carlos snap-fired. The shotgun's blast altered the woman's course midair. She crashed down and slid across the floor but quickly sprang back up to her feet.

Examining the massive wound to her stomach, she tsked. "This was my favorite dress."

"Let's go!" Carlos yelled, grabbing Lisa by her elbow.

"What about Breck?" she asked, clearly shell-shocked.

He spun her around and, with a reluctant glance over her shoulder, saw the children devouring a soon-to-be, if not already, dead member of his crew.

"Where are you going?" Oliver called from somewhere behind them as they ran. "You don't have to go. You're welcome here."

Samson reached the door first, but he was still struggling to open it by the time Carlos and Lisa caught up. "It's . . . stuck." He strained.

"Try the lock," Carlos said, turning to cover their backs.

"It's not . . . the goddamn . . . lock."

"Stay back!" Carlos warned as Oliver charged. He blasted the man in the center of his chest. As Carlos reached into his pocket to reload, Veronica was upon him. She grabbed him by the shoulders and tossed him against the wall. As he collapsed, his head hit the floor so hard his vision blurred.

Struggling to stay conscious, he saw Lisa draw a Taser from her bag and fire it at Veronica. Carlos lifted a hand in warning, but he was too late. Sophie sank her teeth into Lisa's calf. The stun gun fell from Lisa's hand, and she followed it, kicking at the girl.

Carlos passed out as the sound of gunfire ceased and the screaming began in earnest.

He awoke to find a familiar face staring down at him. "Lisa?"

The face smiled, exposing rows of needle-sharp teeth. "She's very pretty," Sophie said from behind Lisa's face. She smoothed out a wrinkle and tucked the skin closely around her eyes, hiding the rotting muscle beneath. "I'm lucky to have such a good one to wear."

"Now, now," Veronica admonished as she worked an iron over a board. "We don't play with our food."

Carlos tried to move but found himself tied to a chair. Samson sat bound beside him, still unconscious. Lisa's headless body lay naked and sprawled out on the table. Huge swaths of skin were missing. The smell of sizzling meat beneath the iron made Carlos's stomach roil.

"What are you?" he asked. "Why are you doing this?"

"The Japanese have a name for us," Oliver said, sitting across from Carlos. "But then again, they think we just go around eating corpses, which is so last century."

"Corpses means dead people, Daddy!" Sophie blurted, meat and sinew filling the gaps in her smile.

"That's right, dear." Oliver laughed and leaned forward, propping his elbows on the table. His mouth formed a thin line, and he whispered, "We found a way to outrun death and the hell that awaited us. Unfortunately, it requires . . . replacement parts sometimes. We are so happy the holiday brought us all together."

With a long black scythe of a pinky nail, Oliver cut into his forehead along the hairline. He circled his face, down the jawline, around the chin, then back up the other side. Black blood oozed from the cut, the smell of infection filling the room.

"You see, when you look like this . . . " He peeled off his face and tossed it to Junior, who snatched it up greedily. Maggots wormed their way in and out of Oliver's exposed face, his true face, purple and gray like rotting hamburger. "Let's just say we had to find a way to reinvent ourselves."

Veronica cackled. "A way to blend in."

Oliver stood and walked around the table toward Carlos, larvae falling from his face like rice at a wedding. "My wife is partial to your face. I think it'll serve me well for the next decade or so."

"No!" Carlos begged, squirming and kicking as Oliver's pinky nail dug into his skin and began its circle.

VIGIL

Chad Lutzke

A‍S WE WATCHED for more bodies, Mrs. Ashton handed me a cup of steaming coffee. It was my second cup that morning, this one better than the first. The first was from my own kitchen. From that percolating piece of shit I couldn't bear to get rid of. Helen loved that thing. But I think she'd love Mr. Coffee even more, with its self-brewing timer and controlled temperature plate. I imagined Mrs. Ashton brewed with a Mr. Coffee. I'd have to ask her. Maybe I'd break down and get one after all.

There were a dozen other people standing around, sipping from cups and watching the abandoned house on Summerdale. Just about every surrounding neighbor—except Mrs. Chisholm, her husband still hadn't built that wheelchair ramp, so she sat in her chair at the bay window. I could see her lips moving, as though she was trying to make conversation, though nobody could hear her. Or maybe she was just going on to herself—or to God—about the poor kids being pulled from the ground at 201 Summerdale.

Some of us were sitting. Lance Ludwick had brought card tables and chairs. And if we weren't so afraid of being frowned upon, I'll bet one of us would have broke out a deck of cards. But that's just rude.

Lance sat in his chair, nudged me. "I could smell that last one. Could you?"

"I think I did," I said. I had smelled it. It was foul. But I didn't say a word. I felt like that was rude, too.

Every so often, Ms. Brininstool would wander over to an officer and ask for a body count. Each time she'd come back with a new number, and each time we'd all look at our laps and shake our heads in disbelief. I think every one of us felt a little guilty. We'd all been in that yard, tending to the lawn, planting flowers, and even hanging decorations during Halloween to lessen the eyesore. And not one of us knew about the kids buried there. Yet there we were, walking about on top of them, only a foot or so of earth between us and them.

It was Charlie Sawyer who found the first one. Charlie's dog, Oscar, had passed, and with the new pool and the deck and the patio taking up most of his yard, he carried old Oscar over to 201 and dug a hole. Except he'd only got down less than two feet before the blade of his shovel cut through the leg of a boy he figured had been there the better part of a year.

That's when the cops were called, followed by the coroner. And within an hour the block was lined with news vans, unidentified vehicles with law enforcement pouring out of them, crime labs and a few volunteer firemen to help turn the yard inside out. That's when the neighborhood showed up for an impromptu wake—though a block party is what it more resembled—for whatever poor souls were buried back there.

It wasn't until Ralph Wygant rolled out his barbeque that any of us suspected one of our own responsible for burying those kids. I knew Ralph better than most, and to me the man was just showing off his goods. I knew he'd gotten a bonus at work and with it bought himself a new grill. In poor taste? Yeah, it was. But I don't think Ralph was insensitive as much as he was an idiot. And once the steak drippings hit the charcoal, there was more than one guy standing around it, asking questions about charcoal this and flame-broiled that. For a while the talk was pure testosterone. A grill tends to do that. Mix it with trying to be strong around your woman while bodies are dug up across the street and you'll sprout hair on your chest just standing nearby.

Still, that's when we all started questioning whether or not any of us on the block was capable of such monstrosities—killing kids and burying them. I overhead more than a few people slinging gossip: *What of Mr. Lincoln? Such a night owl he is, always on his porch reading into the wee hours. Or Rick Wenger and how he seemed to hate kids, always cussing at them for cutting through his back lot to get to school. Or about the McPherson boy who came home early from the Army on account of mental problems. Not sure which ones, but enough wrong upstairs that the government didn't trust him, and maybe we shouldn't either.*

As I listened, I made up my mind that you could have found suspicion in any one of us. Hell, even Mrs. Weimer. She spent more time than any of us over at 201, tending to the perennials, shovel in hand.

And Halloween in particular brought everyone out. Every single one of us made our donation to the late-October decor. Jack-o'-lanterns, styrofoam tombstones, and poster board cutouts. The house was covered in and surrounded by them, thanks to us. It was the one time of year that the chipped paint, broken windows and splintered porch added character to the surroundings rather than stand as an ugly wart in the center of mid upper class Hillfield.

Most of the decorations were up. Except the jack-o'-lantern. Like the star atop a Christmas tree, that was saved for last. Someone, normally Mrs. Weimer, would set a jack-o'-lantern on the porch Halloween day, unlit so no kids would mistake the house for one offering sweets, what with the house glowing in holiday spirit and all. The kids around the block knew better, but sometimes we'd get those from several blocks away with overstuffed bags, on a quest to find more than they could handle, wandering into unknown territory. The thought made me wonder if some of those kids found themselves buried under the lawn of 201.

And here it is, Halloween. Go figure.

The odor hit me again. I couldn't ignore this time. It was stronger, like hot garbage filled with Lord knows what. I stood up, covered my mouth, and headed over to Wygant's barbecue grill where he flipped steaks and drank beers with Steve Lincoln.

"I'll be throwing plenty more on, Richard. I had Suz empty the freezer. Looks like it'll be a long day. Help yourself." Ralph pointed to a red cooler sitting in the driveway near some lawn chairs. I knew there was beer inside. Ralph was big on beer. You'd rarely catch him without, but never drunk. I had my suspicions he'd sip on the same one for hours.

It was a little early to be drinking, but I flipped the cooler lid and pulled out a bottle of Stroh's. Steve was never sold on one brand. He'd try a different kind every time, so what could have been in that cooler was anybody's guess. Steve handed me an opener and I popped the lid. "To the kids," I said, then took a gulp.

"What the hell kind of monster does this, Richard?" Steve asked.

"One that's gonna burn for it, I hope."

"You think he's still out there?"

"None of us know a damn thing, and we may never know."

"Some are saying . . . "

"People are talkin' shit." I cut him off. "We all look guilty in one way or another. But I don't think any of us did it. I think this has been a safe place for someone out there to dump these poor kids for a long time now."

"Seems like one of us would have seen somebody," Ralph chimed in.

"We probably did," I said. "Probably chalked it up as one of our own, keeping up the yard."

That day, among the gossip and the wonderment and the worry, was a bond formed between every one of us, black vinyl bags filled with decomposition the catalyst. With each body removed and loaded into a van, our bond strengthened. The horror we experienced that day would stay with us forever, and it'd be nothing anyone else could ever relate to. There'd never be a shoulder to cry on that wasn't one of our own. And through the years we'd meet other people. Some we'd marry or date or have as friends, and we'd have kids and grandkids and so on. And on those days when we're staring out the window, fighting back tears, they'd ask what was wrong, and we'd lie and say nothing. Nothing was wrong.

"I'll never set foot on that land again," Steve said.

"If I do, it'll be to fetch my lights and that's it," Ralph said.

I knew none of us would ever go there again, and the house would sit buried by overgrown shrubs, the grass would turn to meadow until every few months when the city steps in, cuts it and leaves the foot-long blades scattered about. Mrs. Weimer would never return to the perennials and they'd die away, choked out by weeds, wilted by the piss of roaming dogs. And finally, the city would take it all away, tear it down. And there'd only be a scar in the curb where a driveway used to be. An open lot that would never be used to play catch in or have a pick-up game of ball.

A news reporter had just finished with her hair and makeup and whatever the hell else they do before they go live, then had a test run of their spiel, with Ms. Weimer nearby for an interview. It seemed a little premature yet, that reporter standing there all pretty and composed in front of Summerdale's own hell house. Even worse than setting out chairs for the morbidly curious and grilling steaks for the hungry in waiting. After all, she didn't know a thing about our little neighborhood, the history of the house, the time we'd each take to look after the aging, wooden blemish. Yet, there she stood, microphone in hand, not a hair out of place, getting ready to share our corner of the world with those who'd never know otherwise. All for the ratings, the bragging rights—a little game I knew damn well every news station plays, and I suspect if we could look behind that curtain we wouldn't like what we saw one bit. Well, how's that for digressing?

The reporter spent a good many minutes drilling Mrs. Weimer with questions. She answered them the best she could. She talked about our neighborhood being quiet and about our dedication to the house and how things will never be the same. Then at the end, she looked right at the camera and gave the most enduring condolences I've ever heard. Then the reporter was done with her. And I could tell by the look on Mrs. Weimer's face that she'd felt used and regretted talking to them at all. A quick one-night stand with News 41 was all it was.

I found my coffee again, sipped it to disguise the smell of the late-morning Stroh's, and wandered over to where Rick Wenger stood. I caught a glimpse of his eyes. They were large and glassy and held tears that threatened to drop at the first blink, which was not for a good, long minute.

"My yard's an open road now, Richard," he said.

"What do you mean?"

"I mean if these kids wanna cut through my yard on their way to school, then they're welcome to it. I don't know why it bothered me in the first place. They never mean any harm."

I didn't know what to say, so I just patted him on the shoulder.

"Matter of fact. I'm gonna get one of those Neighborhood Watch signs and put it right on the edge of my lawn, maybe another sign, too. One of those they post near schools where the kids cross, maybe stick a light on it. I just want them to feel safe, ya know?"

He rambled on about plans he had for keeping children safe. None of it made much sense. But I knew he meant well so I listened.

Most of the backyard at 201 was hidden by pine trees, people working the scene, and a few tarps set up, though you could still make out piles of dirt next to holes dug and little yellow flags that poked up from the ground in a dozen different spots. Other than that, it was hard to see much of anything. Until they took to digging in the side yard. Then everyone seemed to shift that way, slow like. We kind of slithered there. Even Mrs. Chisholm wheeled herself to another window to get a better view. Every one of us wanted to see more, yet we didn't. We all pretended that we ended up closer by way of chance and not because we're disgusting humans who peer at things that might keep us up at night for years to come. Human beings are curious creatures. If curiosity kills the cat, it gives humans nightmares.

One of the workers dug about a foot or so into the ground before he stopped, then tugged on what looked like cloth. The crowd grew quiet, a few whispers was all. I looked over at Mrs. Weimer who had her head bowed in prayer, her lips moving frantically, her arms wrapped around herself. Mr. and Mrs. Fields were in each other's arms, Mr. Field with a cigarette hanging from his lips, puffing at it fiercely.

The worker with the shovel called someone over to him and they both tugged at the cloth, then started at it with small garden shovels while another man took photographs.

"If that's another one, that'll be fourteen," I could hear Ms. Brininstool say.

I felt sick. Mrs. Weimer started crying. I could hear Rick Wenger make funny noises, like he just couldn't take it anymore and would break down any second. He turned and walked over to Ralph's cooler and grabbed a beer. He opened the bottle with his bare hands and downed the beer all at once. He burped quietly into his hand, then got another beer. This time he drank only half and sat down in one of the chairs, stared at his feet. I saw his body shaking. He was breaking indeed.

The murmur of voices picked up as we waited for what we'd later regret seeing. The men were careful with their shovels and the digging took some time before they called another person over and more photos were taken. A sheet was laid out on the ground, and a body was lifted from the hole. It wasn't a small body and I don't think it'd been dead for long. It was all intact— skin, muscle, fat. And judging by the short brown hair, I think it was a man. Sadly, it was a relief to see the large, bloated figure rather than the small, frail remains we all anticipated. I watched as it stared at the sky with dirt eyes and knew that any minute we'd smell him.

They covered the body with a sheet quick like—for our benefit—then tried to crowd around and block our view while they poked and prodded and took more pictures. I watched two cops talk and point here and there and talk some more, speculating, ruminating. They scratched their heads and their chins, and looked dumbfounded. They knew as much as any of us did. Shit.

Eventually, detectives questioned us, one at a time. They read the same list of questions from a pad of paper and took down notes, but couldn't answer any of our own questions. Mrs. Weimer begged them for any glimmer of hope that this was over, that it wasn't going to be happening anymore. They said they were doing their best, then shooed her away.

I know we all wished we'd have seen the bastard in action. We would have done something. I'd once seen a movie where the victims of a serial killer came back from the dead for revenge, tearing his head from his body while he screamed in horror. I longed to see these victims do the same to their captor, their murderer. The children skinning him alive, shoving bamboo shoots beneath his nails, slicing the corners of his mouth and filling the cuts with salt, feeding his still attached feet to a pool of piranha. I wanted the satisfaction of seeing them get their revenge. A slow one, where the eyes of the killer reflected deep regret and terror. Grim thoughts, yes. My way of coping, I suppose. The idea that our quaint little neighborhood would never been the same disturbed us to no end. It would strip our children of their freedom. They would be inside well before dark, checking in obsessively, playing close by and never alone. It would taint the memories of their past. There would always be the house at 201, the urban legend we'd all wish was never true. There were more victims than just the ones being pulled from the earth.

Hours went by, more coffee made, more steaks on the grill, and someone finally set a deck of cards on the table. Nobody picked them up. We mingled. We comforted. And we smoked more cigarettes than we should have, puffing away our nerves. Rick Wenger hung his head for another few hours, paced himself a worn path in the grass of his front lawn, then went home, filled with the guilt of every time he'd ever yelled at a child for cutting through the same grass he'd just trampled.

Then Mrs. Weimer went home. After they'd retrieved the body from the side yard, unless she was exchanging words with one of us, her prayers never ceased. And by late afternoon, the last worker was gone and 201 was draped with yellow tape, a sash that screamed keep the hell away, nightmares live here now! Eighteen tiny, numbered flags rippled in the wind—vinyl tombstones marking empty graves that should never have been.

I helped Lance fold the chairs and Ralph with cleaning up, then we all went home. And those of us with kids put on faux smiles, pretending the day hadn't been filled with darkness, that it'd been joyous, like every other Halloween. We helped the young ones with their costumes, taking every moment in, treasuring their youthful smiles and innocence, vowing to always keep them safe. Tonight and every night.

As I led my own children outside, treat bags in hand, the timer Ralph had set on the string of lights at 201 went on and the house turned purple. Then orange. Then purple. A colorful heartbeat where no life dwelled. The little flags and the crime-scene tape glowed green under the lights, and the sheeted ghosts hung just last week by my own hand swayed in the breeze.

And then, Mrs. Weimer walked down her driveway and toward 201, a large pumpkin in her arms. It was lit. With a swift flick of her wrist, she cut through the tape and the flimsy barricade disappeared. She made her way to the porch steps and set the pumpkin down. Its face smiled with an exaggerated grin, unevenly spaced teeth. Large moon eyes.

Feet scuffed the road to my left. Rick Wenger held his own pumpkin, its face growing bright. He carried it, sobbing, to the porch and set it on the steps alongside Mrs. Weimer's. Down the street I caught sight of three more glowing faces bobbing down the street toward 201. Lance, the McPherson boy, and Mrs. Ashton joined the others and added their pumpkins to the growing vigil. If there were appropriately universal Halloween carols to be sung at a time like this, I suppose they would have been heard right then by everyone on the block.

I grabbed my own jack-o'-lantern, my child with his own, and we carried them, lit. As we approached the driveway at 201, I could hear the squeak of Mrs. Chisholm's wheelchair, in her lap a glowing pumpkin, her husband pushing from behind.

Every person there during the day showed up that night to pay respects the one way they knew how, to continue hiding the ugly that was 201. And until the city one day levels the house and leaves behind an empty field, we'll continue keeping it alive.

Especially on Halloween.

MR. IMPOSSIBLE

Gregor Xane

MONKEY CREPT DOWN the road. Suspiciously slow. I would've said something, but I've never known shit about cars or driving. Plus, we were stoned, and I was glad he was paying attention to what he was doing.

I met Monkey back in high school, in a class called Decisions. It really was a class about making decisions. I'm not sure why they waited until freshman year to bother to teach people about such things. Monkey sat in the back of the room next to a girl with braces who was also a champion kickboxer. Monkey was practically her servant.

No, Monkey didn't marry the kickboxer. They never even dated. I'm not sure why I brought her up.

On this Halloween night, on our way to Mr. Impossible's place, we were old friends. Old friends getting older. Both in our early thirties, unmarried. I was unemployed. Monkey worked in an office. Well, mostly he just pretended to work. Every job he ever had, he did his very best to do very little.

I used to think he was lazy.

Now, I think he may have been rightfully sticking it to the man. Kind of like how I used to think he was a mingy freak, and now I'd say he's always been responsible with his money.

Monkey doesn't look like a freak. We used to say he did

though. When we were teenagers. We used to say he looked like a monkey. We were a bunch of assholes who thought we were funny.

But I don't think Monkey thought it was funny.

I know he didn't.

No one calls him Monkey anymore. We haven't in years. But I still did, back then, when we went to Mr. Impossible's place for the Halloween block party. We called him Monkey, and since we were adults, we even sometimes called him Steve.

I didn't call him Steve all that much, though. And I know he was Monkey that night, for sure.

He was even dressed like a monkey. Furry body suit with a tail. Floppy shoes that looked like monkey feet.

He didn't wear a mask.

That was the joke.

But I knew he didn't think this was funny, either. He'd worn the monkey suit before, and he mocked anyone who even mentioned his costume.

"Oh, yeah. Ha, ha, ha. Yep. I'm dressed as a monkey," he'd say with a condescending disdain. That costume became his litmus test.

I never said Steve wasn't a weird fucker.

I mean Monkey.

Monkey dressed as a monkey that night, and I wore a wrestling singlet. I was not in good shape and looked like an idiot. But I didn't care. At least I didn't care when Steve picked me up—I'd started drinking an hour before—but once we were higher than shit, I felt self-conscious about it.

My mouth dried out, and I had difficulty swallowing. We had nothing to drink in the car, aside from beer and bourbon, and we weren't going to break the seals. We were, after all, on the border of becoming responsible grown-ups.

"Fuck," I said.

"What?" Monkey said.

"I need something to drink."

"Cottonmouth?"

"Bad."

"Me, too."

I never said Monkey and I were brilliant conversationalists.

"I hope he's got something to drink," I said.

"We've got shit," Monkey said.

"That's not what I mean."

"I'm sure he's got water."

"I mean, like pop."

"Pop?"

"Soda."

"Ask him."

"I will."

"He'll probably have some cougar piss."

"He might."

"He is Mr. Impossible."

And he was. Back in the day, Mr. Impossible loved to drop acid and run for miles. He'd drop acid and go rock climbing. He'd drop acid before attending Sunday mass with his grandparents. He loved to drop acid and solve chemistry problems for fun. Mr. Impossible just loved to drop acid.

I'm pretty sure he doesn't do that anymore. And I doubt he did the night of the Halloween block party. I don't think he'd do it around his kids. But with Mr. Impossible . . .

The Impossible One graduated high school with Monkey and me. His son, Chapman, born in the summer between our freshman and sophomore years, was seventeen the night of the Halloween party. Everyone called him Chap. Chap's mom was a girl Mr. Impossible hooked up with at a Christian youth retreat. I don't even know who she is or if she's even still alive. No one talks about her. And it's none of my business.

Sandy, that's Mrs. Impossible, has been Chap's step-mom since he was maybe eight or nine years old. He calls her Mom, not Sandy. And he doesn't say 'my step-mom' when he talks about her when she's not around.

Chapman is a shitload of trouble, and most everything that happened that night was Chapman's fault.

No, everything was.

But back to his dad, Mr. Impossible. After graduating high school, he went to college, did drugs, jumped off bridges, did more drugs, ran triathlons, and cooked up illegal experimental pharmaceuticals in his garage, the whole time earning his master's in chemistry.

He accomplished all this as a single dad.

He became a pharmacist and got married to another pharmacist (that's Sandy). When they returned from their honeymoon, they became researchers for GorKor, the world's largest pharmaceutical multinational corporation. All the while, Mr. Impossible was smoking weed, tripping balls, and throwing together insane chemical cocktails in his free time.

And I forgot to mention that somewhere in there he'd also become a world-class snowboarder.

We called him Mr. Impossible for a reason.

"What's he dressing as, do you know?" Monkey asked.

"I never talked to him."

Monkey saw Mr. Impossible more often than I did. They both lived in the same metropolitan area. I still lived in Medium, Ohio. Our home town. With my parents. In their basement.

I know what you're thinking, and you're probably right.

Lazy.

But this story isn't about me. It's about Halloween with Mr. Impossible.

And Monkey.

When Monkey pulled into the subdivision, it was dark, and we could see a halo of light over Mr. Impossible's block.

I'd never been to this Halloween thing before. Monkey had. A couple of times. He claimed it was great.

I don't like crowds, but I liked the idea of getting fucked up and looking at people in costumes.

"Do a lot of people dress up for this thing?" I asked.

"Oh, yeah. Lots of people. But mostly the kids."

"And there's a fireworks show?"

"Yeah. Neighborhood backs up to Maedall Park."

"I've never heard of anyone ever shooting off fireworks at a Halloween thing."

"That's where they set off the Fourth of July fireworks."

"Where?"

"Maedall Park. But this is nothing compared to that."

"I wouldn't think so."

"Not even half the size. Mr. Impossible pays for it."

"Of course he does."

"Well, he puts in on it, I think."

"Either way."

"You think his kids will be there?"

"Billy and Betsy will be trick or treating, I'm sure."

When we were in school together, we didn't want to be around our friends' parents when we were high, as grown-ups, we didn't want to be high around their kids.

"What about Chap? You think he'll be there?" Monkey asked.

"I hope not."

"I guess he's all right."

"He's always asking me to spot him some weed. It's like some dumb way of trying to cover up for the fact that his dad's growing."

"That's what I think, too. I don't mind that as much as the throwing up."

"Yeah, he can't drink. And when he does, he wants to fuck with me. Especially when he thinks I'm high."

"Don't you have eye drops?"

"Yeah."

"Well, use them."

"I do. I'm just telling you what he does."

"I know what he does."

"I hope he's not there."

"Me, too."

"He will be."

"I know."

"I mean, why would you go get high with your friends if your dad was Mr. Impossible and you could get high with him?"

"Exactly. He'll be there."

"Fuck."

"What?"

"Chap."

"Oh. Right."

The neighborhood, a circuit of cul-de-sacs, had a single entrance, and two sawhorses and a cop car blocked it off.

We rolled past. Monkey didn't turn his head to look at the cops standing outside their cruiser holding big plastic pumpkins filled with candy. If he looked at them, they'd notice him. They'd know he was high and take up pursuit. It was much safer to pretend they weren't there.

"Fuck the police," Monkey said—after we were more than a block away—with the windows rolled up.

Monkey parked, and we made sure we had everything we needed. Cigarettes. Rolling papers and weed tucked in the bottoms of our socks. Lighters (we both carried more than one). Beer and bourbon.

"Wait," Monkey said.

"Wait for what?"

"We don't have a bag for this stuff."

"So?"

"Don't you have to carry alcoholic beverages in a bag?"

"No."

"I think it's a law."

"We don't have open containers."

"I don't think it matters."

"It's a block party. Didn't you say there were kegs and shit?"

"Yeah, but still. We'll be carrying this outside the fences."

"Fences? What fences?"

"The barriers."

"Barriers?"

"You know what I'm talking about. We'll be outside the zone."

"The zone?"

"The zone in which alcohol's allowed out on the streets."

"I don't think they call it a zone."

"You know what I mean, man. And you can't carry bottles of beer around either. Nothing with a label. It's got to be in an opaque plastic cup, too, I'm pretty sure."

"You're high." I said.

Monkey agreed. He checked to make sure the windows were rolled up. He rooted around in his fanny pack, zipped it up, patted it a couple times and said, "What's that smell?"

I sniffed. "Something's burning."

"Shit," Monkey said. "You're on fire."

I jumped. "What?"

"Your dick's on fire!"

Smoke curled up from my crotch into my face. I made a series of embarrassing noises and jumped out of the car. I danced in the grass, beating myself in the groin, whimpering and dancing like an idiot, less than a hundred yards from where the police cruiser was parked.

"Stop," Monkey said. "I'm sure you're all right now." He looked at the police car, then back at me, and frowned.

"Can you see a hole?" I said, rubbing both hands over my crotch.

"Stop that," Monkey said. "Let me see." He crouched down in front of me and had a look. "Fuck," he said, laughing.

"What?"

"That's where that cherry went. You burnt a big-ass hole in your leotard."

"Singlet."

"Whatever."

I felt around again, and it took me a moment to find it: an almost perfectly round hole about the size of a quarter. I could feel the cotton of my red jock strap underneath. "I'm all right," I said and rapped my knuckles twice on the cup I'd worn out of self-consciousness.

I looked up and saw the cop. Just one officer hung around the cruiser then. He was staring at us.

"Monkey," I said. "You better get up. That cop thinks you're giving me a blow job."

Monkey shot up, turned, looked around on the ground, crouched down again, ran his fingers through the grass. Then he dropped to his hands and knees and crawled in a circle.

"What the hell are you doing?" I asked.

Monkey stood and waved his car keys high over his head and shook them in my face.

"What the fuck?" I asked.

"I didn't want that cop to think I was blowing you, man," Monkey explained. "So I made it look like I was searching for my car keys."

"I think you overdid it."

"I don't think so."

"You just made it look like you dropped your keys while you were blowing me."

"Fuck you."

"All right. But I'll need about an hour or so refractory period after that sweet BJ."

Monkey started off toward the cop car. He seemed to be walking way too slow. I figured he was trying to give the impression that we were in no hurry to get past the police. But he was overcompensating. I kept pace with him, and I felt like the cop was thinking we both might have some developmental challenges. Monkey kept his eyes on the sidewalk, and I kept my head turned toward the flashing lights coming from the Halloween block party.

When we approached the entrance, the police officer was leaning against his car, arms folded, looking down at his feet, bored. He didn't give two shits about us. His plastic jack-o'-lantern was on the roof of the car.

"You think we smell?" Monkey whispered.

"Dude, shut up," I said. I don't think we were close enough for the cop to hear us, but we were trying to be inconspicuous.

When we arrived at Mr. Impossible's subdivision, we stayed as far away from the cop car as we could and looked down the street. It was mostly empty. The next cross street was where the action started. The place was packed with people in costumes. Parents held plastic cups and the hands of kids clutching trick or treat buckets and bags.

A teenage couple walked toward the party on the side of the street opposite Monkey and me. They weren't wearing costumes. Too cool, I guess.

We were about to turn the corner and head down into the crowd when a kid ripped free from his mother's grasp and sprinted up the street toward us. The kid wore a black jumpsuit, black sneakers with bright white lightning bolts on the sides, and a gas mask. He waved a crowbar over his head.

"What the hell?" I said.

"Wow," Monkey said. "That's a great Kid Crowbar costume."

"Who's Kid Crowbar?" I asked, but before Monkey could answer, the kid climbed up the back of the police cruiser and screamed at the cop. I'd assumed it was a boy in the costume, but after hearing the kid's voice, I wasn't so sure.

The kid raised his crowbar and said, "Stop, police!"

The police officer laughed, took a step back from his vehicle, held up his hands and said, "Funny, kid. But that's enough. Get down from the vehicle now, please."

"You have the right to remain silent!" Kid Crowbar said.

The cop waved to the kid's mom, who was running toward him in high heels. She looked like an accountant type who dressed up in a skirt and heels once a year.

She wasn't good in heels.

The cop shouldn't have looked away because Kid Crowbar wasn't messing around. He reared back and whacked his crowbar against the side of that police officer's head.

The officer's hat flew off. And the crowbar snapped in two.

The officer staggered and felt all over his scalp.

The crowbar had been a plastic toy. If it had been the real deal that cop would have been dead.

The kid's mother left her shoes behind and ran to her child.

"Holy shit," Monkey said.

The kid jumped from the trunk of the car and kicked the police officer in the neck.

The cop stumbled again, but didn't fall. "Son-of-a-bitch," he said.

Kid Crowbar fell to the pavement and wailed, his arm trapped beneath him. It had to be broken, the way the kid was screaming.

Then the kid's mother was there. "Ryan," she cried. "Ryan, what the hell has gotten into you?"

Ryan? I still didn't know if Kid Crowbar was a boy or a girl. I guess it didn't matter. I didn't want to mess with that kid.

The mom scooped her kid up, but despite his injured arm—it was obviously broken, bent at a wrong angle—the kid fought to get free, so he could resume his attack on the officer.

"We enforce the law now!" the kid screamed. "We'll liquidate you. We'll liquidate all of BizCorp's assets!"

"Jesus, lady." The cop dabbed at a cut on his forehead. His fingers came away bloody. "Maybe you shouldn't use the boob tube as a babysitter."

"Don't you tell me how to raise my child! Who the fuck do you think you are?"

The cop raised his hands in surrender. "Take it easy. I was just joking."

"No, you weren't."

"Hey, your kid just clocked me. Give me a break."

"Your law is crime," the kid said through clenched teeth. "Your justice is tyranny."

"Ma'am, do you have meds this kid can take?"

"He's not on any medication."

Ryan was a boy! I kind of figured that all along.

"Then, ma'am," the officer said, "no offense, but maybe you should—"

"Maybe you should shut the fuck up," the kid's mom said. "Can't you see he's hurt?"

The cop stepped closer, leaned in, not too close. He had his hand on his holster. "Shit, that arm looks bad. I'm calling an ambulance."

"No," the woman said. "You've done enough." She stomped off with her boy hugged close to her chest, and Kid Crowbar wouldn't stop screaming, "We're coming for you! Every last one of you. We see you in your uniforms. Easy targets. Every last one!"

"Ma'am," the cop called after her. "I'm not sure that's such a good idea."

"Fuck off," she said. "Fuck right the fuck off!"

The cop shrugged, squatted, snatched his hat off the ground and dusted if off. When he stood and donned the hat again, he noticed us standing there like spooked rabbits, and said, "What are you two stoners staring at?"

We didn't move. We didn't answer. We were petrified little bunny rabbits.

He shook his head and waved us on. "Go on. Get the fuck out of my face."

We didn't need to be told twice.

I don't like crowds, especially when I'm high, but disappearing into the throng of bodies after that scene felt great, like a return to the warren and the reassuring safety of a hundred warm bunny bodies huddled all around us.

"What just happened?" Monkey asked.

"Who is Kid Crowbar?" I asked.

"What do you mean, who is Kid Crowbar? Oh, that's right, you don't have a TV."

"Well?"

"He's a cartoon character. Pretty popular."

"What the hell's it about?"

"I don't know. I don't watch it. It's for kids."

"You watch Belly Ape."

"Belly Ape's different."

He was right. Belly Ape was different.

We pressed through the crowd, checking out the costumes. I've got a thing for ladies in sexy cat outfits, but I didn't see any. I saw plenty of people dressed like vampires and zombies. Lots and lots of zombies.

Zombies will never die.

Most of the kids wore costumes I didn't recognize, and I figured they were like Kid Crowbar, characters from current children's shows I'd never heard of. For the first time in years, I kind of regretted not having a television. I liked knowing about cartoons and superheroes. Some kids wore classic costumes. Robots made of cardboard boxes and aluminum foil. Ghosts. Vampires and vampire hunters. Werewolves. Mummies and pirates. Wizards and firefighters. Army men and princesses. Barbarians and priests.

Who lets their child dress up as a priest?

The teenagers and parents were mostly not dressed up. But there were enough wearing costumes for me not to get indignant about it. Many people were just dressed in black, wearing masks. Ghouls and politicians. Melting madmen. Screaming women with axes lodged in their foreheads. Burn victims. More zombies. And cartoon character heads that, in 3D, just looked creepy. I saw squid masks and shark masks. Even a cockroach mask and a microwave oven mask with the guy's head lit up and cooking inside. There were demons and drag queens. Medusas and auto mechanics. Frog men and jungle queens and everything in between.

Everyone seemed to be having a great time. I'd calmed down a little from the encounter with the cop and was feeling the negative effects of the crowd pressing in all around me. The stale beer smell, the body odor, the occasional fart, the bad breath, people coughing next to me, brushing up against a sweaty arm. People laughing right next to my ear. People shouting something stupid that was supposed to be funny.

I imagined getting stampeded, trampled to death by hundreds of costumed assholes and dying in a pool of blood on the street, staring into the blank eyes of a discarded, smiling Lolli Tuesday mask.

"Do kids still watch Lolli Tuesday?" I asked Monkey.

"What the hell are you talking about?"

"Lolli Tuesday."

"Why?"

"Is that creepy-ass shit still on?"

"Why?"

"Just curious."

"I don't think it's on anymore."

"Do you know where we're going?"

"Yeah."

"Are you sure?"

"Yeah, it's right up there." Monkey pointed to a flashing neon sign mounted on the side of one big-ass house. The neon sign flashed three images; a smiling jack-o'-lantern with spindly arms and legs, with one hand held over his head in a friendly wave, the other hidden behind his back; a surprised jack-o'-lantern who has just pulled a meat cleaver from behind his back; a frowning jack-o'-lantern who has just sliced his own head open with said meat cleaver.

"That's new," Monkey said, pointing at the neon sign.

"I wonder how much that thing cost."

"He probably rented it."

"Still."

Monkey and I wouldn't admit it, but we were bums, jealous of Mr. Impossible's affluence.

The crowd pressed tighter around us, and we could barely squeeze through the bodies. People laughed and cheered, some cried out in alarm.

"What the hell is going on?" I asked.

136

Taller than me, Monkey looked over the heads of the crowd and laughed. "Holy fuck!"

"What is it?"

"Some kid in a cape is running on top of everybody."

"What do you mean?"

"He's running on top of the crowd. Oh, shit."

"What?" I asked. "What's happening?"

"There are two of them. Running after each other, man."

I jumped up to see what he was talking about, and it took me a few jumps to put a complete picture together. A kid dressed in spiky black body armor with a sinister-looking helmet and face mask ran across the heads and shoulders of the tightly packed crowd. People screamed at him, reached up to grab him, but he was too quick. He stumbled and rolled once, and got right back up, launching himself forward with a boot to some fat goblin's face.

Coming up behind the kid in the spiky body armor was another kid in a purple jumpsuit, purple domino mask, and a purple cape trailing off behind him. He had a tougher time making it across the crowd because it had thinned out in the spiky body armor kid's wake. This purple superhero had to cross gaps in the crowd with leaps and bounds. He was in hot pursuit of the bad guy, and he wasn't slowing down for anything.

On my fourth or fifth jump, I saw the spiky body armor kid was right up on us, then one of his black boots drove down hard into Monkey's shoulder and the other boot kicked him in the face. But, before Monkey could react, the kid was gone.

Monkey turned toward me, blood dripped from his eyebrow. "What the fuck?" he said. His voice was shaky, and I could tell he was trying not to cry.

"Are you all right?" I asked.

But before Steve could answer, a purple boot stomped down on his neck and the little purple hero pushed off and propelled himself over my head to land somewhere in the sea of bodies behind me.

It was kind of cool watching that little kid in that purple superhero costume flying over me with his cape waving in the night sky.

But I'd never tell Monkey that.

The kid in purple had pushed off Monkey and drove him backward into the arms of a large person, presumably a man, dressed like a grizzly bear in a tutu. Grizzly held Monkey up under the armpits. Monkey appeared to have been knocked out cold, but he soon recovered and pushed himself out of Grizzly's arms in a manner that seemed a bit ungrateful.

But Grizzly didn't seem to notice, and, without saying a word, he patted Monkey on the shoulder consolingly, turned away, and slung his arm around a petite brunette dressed like a big game hunter.

I grabbed Monkey's arm and asked him if he was all right.

He nodded, turned around, and pushed through the crowd. I figured he was hurting more than he wanted to let on.

I kept close behind him and offered apologetic shrugs to anyone who turned around to scowl at us.

We made it about another thirty yards and stopped at the edge of a clearing in the crowd. Monkey blocked my view, and he wasn't moving. Men laughed and shouted, and women screamed, and I heard a lot of 'holy shits' and 'what the fucks.' Then a kid growling, and another kid screaming.

"Monkey?" I said, trying to push forward, but he was pushing back into me. Hard.

"Holy fuck," he said. "Jesus Christ!" He pushed back even harder, turned, and caught me in the gut with his elbow, knocking the wind out of me, then he was behind me, and I was facing the clearing.

A man dressed as a five-star general crouched beside a boy

dressed in camouflage. An orange plastic assault rifle lay at the boy's side. The kid's face was covered with blood. Another child, a girl dressed like a zombie, snarled in the clearing. Fresh blood coated the front of her ragged pants suit and clotted on her face. Two women dressed like nuns held her arms, but the girl kicked and growled and moaned, doing her best to escape their grasp and resume her attack on the boy in combat fatigues.

Or at least that's what I thought was going on. And I guessed that a few moments before a circle had formed around these two kids and a bunch of assholes had been cheering them on as they fought each other. They probably thought it was cute. They likely let it go a little long because it was a boy versus a girl.

So funny.

So cute.

It's all fun and games until someone gets hurt.

My dad's favorite phrase.

Speaking of dads. The general's cell phone lit up his face. This guy was likely the army kid's father, and he was probably calling an ambulance.

I didn't want to stick around. The parents might start fighting next, and I didn't want to get in the middle of that.

Violence and weed just don't go together.

I turned away, in the mood for the booze I held clutched in my fist. I even thought about twisting it open and taking a swig right there. But I didn't. And I didn't see Monkey anywhere.

It didn't matter. All I needed to do was walk toward the happy jack-o'-lantern chopping a meat cleaver into its own forehead.

The crowd got rowdier after witnessing a little kid-on-kid blood sport. I passed teenagers sucking each other's faces like it was the end of the world, hands down each other's pants, grinding hips. A man held both of his kids in a head lock, one under each arm. An old woman dragged a hogtied toddler behind her. Two soccer moms grabbed my ass.

I pushed through a group of about eight adults in lame white bedsheet ghost costumes and stumbled onto the sidewalk in front of Mr. Impossible's house.

Man, I was high as fuck—marijuana mixed with adrenaline.

Monkey stood among a gathering of costumed children on the porch and looked like a dejected overgrown kid himself, a mentally challenged adult who doesn't understand that he's too old to go out trick or treating with the neighbor kids.

I walked to the bottom of the porch steps—there wasn't any room on the stoop. "Steve?" He didn't look like he was in any mood to be called Monkey. "You been out here waiting long?"

Steve didn't answer. A girl in a Dalmatian costume turned and gave me a dirty look. A boy dressed in a three-piece suit said, "We runged the doorbell about eight times."

A boy in a saggy pumpkin costume pressed the doorbell, again.

"Try knocking," I said.

Saggy Pumpkin took this as his cue to beat the shit out of the door with both fists.

"That's probably good," I said, and the kid started kicking the door. I just let him go at it.

"I don't think anyone's home," a woman's voice called from the sidewalk. She was probably chaperoning the band of beggars. "Come on now."

Saggy Pumpkin stopped banging and kicking, turned around, and looked extra saggy. He pushed through the other kids on the porch, knocking a toddler dressed like a cowgirl into a bush, and stomped out to the sidewalk next to his mother. She reprimanded him for knocking the girl off the porch but didn't check to see if the girl was all right. She grabbed Saggy Pumpkin's hand and dragged him off to the next house.

The cowgirl didn't seem put out by getting knocked into the bushes. She just laid there, eyes wide and smiling. It was kind of spooky.

Then the front door opened and Mr. Impossible was standing there in a candlelit foyer. He wore an orange prison jumpsuit and held a black witch's cauldron cradled in both arms. He looked at Monkey and I and said, "Aren't you two a bit old to be out trick or treating?"

Monkey didn't answer.

I told him to hand over the candy. He laughed, gave Monkey a concerned look, then leaned over to let the kids reach into the cauldron and grab their treats. Once the kids cleared off the porch, I pointed to the cowgirl still lying in the bush, still smiling up at the stars.

Mr. Impossible sauntered out onto the porch, passed the cauldron to Monkey, and looked down at the girl, hands on his hips. "Gracie, is that you?"

The girl giggled.

"Why are you napping in my bush?"

"I'm not napping," the girl said. "Those boys pushed me."

Mr. Impossible turned and glared at us. "These boys?"

"Those aren't boys," Gracie said.

"You're right," Mr. Impossible said. "They're not. I don't know what they are."

"One's a monkey," Gracie said.

Mr. Impossible got a chuckle out of that.

Steve didn't.

"Well, Gracie." Mr. Impossible reached into the cauldron and grabbed a handful of candy. "You want some homemade Halloween buckeyes?"

The girl's eyes lit up. "Yes!" She moved her arms and legs in a way that reminded me of a wind-up doll that's fallen over.

"You need some help?" I asked the girl.

She shook her head and kept on moving her arms and legs.

I offered her my hand. She turned her head away as if it were Brussels sprouts.

"It's all right, Gracie," Mr. Impossible said.

"Fine," Gracie said. She grabbed my hand, and I pulled her up and to her feet. It was like lifting a balloon.

"There you go," I said.

Once she was upright, she snatched her hand away and held it out along with her other one, forming a bowl for Mr. Impossible to fill up with Halloween buckeyes.

She picked up her bag and plopped the candy inside and ran off without a 'thank you.'

"Happy Halloween," Mr. Impossible called after her.

Gracie ran to the next porch and stood behind the gang of waiting kids, ready for more sugary goodness.

"How the hell are you guys doing?" Mr. Impossible asked.

I pointed at Monkey.

Mr. Impossible grabbed Monkey by the shoulders. "What the hell happened to you?"

Monkey looked away. "Kid stomped on me."

Mr. Impossible laughed. "What?"

"Yeah," I said. "It was crazy. These two kids, maybe five or six years old, were running on top of the crowd. Steve got stomped."

"Cool. Sounds like something I would have done as a kid." Mr. Impossible looked at the crowded streets, then back at Monkey. "You need a little Band-Aid or something?"

"No," Monkey said, pouting. "I don't need a little Band-Aid."

"Well, then stop acting like a pussy and come inside." Mr. Impossible slapped Monkey on the chest. "Let's go."

We followed Mr. Impossible into his big-ass house. I'd never been there before. The foyer was huge. A winding staircase led up to an open second-story landing. Aside from the Halloween decorations, there wasn't much in the way of wall hangings or adornments. This place, like all his previous houses, looked like a model home.

"Monk," Mr. Impossible said. "Looks like you need to crack open one of those beers and chug the fuck out of it."

"Where's the fridge?" Monkey asked.

"Dude, you need to lighten up," Mr. Impossible said.

Monkey touched the cut over his eye and frowned.

"All right, come on." Mr. Impossible waved for us to follow him.

"What about the buckeyes?" I asked.

"You guys want one?" Mr. Impossible asked.

"I can't eat peanut butter," Monkey said.

"You allergic?" Mr. Impossible asked.

"No," Monkey said. "Just don't like it."

"How about you?" Mr. Impossible looked at me.

"I don't like chocolate," I said.

"Really?" Mr. Impossible raised his eyebrows.

"Really," I said.

"That's not right."

"That's what I hear."

"Then why are you asking about the buckeyes?"

"Who's going to hand them out to the trick or treaters?"

"Right. I almost forgot. I got started with the celebrating a couple hours ago." Mr. Impossible picked up the cauldron, flipped a sign taped to the lip so it faced outward. The sign read: TAKE ONE.

He placed the cauldron on the front porch and closed the door.

"You think they'll take just one?" Monkey said.

"No way. And I don't care."

We walked up the winding staircase, down a long hallway to his office. Built-in bookshelves were filled with textbooks and academic journals. Mr. Impossible wasn't a big fiction reader. He had the periodic table of elements hung on one wall and on another wall there was a poster of some naked supermodel sitting on a toilet, reading a book about quantum physics. The book covered up her tits.

Mr. Impossible opened what I thought was a closet door and revealed a flight of stairs. We climbed the stairs into an expansive third floor recreation room lit with lava lamps, neon beer signs, and strings of Christmas lights. A massive television hung on one wall. Along the wall opposite was a wet bar and shelves lined with booze and collectible beers. There was a pool table, a foosball table, a dart board, a workout bench, and some free weights. A couch shaped like the letter C sat facing the TV, along with two comfy looking recliners. A card table stood in the middle of the room with four metal folding chairs. On the card table sat a plastic tray with a pile of weed on it and some rolling papers. Next to the tray was one of those fancy root beers that come in a glass bottle. The hand wrapped around the root beer belonged to Mr. Impossible's son, Chapman.

Chapman was tall and thin and handsome, which was weird, because his dad was short and not good looking. He wasn't ugly. Mr. Impossible looked like what a squirrel would look like after a fairy godmother transformed it into a human being.

Maybe the kid took after his biological mom? I don't know.

Oh, and Chapman's teeth are all perfectly straight and white. Mr. Impossible's are not, and we'll just leave it at that.

"Hey, Chap," I said. "How's it going?"

Chap nodded, smirked, and returned his attention to his phone.

Mr. Impossible rolled his eyes and said, "Don't mind him. He's forgotten all the social skills he learned in childhood." He placed both hands on the bar and looked Monkey in the eye. "I think you need a shot."

"Yeah, he really does." I grabbed a nearby shot glass that

looked fairly clean, set my bourbon on the bar top, broke the seal, and poured a hearty dose. "Here you go, Steve." I slid the shot toward him.

Monkey frowned.

"Suit yourself," I said, and slammed the shot. It was mid-shelf shit and burned going down, but I didn't mind. It was what I was used to.

"I don't know how you do it," Mr. Impossible said, shaking his head at my bottle. "Greene Angry? I haven't had that since college."

"I like it," Chap said.

Everyone ignored this.

"Monkey," Mr. Impossible said, "you want a swig of Gainsail Black?"

Monkey's eyes lit up. "Shit, yes, I do."

Neither Monkey nor I could have afforded the Gainsail. That was for celebrities and Internet billionaires.

Mr. Impossible produced a sparkling clean shot glass and poured. He smiled and pushed it across the bar.

Monkey slammed it and gasped. "Ah," he said. "Ahhhhh!"

"Good shit, huh?" Mr. Impossible said.

Monkey coughed.

Mr. Impossible turned and asked me, "Want one?"

"Why not?"

He poured another shot, and I drained it in two gulps. I wanted to savor it. The shit was delicious. Not go-into-debt-to-drink-it delicious, but damn good.

"That's some fine, fine shit," I said.

"Oh, yeah," Mr. Impossible said. "It's great to see you guys. Let's get high."

And with that we started in with the small talk and caught up on where we worked or didn't work, where Mr. Impossible went on vacation, music, and movies, and other sundry bullshit. Mr. Impossible rolled a giant joint using two rolling papers. He took his sweet time lighting it up, and Monkey kept his eyes trained on that thing like a dog waiting for a Bacon Chewz.

Mr. Impossible noticed this and handed the joint to me first just to mess with the Monkey.

I took my time with it, too, even made a conscious effort to strike up a conversation while holding the burning thing in my hand. "Hey, Mr. Impossible, you know anything about Captain Crowbar?"

"Huh?" Mr. Impossible said.

I poked the joint toward Monkey but didn't hand it to him — a real asshole move, I know — and said, "Steve says it's some kind of Saturday morning cartoon."

"Kids don't watch cartoons on Saturday mornings anymore," Mr. Impossible said.

"When do they watch them then?" I asked.

"Anytime they want," Chapman chimed in.

"Captain Crowbar?" Mr. Impossible drummed his fingers on the bar top and looked up and to the right, biting his lip. He shook his head. "Never heard of it."

"It's *Kid* Crowbar," Chapman said.

I turned to Chapman. "Oh, you know what it is?"

Chapman shrugged. This style of shrug said 'yes.'

"What's it about?" I asked.

"Can I get a hit off that?" Monkey asked, pointing to the joint still blazing in my hand.

"Oh, yeah, sorry." I handed it over, then turned back to Chapman. "So, what's it about?"

"Kid Crowbar?" Chapman said, his fingers pinching on his phone's screen. I was too far away to see what he was looking at.

"Yeah, what's the deal? We saw a kid dressed like him, going absolutely batshit."

"The show's set in a future totalitarian state," Chapman said, "and all the adults are corrupt. The only good people left are the

146

kids. Kid Crowbar's a freedom fighter who leads a band of rebels. They mainly fight corrupt super cops."

"Super cops?" I asked.

"Yeah." Another shrug. "The super cops have all kinds of high-tech gadgets and shit, and they're always giving some kid the beat-down."

"And you watch that?" Mr. Impossible asked.

"No, I don't," Chapman said. "Not anymore. Betsy and Billy do though."

"Hmmm," Mr. Impossible said. The 'hmmm' meant that he'd have to see about that.

"Where are Betsy and Billy?" Monkey asked.

"They're out making the rounds with Sandy."

"Ah," Monkey said.

"So, what happened with this Kid Crowbar kid?" Mr. Impossible asked.

Monkey relayed the story.

"What the hell?" Mr. Impossible said. "That's crazy? He actually jumped up on the car and whacked the cop in the head with the crowbar?"

"It was plastic," I said.

"Yeah," Monkey said.

"Still." Mr. Impossible looked very concerned about this. "Now tell me again, what happened to your head?" He gestured at Monkey with the joint and Monkey almost grabbed it.

Monkey retold the story about the kids chasing each other across the crowd, this time with more details and embellishments.

"That sounds like Jackie Saturn and Kill Machine," Chapman said.

"I'm out of the loop when it comes to cartoons, I guess," Mr. Impossible said.

"Me, too," I said.

"I've heard of them," Monkey said. "But I didn't know these kids were supposed to be them. And I didn't give a shit."

"Yeah." Chapman lit up his own joint and took a drag. "They're sworn enemies," he said as he exhaled. "And they're not from a cartoon. They're from a live-action movie."

"Oh," Mr. Impossible said. "God, I'm getting old."

"Magmanauts," Chapman said. "It looks cheap as shit, but it's popular as fuck."

"Watch that mouth," Mr. Impossible said, with zero conviction.

Chapman ignored him.

Something was bothering Mr. Impossible, and it wasn't his teenage son cussing and smoking a joint in his presence.

"I've never even heard of that," I said. "It's a movie for kids?"

"Sort of. Not really. It's PG-13, but the comic it was based on was for adults. Allegedly. Well, adults that are fat creepy guys." Chapman snickered.

Monkey turned to him and held out the joint. "Don't you want some of this?"

Chapman shook his head and took a hit off his own joint. "Germs, man."

"Kids today don't pass joints around," Mr. Impossible said. "They all smoke their own. They say it's unsanitary."

Monkey and I didn't have a thing to say about that.

We made it through about half of the giant hog leg before we had to quit. Mr. Impossible pinched it out and slipped it into a sandwich baggie. He reached under the counter into a mini-fridge and pulled out a Hippo IPA—the expensive shit. He took a swig and said, "Preventive measure." He winked. "For the cottonmouth."

Monkey cracked open a beer. I poured my cheap bourbon over ice, and we took a moment of silence to drink and to gauge how high the weed had gotten us.

Then Monkey said, "Shit!" He pointed at Mr. Impossible. "I forget to tell you about the kid who got his nose bitten off!"

"What?" Mr. Impossible said.

"Yeah, what?" I said. I didn't see any kid get his nose bitten off. "What are you talking about?"

"The army man," Monkey said.

"What army man?"

"The kid dressed up as an army man. You saw him. In the street, blood pouring out of his face."

"Oh," I said. "Yeah, I know who you're talking about. He wasn't missing a nose."

"The fuck he wasn't. That little zombie girl bit that shit clean off. I saw her spit it into the street."

"Bullshit," I said, but I had a feeling Monkey was telling the truth as he saw it.

"Yeah," Mr. Impossible said, "that sounds pretty unbelievable." He took a long draw from his beer, set it down on the bar, and stared at his son.

Chapman turned to meet his dad's glare and laughed.

"What's so funny, Chapman?" Mr. Impossible asked.

Chapman tried to suppress his laughter, but failed. His was the loud, sinister laughter of one guilty son-of-a-bitch.

"What did you do?" Mr. Impossible asked.

"Nothing." Chapman stopped laughing long enough to take another puff. "Nothing at all, Pops."

Mr. Impossible took another swig of beer. "Tell me what you did. Now."

"Well," Chapman took a long drag off his joint, by this time a fat roach glistening with black resin, "I may have injected some buckeyes with a little bit of the spirit of Halloween." He sniggered like the devil and coughed out a cloud of smoke.

"What's he talking about?" Monkey asked.

I looked to Mr. Impossible for an answer.

"Unacceptable," Mr. Impossible said. "Unacceptable." He came out from behind the bar, clenched his fists, but didn't approach his son. He kept his head down and tried to control his breathing. His rage. "How many?"

"Hmmm. Let me think." Chapman touched his chin and rolled his eyes. "All of them."

"This is bad," Mr. Impossible said. "Very bad."

"What the hell is going on?" Monkey asked.

"What did Chapman inject the buckeyes with?" I asked.

"Larpinol," Mr. Impossible said. "It's a side project of mine."

"Oh, yeah," Monkey said. "You told me about that. I even read something on the web about it."

"Yeah," Mr. Impossible said. "It's been getting some attention. The FDA is involved, and it's getting a little hairy. But until they close a couple loopholes, I could still sell it with no worries." He looked at his son. "Until now."

"What is it?" I asked.

"It's controversial because a couple of big shot actors are taking it, right?" Monkey asked.

"Right," Mr. Impossible said. "People are claiming unfair advantage. They're calling it steroids for movie stars. Method acting in a pill. It's not illegal." He looked at Chapman again. "Yet. So there is nothing unfair about it. Anyone can order it from the website."

"I'm still not getting it," I said.

"Larpinol is a chemical compound I put together, a drug which helps an actor get into character. It stimulates centers in the brain that naturally light up when a person gets into costume. Or dons a particular accessory. Like a mask. Take glasses for instance. You may have read about this one study—it's pretty well-known—which shows that people perform better on tests when wearing eyeglasses. Not corrective lenses. Just clear glass. It's the associative power of the artifact that sets the mind, frames it, and enhances the performance. Our cultural notions about people who wear glasses are all tied up in it. But you get the picture. Larpinol enhances that effect."

"How?" I asked.

Mr. Impossible glared at me. This glare said 'I'm not going to waste time explaining the science to someone who will not understand it.'

I held up my hands in surrender. "Yeah, don't tell me how it works. So, the problem is that some kids may have already eaten these buckeyes, and they'll be pretending really hard that they are whatever it is they've dressed up as for Halloween?"

"Probably not," Mr. Impossible said.

"What do you mean?" Monkey asked.

"Obviously, I never tested the stuff on children," Mr. Impossible said. "But my guess is that it'd go beyond just pretending really hard. I'd say any kid who's ingested Larpinol would completely and totally believe they *are* whatever they are dressed as. With absolute conviction. Children don't have the same wall adults have built up between fantasy and reality. Larpinol helps the geeks reenacting the Civil War really, really get deep into it, but they still know they're pretending. I don't think kids will."

"Shit," Monkey said.

"Plus," Mr. Impossible said, "overdosing could be a problem. It's not like kids eat just one piece of candy."

"Aren't kids supposed to be waiting to get home to have their folks inspect their candy?" I asked.

Both Mr. Impossible and Monkey glared at me.

"Yeah, okay," I said.

"Besides," Mr. Impossible said, "these buckeyes are a tradition. The parents all know who makes them. They'll be letting the kids eat them without a problem."

"Shit," Monkey said.

"Shit, is right," Mr. Impossible said and stormed out of the room.

Chapman smiled down at the new joint he was building.

I couldn't believe the kid thought this was funny.

"This is totally fucked up," Monkey started pacing. "I need a smoke."

"You quit," I reminded him.

"This is a special occasion. Can you bum me one?"

"Sure."

"You guys can't smoke in here," Chapman said. "Cigarettes."

Monkey and I both knew that, so we ignored him. But before we could head outside for a smoke, Mr. Impossible stomped back into the room, holding a wooden case about the size of a cigar box. He rushed around to the back of the bar, set the case down, and fixed himself a stiff drink. Gainsail Black on the rocks. A double. He slugged it and slammed down the highball glass. Hard.

We all jumped.

He then fished around in his front pants pockets and produced a key chain with a single key on it. He unlocked the wooden case.

Monkey and I both stepped back when we saw what was inside.

"We've got to take care of this problem," Mr. Impossible said.

"With a gun?" Monkey asked.

"No, I'm not going to run around shooting doped-up kids," Mr. Impossible said. "It's not like they've transformed into zombies. They'll come down. Eventually. I think."

"What's the gun for?" I asked.

"It's a tranquilizer gun," Mr. Impossible said.

"Dad?" Chapman said. His voice cracked.

"Sandy wouldn't let me keep a real gun in the house," Mr. Impossible said.

"Dude," Monkey said, "you can't run around shooting other people's kids with a tranquilizer gun, either."

"I don't plan to." Mr. Impossible picked up the gun, aimed it at Chapman, and squeezed the trigger. "Not other people's kids."

I jumped, ducked, and when I looked up, I saw a tiny dart poking out of the side of Chapman's neck.

"Dad?" Chapman said again in a strangled voice. His eyes went wide, and he slid out of his chair and under the table, out cold.

"Fuck!" Monkey said. "What the fuck?"

Mr. Impossible waved the gun dismissively. "He'll be all right."

Monkey had both hands on his head, pacing back and forth, and he kept saying, "Fuck."

"Settle down, Steve," Mr. Impossible said. "He'll be fine."

"What about Sandy?" I asked.

"I'm not going to shoot her," Mr. Impossible said.

"No," I said. "Won't she be pissed when she finds out you shot your kid with a tranquilizer dart?"

"She'll be more pissed about the Larpinol," Mr. Impossible said. "I might be a bachelor here real soon, fellas. Now, help me get Chapman on the couch."

Monkey didn't seem to have heard this exchange. He poured himself a stiff drink and gulped it while Mr. Impossible and I grabbed Chapman by his wrists and ankles and flung him onto the couch.

When the deed was done, Mr. Impossible clapped his hands together like he'd just finished digging a grave and said, "All right. Let's get out there and warn folks about the buckeyes. They have a PA system we use for announcements. Raffle winners and shit like that."

"I need a smoke," Monkey said.

Then the world exploded.

We dropped to the floor.

Outside it sounded like a war zone, like bombs going off, and a hundred people had decided to just start shooting guns at one another. Women and children screamed, and I heard things bursting into flames and heavy things falling and crashing into other things and busting them up.

The window over the pool table shattered, and the room filled with smoke and sparks and a deafening roar.

I think I was knocked unconscious for a second, maybe longer, because when I woke up I heard a loud hissing noise. Mr. Impossible ran around the room, spraying a fire extinguisher. I didn't remember him grabbing it, and it looked like he'd been spraying the thing for a while.

All the bottles behind the bar were shattered. The bar itself was charred. All the movie and sports posters on the walls were burnt away or smoldering. The card table that Chapman had been sitting at was gone. The folding chairs were twisted scraps of blackened metal.

If Mr. Impossible hadn't shot his son with the tranquilizer dart and moved him to the couch, he would have died in the explosion.

Monkey was on the ground, kneeling, with his hands over his head, like he was in a tornado drill, repeating the phrase, "What the fuck?" over and over again.

"Shut up, Monkey!" Mr. Impossible said as he continued to put out fires. "Please, shut the fuck up!"

I got to my feet, held on to a wall for balance, and asked, "What the hell just happened?"

"Someone set off the fireworks early," Mr. Impossible said. "After aiming them all into the fucking neighborhood first."

"Holy shit," I said.

Monkey removed his hands from his head and sat back on his haunches. "Who the fuck would do that?"

"Who do you think?" Mr. Impossible threw the fire

extinguisher down. All the flames had been put out, but it was still hard to see, to breathe, through the smoke.

"Kids," I said. "Crazy fucking kids."

Mr. Impossible ran from the room, and I heard him leaping down the stairs like a madman.

"Where'd he go?" Monkey asked.

"His kids are out there with Sandy," I said.

"Shit," Monkey said and jumped to his feet.

A second later we were running down the stairs like madmen, too.

When Monkey and I made it out of the house, Mr. Impossible was nowhere in sight, and the block was on fire. Fireworks exploded in the night sky. We saw blood in the street. Shattered windows blighted cars and houses. A scarecrow burned face down on the neighbor's lawn. People, the grown-ups, screamed in pain, screamed for missing loved ones.

Across the street, a group of kids dressed in sci-fi combat body armor moved like a trained military unit. It would have been cute as hell if it hadn't been so damn scary.

A mob ran back and forth between us and the space marines.

A dog bit a woman dressed like a gypsy.

A girl dressed like a koala bear scurried up a light post and perched on its lamp.

Another Kid Crowbar took down an old lady by smashing his crowbar into the backs of her legs. Then he turned and swiped at an EMT—it wasn't a costume—and the guy was quick, which was good, because the crowbar smashed through the passenger side window of an economy-size car.

I elbowed Monkey and pointed to the Kid. "Watch out. That one's got a real crowbar."

"Oh, shit," Monkey said. "Let's go." He jumped off the porch and raced down the sidewalk.

I took off after him.

We ran past parents hugging kids as the little ones kicked, screamed, and struggled to break free of their embrace.

We found costumed children on the ground, unconscious. Monkey made us stop to make sure none of them were dead.

Not like I didn't want to.

Well, I didn't want to run across a dead kid. Luckily, they were all breathing. They all had a pulse.

But some of those faces scared the living fuck out of me. I convinced myself that the worst of them had to be Halloween makeup.

So many parents raced past us without kids. I knew they were parents because they were screaming out names, and I could tell they weren't screaming for their husbands or wives—no irritation in those voices.

And what I did hear in those voices, I didn't want to hear again.

We stopped at a street corner, and Monkey looked both ways, but not because he was worried about traffic; he was trying to figure out which way to go. I noticed then he had tears running down his face.

I tried hard to catch my breath, had trouble asking, "Where we going?"

We were breathing heavily. We were both smokers, despite Monkey saying he'd quit. Quitting cigarettes meant that he quit buying them, is all.

Monkey coughed out, "Haunted Gardens," before bending over to put his hands on his knees. He huffed for a bit, then stood upright again. His breath hitched, and he said, "Mr. Impossible's kids love that place. Went through that thing about ten times last year. I'd say that's where he was headed."

I looked around for some giant-ass sign with an arrow pointing to a place called The Haunted Gardens. I didn't see one.

"That way." Monkey pointed to a mansion at the end of a cul-de-sac. Upward of two hundred carved jack-o'-lanterns cropped up across its lawn and 'grew' from two giant trees to either side of the driveway. With all the smoke in the air, it was a wicked sight.

Monkey took off running in that direction and I followed, lagging behind. He didn't smoke as much as I did, and he's taller and not fat. I didn't have a chance at keeping up.

We had to take a serpentine path around bodies lying in the street, discarded burning costumes and Halloween decorations.

When we were about a hundred yards from the mansion, Monkey was knocked flat onto his back in the middle of the street. The upper torso of a scarecrow kept the back of his head from cracking on the blacktop.

Monkey's chest was on fire.

I sprinted to him, but when I got there, he'd already rolled around to put the flames out. He stayed on the ground, on hands and knees, and I couldn't read his expression.

"That could have killed me," Monkey said.

"What the fuck happened?" I asked.

"Watch out!" Monkey screamed, and I looked up to see the evil grin of a jack-o'-lantern flying through the smoke toward us.

I jumped to the ground, covered my head, and the flaming pumpkin came down with a heavy thud behind me.

"What the fuck?"

"Kids are throwing jack-o'-lanterns, dude," Monkey said.

"I get that now," I said, but I didn't *really* get it. "A kid couldn't throw a pumpkin that far."

"You think some adult is doing it? Like maybe some dude ate a ton of those buckeyes and OD'd or something?"

"I don't think so. That's pretty far. I don't know if even an adult could throw a pumpkin that distance."

"Maybe it's some guy on PCP?"

"Could be. But I think we need to find another way. The Haunted Gardens is behind that big house, right?"

"Yeah," Monkey said.

Another blazing jack-o'-lantern smacked down about ten feet in front of us. The thing smelled fucking awful.

"Shit," Monkey said.

Two more sailed toward us and we rolled out of the way. They crashed down and belched flames.

"Fuck," Monkey said. "There's got to be a *bunch* of dudes hopped up on PCP."

"Let's get out of the street. Cut through backyards."

"I don't know."

"What?"

"Dogs."

"Right." I didn't like dogs, either, at least not strange dogs protecting their territory. "Then let's cut through the front yards and stay close to the houses."

Monkey jumped up and raced to the nearest house. He was on the porch before I even regained my footing.

When I got to the porch, I found him hiding behind a curtain of phony cobwebs populated with huge plastic spiders. The front door of the house was open, and I could see through the screen door a body lying in the hallway—an old woman in a bathrobe.

I pointed through the screen and whispered, "Should we go in and see if she's all right?"

"It's gotta be a trap," Monkey said. "You know there's a kid in there with a machete, wearing a goddamn paper bag on his head."

I couldn't argue with that.

"All right," I said. "We need to dash from porch to porch. I think that'll provide us enough cover."

Three flaming pumpkins smashed down in the street, one right after the other.

A woman screamed. It sounded like it came from inside the house. We jumped and ran over to the neighbor's porch.

This house wasn't decorated and there didn't appear to be

any lights on inside. A metal sign screwed to the red brick beneath the house number read: No Solicitors.

I guess that included trick or treaters.

"Ready?" Monkey said.

"Yeah."

And we ran to the next porch, and the next, while pumpkins smacked down in the street.

When we reached the screened porch of the house two away from the mansion, we saw through the smoke who was throwing the jack-o'-lanterns.

A half-dozen kids, all dressed as pirates, clustered in the mansion's front yard. They'd set up four makeshift teeter-totters they were using as catapults. One kid hefted a glowing pumpkin onto one end of the plank, then two pirates jumped onto the other end and sent the pumpkin sailing through the air.

"Fucking pirates," Monkey said.

"I used to love pirates," I said.

Monkey gave me a grave look.

"When I was a kid."

Monkey turned back around. "What do we do?"

"We're close enough now that they can't hit us with the pumpkins," I said. "Let's just truck it past them."

"I don't know."

"There's too much light for us to sneak past them."

A knife blade stabbed through the screen.

Monkey jumped back into me, and we both fell onto a potted plant that was little more than a barrel of dirt with a bunch of sharp sticks poking out of it. That hurt like hell.

The knife sawed through the screen. It was one of those pirate kids holding the knife, and he wasn't playing.

We jumped to our feet, smashed through the screen door, and raced down the sidewalk just as two flaming pumpkins smashed down behind us.

We sprinted through the mansion's front yard, tripping over pumpkins, sending their flaming faces rolling.

Around the side of the house, a wooden fence stood decorated with blinking bats, witches, and spooky skulls. The gate was open and hanging on one hinge. We raced through the gate and heard the pirates giving chase behind us.

A long table, like what you'd find in a high school cafeteria, sat on the other side of the fence. A paper sign taped to its front read: DONATIONS. A lockbox was toppled over in the grass, bills and coins spilled around it. Two metal folding chairs sat empty.

A wall of tall, spindly bushes loomed in front of us. At the center of the wall was an archway with a grinning plastic skull up top. A beaded curtain hung from the archway, and all the beads were tiny bones.

I ran through the curtain and heard Monkey say "wait" behind me. But he didn't hesitate for more than a second. The beads rattled, and he was next to me in the semi-darkness.

We found ourselves in a long, open-air tunnel made of plywood that went on for about twenty feet and ended at a T intersection. Lights were strung along the tops of the walls, and each little light bulb was a goofy skull. But only half of the lights were lit. There must have been an event at some point where the neighborhood kids had been invited to a painting party. Movie monsters and mythological creatures were smeared and splashed all around us. I noticed several creatures with enormous hands and thought back to something I'd heard in a psychology class about how kids often drew pictures of their parents with giant hands if they'd been abused.

"Let's go." I headed toward the intersection and turned left. We found ourselves in a similar plywood passageway, surrounded by more unsettling artwork. More monsters with large hands.

I felt sick to my stomach.

The hallway led to a maze of bushes, walls of flowers, latticework overtaken with crawling vines. We followed twists and turns in the haunted maze. All the spooks who'd volunteered to haunt the place had abandoned it. The sounds from the surrounding neighborhood, of screaming children and weeping parents, of burning homes, and crackling police radios seemed far away, like sound effects from a loud movie playing inside someone's house.

The volunteer spooks were gone, but we were not alone in the maze. We heard the pirates creeping behind us. Branches snapped to our right. A plywood wall collapsed with a *whoof* to our left.

"Mr. Impossible and his kids aren't in here, man," Monkey whispered.

"We don't know that yet," I whispered back. "We need to keep going."

"We should bust right out of this maze," Monkey said. "It's creepy as hell."

"Let's keep going." I turned a corner and found a headless woman sitting in a rocking chair, her severed head resting in her lap. I jumped back into Monkey. He stumbled and gasped.

I laughed at myself for letting such a goofy-looking prop scare me.

And that's what drew the pirate to us.

A round kid in tricorn hat broke through a wall of bushes and started hacking at Monkey, a butcher's knife in each hand.

Monkey went insane. It looked like he was slap-boxing the kid. It would have looked humorous, like wussified slap-boxing always does, if I didn't know the kid had two knives and Monkey just had his forearms to block with.

Monkey screamed 'fuck, fuck, fuck, fuck' as the blades cut and stabbed away at his flesh, and before I could move in to kick the little bastard, Monkey decked him, and the kid slammed to the ground and stopped moving.

Monkey held his hands up in front of him like Doctor Frankenstein waiting for Igor to pull his surgical gloves down over his fingers and said, "I killed him."

"You didn't kill him." Blood dribbled from Monkey's elbows and pattered into the dirt at his feet. A lot of blood was collecting there, and I stared at the black pool. Blinking skull-shaped lights reflected in its surface.

"Can you check?" Monkey asked. "I'm . . . I can't."

I never liked the sight of blood. Seeing this much of the stuff stunned me. Seeing it pouring out of my best friend stopped me from breathing, from thinking, from being present in the world.

"Yeah," I said, my voice thick and sleepy-sounding.

I stumbled over to the kid and surprised myself by being smart enough to kick the knives far from his body before I knelt down to examine him.

"He's breathing," I said. The chubby little guy was even snoring. I touched his neck. "And his pulse is strong." I didn't know a strong pulse from a weak one, and I only said this to make Monkey feel better.

I stood and looked at Monkey. He was staring forward into nothing. His arms were wet with black goo. His blood.

"I could have killed that kid." Monkey sounded like a hypnotized killer in some cheapo political thriller.

"It was self-defense, man."

"It doesn't matter," Monkey said. "He's just a kid."

"He's fine," I said. "But we better go. Get you fixed up before his buddies show up."

I kicked through a plywood wall and stomped over it into the next hall of the maze, not caring about being heard. I needed to get Monkey somewhere where we could see how bad off he was, under some light, get him bandaged up.

162

"Come on." I waved him forward and smashed through a section of old wooden fencing, stomped through bushes, kicked stacked milk crates, toppled over more plywood walls, until we arrived at a spot outside the maze, next to a birdbath and a woman holding a small limp form in her arms, a toddler dressed as a bumble bee.

When the lady looked up, I saw it was Sandy, Mrs. Impossible. Tears streamed down her face. Her eyes widened with recognition when she saw us, but she didn't greet us. She didn't smile. Her bottom lip trembled, and her tears splashed down on the child's yellow and black stripes.

"Billy stung me," she said. "And now he won't wake up."

Monkey moved past me, still holding his arms up in front of him. They still drizzled blood, but Sandy didn't appear to notice.

"Is he . . . ?" Monkey couldn't bring himself to finish the question.

Sandy looked down at her child, his sweet, still face and said, "I told him this summer, what happens to a bee when it stings you. He thinks he's dead."

I cleared my throat and asked, "Is he breathing?"

Sandy nodded her head. "But he won't wake up."

"It'll wear off," I said.

"Yeah," Monkey said.

Sandy issued a sharp, derisive laugh. "Leif said that, too. That he'd come down." Her face changed when she said 'come down.' She was angry as hell, to think of her baby on drugs, having to 'come down.'

Mr. Impossible wasn't going back to a happy home.

"I pressed him on it," she said. "And, like I figured, he said he couldn't be sure of that." She squeezed her boy, held him tight against her chest. "My baby's in a coma. He might never come out of it."

I stepped up next to Monkey, put my hand on his shoulder,

and it came away gummy with blood. I wiped it on my singlet, and we stood there looking stupid for a while before Sandy looked up and noticed Monkey's arms. She gasped when she realized what she was looking at. "Steve, what happened to your arms?"

"Pirate," Monkey said.

She nodded her understanding and returned her attention to her boy.

"Where's Leif?" I asked.

Sandy sniffled. "He just now ran after Betsy." She cocked her head toward a wall of trees behind her. "Through there."

The trees were giant conifers strung from top to bottom with more strings of skull lights. Witches and goblins, and other monstrous decorations hidden in the branches.

"I'm going to find him," I said. "Steve, you should probably go get fixed up."

"No," he said. "I'm coming with."

I walked into the trees, amazed to find that someone had spared no expense decorating what looked like a hundred great firs with lights and spooky creatures.

Steve followed, and so did Sandy, her bumble bee cradled in her arms. We stopped at a tree taller than the rest. It stood at the center of a clearing. Skulls blinked. Monsters winked and snarled in its branches.

Sandy cried out behind us. Her face turned up to the sky, new tears streaming down her cheeks. I followed her gaze and saw, perched at the top of the giant tree, a girl dressed like an angel. The glitter in her white dress danced, the teeny LED lights in her wings flashed, and the halo over her head glowed bright against the night sky. She held her arms out and her head tilted back as if she were blessing all of creation.

"Betsy," Sandy whispered. "No."

"Shit," Monkey said.

And I almost shit my pants.

Betsy was no older than four, and she stood at the top of what looked like the devil's Christmas tree, at a height of thirty feet.

I did not understand how she was balanced up there, what she was standing on, but she didn't waver. She stood perfectly still, just like an ornament is supposed to do.

"Betsy," another voice whispered through the night. It came from above. It was Mr. Impossible's voice.

Branches ruffled just under the apex of the tree. Mr. Impossible had climbed up after his daughter. He was trying to talk her down.

"My work here is done," Betsy said in a voice that truly was the voice of an angel. "It is time for me to fly up to heaven. May God bless you all."

And with that, she leapt into the air.

I think we all stopped breathing. I know I did.

Monkey and Sandy both gasped when Betsy jumped.

And Mr. Impossible sprang from the branches and wrapped his arms around his little girl. He twisted in the air so that his back would hit the ground first. He'd not given a second thought to giving his life for that of his daughter's.

And the angel fell in her father's embrace.

Mr. Impossible's body hit with a thud, and I swear I heard bones break.

Okay. I guess it might have been branches snapping beneath them.

Then the world went silent. It even seemed that the chaos in the neighborhood had paused for this moment. I heard nothing but my heart pounding in my chest.

Three angry beats. Like an ogre pounding at a castle door.

Then the angel cried, and it was the most beautiful sound in the world.

We all rushed forward, and the sound rushed back into the

world. Sirens and screams and burning homes and fireworks. More fireworks.

And that wonderful wail from that little girl that told us she was alive.

Sandy handed me her bumble bee and scooped her angel up into her arms. "Are you okay, sweetheart?" she asked. "Are you okay?"

"We are made of sterner stuff than mortal men, my lady," the girl said, and her mother cried harder. But there was laughter mixed in there, too. But just a little.

Monkey and I stood over Mr. Impossible. I winced when I saw his leg twisted up, snapped in two, and trapped behind his back.

"Fuck," Monkey whispered. "He's dead, man. Gotta be."

"No, I'm not." Mr. Impossible blinked. "And you're bleeding all over me. Back the fuck off, Monkey."

Monkey and I laughed.

Then Monkey collapsed at my side. He didn't have enough blood in him to keep him upright.

A single pool, almost a pond, of Monkey and Mr. Impossible's collective blood formed around their fallen bodies, and I thought to myself that couldn't be sanitary.

And I also thought my friends were about to die in my presence, and I was helpless to do anything about it.

But they didn't die.

Monkey almost bled out, but he got a series of transfusions just in time and spent a few weeks in a hospital getting his strength back.

Mr. Impossible had cracked a few ribs and punctured a lung.

And he had that brutal compound fracture. He spent a month in the hospital and more months in physical therapy, but he still walks with a limp. And on rainy days, he uses a cane. But this hasn't stopped him from playing Ultimate Frisbee or rock climbing or from doing any of the crazy shit he does.

While tripping balls.

He is Mr. Impossible after all.

And his kids, and all the kids in the neighborhood, wound up coming down from their Larpinol highs, and being mostly all right. Billy woke up. And Betsy stopped believing she was an angel.

Luckily, no kids died that night.

I know what you're thinking. Didn't Mr. Impossible's ass get sued? Didn't he go to prison?

And the answer to both questions is yes. He spent a year in prison and lost a lot of money in a series of lawsuits.

And Chapman, too, got locked up for a while. But he doesn't seem to have shaped up. He even brags about what he did on that Halloween night.

Hell, even all these years later, he's still a kid. He might grow up one day. But when he does, I kind of think he'll just be a grown-up asshole. I'd never tell Mr. Impossible that though.

And, yes, it doesn't seem like a year in prison is much time at all for what Mr. Impossible was responsible for. Most of his sentence was suspended. His new employer had a lot to do with that. As soon as Mr. Impossible got out of the can, he started working as a civilian contractor for some shady military intelligence outfit. He doesn't talk about it.

He can't.

But I know what kind of things he's doing for them.

Impossible things.

BETWEEN

Ian Welke

SHE WIPES HER foot across the wet sand erasing a triangle someone has etched into the mud with a stick. Finding a stick of her own, Yolanda replaces the triangle or delta with a long integral ∫. It was the delta that initially attracted her to calculus. The delta is the mathematical representation of rates of change, but tonight's ritual is all about the past. The integral reverses the derivative, in this case symbolically reversing her history. She draws a sigma next. For she'll need the sum total of the variables working for her, even the marks on the sand.

The letters for the variables . . . t for time? The hours between sunset on Halloween and the end of Dia De Los Muertos. She's piggy backing on the shared belief that the veil is thinnest these two nights, this night specifically since there are more unwitting participants, the greater the effect. She is x in the equation. The observer is part of the ritual. She giggles. How's that for an Uncertainty Principle? There must be a variable for place, as she fully believes this ritual can only work here, the city that substitutes so often for so many other places.

A man with an unbuttoned shirt and his pant legs rolled up to his knees, stands in the surf ahead. She follows the trail of hair up his chest, neck, and muttonchops, and realizes that he is staring back at her.

His eyes are bloodshot, but his pupils are as immense and saucer sized as her own. She's certain that the spirit staring at her is a young, Los Angeles-years Jim Morrison. And he should stare at her, for she is the L.A. Woman. She is Los Angeles. Born to a Hispanic mother and a half-Korean half-African American father, she worked two jobs while going from LACC to UCLA to grad school at Cal Tech, all while painting and working theater crews and never ever sleeping. She grew up on this beach and in traffic between this beach and her parents' home in Boyle Heights. She's seen the absurd wealth in the estates just blocks from people sleeping beneath overpasses. She's seen her streets double for countless other cities on the movie and television screens. If anyone would know that the barrier between worlds is thinnest in Los Angeles, it's her.

Los Angeles, Halloween night, she has her coordinates in space time.

She feels the pull of a thousand dark suns as she's drawn into Morrison's eyes. But before her vision is engulfed in the black of those immense pupils there's a light, yellow and pink, she realizes it's the sun reflected off the waves in front of her. There's no sign of the man she thought was Morrison's spirit, it's faded like so many shades before her, leaving the trace of cigarette smoke on the wind.

How long has she been staring at the ocean? How long has it been since the spirit passed her by? Maybe she shouldn't have eaten all three-and-a-half grams of the mushrooms. No. She shakes her head and the world shakes in jangled frames in front of her. It had to be the whole eighth and it had to be tonight.

It can't be as long as it seems. The sun is still above the horizon, if only just. She trips out on its flicker across the waves, but forces herself to stop and concentrate for one moment. The time dilation effect is a double-edged sword. It buys her more time to think and to explore, but there's the danger that she could forget her task, get too buried in the rite to remember its purpose.

That's just one of the dangers. Every time she's taken psychedelics there's been that fear in the back of her head, the one where she worries this is the time it lasts forever, this is the time she doesn't come back. And it's more important not to give power to that fear tonight, with the greater effects of the ritual, she doesn't want her own mind to give her power over to any of the dangers. With the barriers between worlds down, there's the rift wraiths to contend with, and not all the spirits she'll encounter will be friendly, and of course she needs to do all she can to not mess with Mr. In Between.

She shakes her head like she can rattle the notion out through her ear. At least she went with mushrooms instead of LSD. She's taken enough chemistry to know she prefers the simple organic compounds over the complex chemicals.

Several chemical formulas are etched into the sand underneath her integral $\int$. She realizes she's giggling before she knows what she's laughing at. Trying to be consistent while mixing weird mathematics with magical ritual. Do the formulas work as well as her tia claimed? Jack Parsons sure thought so when he combined magic with rocketry, and he didn't have half the math available to him that she does. He didn't have half the theory of the multiverse, or of the simulation nature of the universe. He did understand that belief informs reality, but he could not have understood the importance of this location on this night.

Or did he? The man was a black magician as well as a rocket scientist. He cofounded JPL. Was there a reason JPL was founded on Halloween?

She wonders if she made her way back to Pasadena if she'd see his shade there. He blew himself up not too far from where she lives today.

There are plenty of spirits out on Halloween night through to the end of Dia De Los Muertos, but Yolanda is looking for two in particular.

Shades move past her in the windswept sand, but none of them are her parents. She'd hoped to find them here, in an echo from their time together at the beach from her childhood, but no such luck. If she can find them, will they be able to tell her what she should do? Should she stay where she is and take the job she wants researching, or take the better paying engineering job and have to move away? If she stays, her life will be beset with costs she can never afford. If she leaves she will miss her home and will forever wonder if what might have been if she'd remained in academia. Security or achievement. And of course there's the fear of leaving Los Angeles. For all its faults, it's her home, and it's a city with more to offer her than anywhere else. She's thought about it for so long, she just wishes that she didn't have to choose.

She hoofs it up the road. It's hard to tell some of the more opaque spirits from the living people she sees. People, especially the fast moving little ones already out in their costumes, smear and blur past as the mushrooms do their work, leaving bright trailers behind. Peering harder, she can tell the shades from the people by their faded colors.

Yolanda passes the Abbot Kinney Library, and he's there out front, the founder of Venice By The Sea, he tips his hat to her as she passes.

A trio of jack-o'-lanterns are on the top step. The tall one has the sideways eight, the infinity symbol carved into its forehead. The magician jack-o'-lantern. The other two have spirals for eyes, reminding her of the Indian petroglyph she's always assumed means gate or portal. She's on the right path.

Birds chatter around her. No. It's the cackle of seven, eight, then nine small children. Tiny ghosts and goblins parading the street, encircling her and dancing around her like a May Pole. This is not Beltane, this is on the opposite side of the linear time axis. She'd be stunned that they're so fearless with a stranger, but she realizes this too is part of the rite. Even on a standard Halloween the children practice the sympathetic magic of transformation when they don their costumes. At the doorsteps of their neighbors, the children recite the evocation of the spell with "Trick or Treat" and they are rewarded with sacrifice in sugar.

She passes two shades, definitely not with the trick or treaters. One she's certain is Pio Pico, the last governor of Alta California. The other is an African American woman. Is that Biddy Mason? Or is Yolanda's hero worship of Mason's history playing on the psilocybin and the disorienting overall nature of the rite? Is this confirmation bias in action?

"Excuse me, ma'am. Are you Biddy Mason?" she hears her own voice say. It's a shock to her. Did she mean to speak? If she's just hallucinating and she's said this to a random stranger how embarrassing would that be?

The woman smiles kindly. When she speaks it's barely audible, a whisper on the wind. "It doesn't matter, does it, dear? You can't let yourself be distracted along the way. If I learned anything, it's that you need to be focused on what you really want."

Before Yolanda can ask another question, the woman fades to shadow. The ghosts of Los Angeles rise and fall and rush away like the white foam of a broken wave.

Yolanda looks up to see that her bus has arrived. She steps onto the 33 Downtown and is surprised that she has the fare already in hand. Maybe the spell is stronger than her. She's not sure if that's a good thing.

IAN WELKE

The Central Library is Yolanda's favorite building in the world. The mosaics on the outer walls and busts of great thinkers symbolize the theme of the light of learning. Climbing the steps many times she's felt the power growing around her, coming closer into the building that embodies not just learning as a goal and concept but also a wondrous architectural achievement, a symbol of what society can do when they're motivated by the public good more than individual greed.

As she forces herself to walk past the steps, to continue tonight's mission, she wonders if she should have spent more time inside prepping for the evening. Is she knowledgeable? Isn't the thing she learns most often when she researches, how much there is she doesn't know? An equation appears on the wall in front of her, glowing in hot red, the limit as K approaches infinity. K must be knowledge. She wonders if the rest of the equation is research or her ability to understand it, then she shakes it off and tries to maintain her focus on her purpose. There is little time. It has to be tonight.

If she does meet the spirits of her parents, does she have the question worded properly? Will she make the most of the situation, or will she stammer or confuse them until they can't provide her with any help after all?

Her parent's first apartment was in Korea Town. She wades through crowds of drunks stumbling out of restaurants and bars. She waves her hands to balance herself as if she's surfing an imaginary wave and bending the board around the rocks coming up fast ahead. No not rocks, loose jack-o'-lanterns bouncing and twirling levitated ahead of her. That can't be real, she tells herself, but whether she believes or not, she takes the time to find the one with the infinity symbol etched in its forehead to make sure she's on the right path.

A thousand separate bird chirps chatter around her. She covers her ears. Too many voices at once as the crowd thickens.

This is nothing. If things go badly she'll have to brave the multitudes in Hollywood. The thought sends a shiver down her spine. She's not ready for that. A Hollywood Halloween Night while she has a head full of mushrooms.

This crowd is bad enough.

"The overlay of the worlds, tonight that barrier is the lowest." The voice sounds familiar, but she can't place it in the crowd.

"Is it tonight that it's lowest, or is it the belief that makes it so?"

"Does it matter in practicality?"

The first voice is her physics professor from UCLA, but she doesn't see him in the crowd, certainly not close enough to hear him speaking. The second voice sounds a lot like her own, but older, merged with her tia's? It seems like there's something she's forgotten, probably she should consider how many mushrooms she ate on the beach, but no, that's not it. She's sure of it.

As if they know she's trying to concentrate on them, the voices die back down to dull crowd murmur.

Olvera Street to her left is home to some of Los Angeles' most famous and oldest ghosts, but she keeps moving. It's her folk's apartment she needs to check out, her last chance at sparing herself the chaos of Hollywood on Halloween Night.

A man in an out of fashion suit wearing a hat stands in front of her.

"My walks are beset with difficulties. It was easier before the freeways. How can I hope to find Cissy now?"

She looks over her shoulder, but the shade is definitely speaking to her. "I guess we're all looking for someone. Is Cissy still among the living?"

He stops and ponders and flickers as the realization passes over him. "No. She passed before I did. I died, and far from here. What am I doing back on these streets?"

"I think it's an echo. I think it's unique to Los Angeles, and possibly elevated by the Halloween and Dia De Los Muertos traditions."

"Los Angeles is unique. Thank the Gods for that. At least the Santa Anas aren't blowing in force tonight. I've said it before, on nights like those, every party ends in a fight." He stops walking and smiles at her.

Or so she thinks. She turns around to see who he's really smiling at, but there's just the empty sidewalk leading down 7th Street.

"Is that the Athletic Club? At least some things never change. It's been so many years . . . I hope you find who you're looking for."

She looks back to see if she can read the text over the door, but it's too far and she's at too sharp an angle. She turns back around, but the spirit of the man is gone.

Yolanda spins in place and realizes she's come off the beaten track and into an alleyway. Spirals the same as the petroglyphs are etched into the sides of the alley dumpsters. But because they're on either side of her, she's not sure which way to go.

The dumpsters start to shake. After a moment the three closest to her are hopping around like an unbalanced washing machine. Wind swirls forming a cyclone of rubbish, and an unearthly howl roars from the sky above. Black smears pinwheel in smoke on the alley walls. The temperature drops around her and the howl jumps up an order of magnitude of decibels. The ground shakes and car alarms blare in the distance, but the shaking feels less like an earthquake and more like an oncoming train.

She picks a direction and sprints away, unsure of what she's running from precisely, but she doesn't stop and she doesn't turn around to look and find out.

BETWEEN

Yolanda's surprised to find that she's able to cope with so many people around, despite the mushrooms. She's not sure it will last. Her fear may grow and the shadows that chased her here may grow braver, but for now, the teeming multitude of celebrants seem to be holding the darkness at bay.

The first Ishtar Gate in Los Angeles was built for D.W. Griffith's 1916 film *Intolerance.* Like many landmarks from Hollywood's earliest films, it stood in place for decades until it fell into disrepair and had to be torn down. According to the author Ray Bradbury, rebuilding it to its present height as part of a shopping mall was his idea.

Yolanda stares at the gate now. On a night like this more than shoppers are likely to travel through such a thing.

The shadows seem to sense this. They scurry around the periphery of the Halloween crowd, flickering in and out of the light, until they glom onto the wall of the gate and instead of an empty space at the bottom a purple reflection starts to shimmer into being.

Yolanda's not sure what's coming, but she knows she's not going to stick around to find out. She takes off down the side street and keeps running until the crowd starts to thin, but then she realizes she's vulnerable to the shadows and she ducks into a diner. The place is packed, but a man with a scruffy goatee and a Porkpie hat, waves at the empty seat on the other side of the table from him.

Something about him looks familiar. She's seen him on album covers, a younger version of one of her favorite musicians. She stammers, "Aren't you . . . ?"

He nods and exhales tobacco. She's sure no one was smoking when she came in. "I am."

"But . . . You're not dead."

"No. Not the version of me in your present day. But the spirits you speak to, it's not the same as speaking to the dead. It's just memories. And this memory of this time is just as gone to you as any of the dead. Past versions of yourself are just spirits now, maybe more accessible to you because you remember them the best. Oh yeah you could talk to past versions of yourself tonight. Future versions too, but don't think about it too much. In your condition you might just bodhisattva out of control and fill the diner with a horde of yous. And then I'll never get a refill." He holds his coffee mug up in the direction of the waitress.

A waitress with a chain clipped to her rhinestone glasses lopes to the table carrying a coffee pot. Her nametag says "Irene." She doesn't take Yolanda's order or even acknowledge her presence. The moment she finishes pouring the coffee she fades away into nothingness.

"I'm dead." A young man with short-cropped hair materializes on her right.

"You've no one to blame but yourself for that, Darby." Her favorite singer in the porkpie hat grins and takes a big gulp of his coffee.

"But if we're stuck in the 70s, shouldn't I be alive?"

"Memory is as unstable as reality, particularly tonight. Things overlap. That's sort of the point."

Yolanda smells something. Could be spoiled bacon, but no, she looks more closely at the young man next to her and discovers that he's putting out a cigarette on his arm.

"Knock that shit off, Darby. No one cares. No one's interested in your crap. You got to grow up."

"I never did. I thought that was my point."

Their bickering fades into the background. The chatter of the diner, clank of silverware hitting plates, and the hiss of the coffee maker take over as Yolanda ponders growing up. Has she ever grown up? If so, why does she need so badly to speak to her parents? Hasn't she learned enough? And if not, why is growing up so important anyway?

She's not sure when she stops talking to the two men, if she left the diner first, or if they did, but by the time she's stopped thinking about the singer's words, she's bewildered to find herself sitting on another bus. Streetlights warp past. The brakes squeal and the door opens.

The spirit of the singer she likes is in the driver's seat. "I'm afraid this is where you get out. You see, I have to be making a turn up ahead." He chuckles and mutters something to himself she can't quite hear.

She knows better than to ask. She steps off the bus, turns in place to get her bearings. She's near her tia's home in East L.A. When she turns back to the street, she watches the bus evaporate into mist in the intersection ahead.

Walking up Whittier Boulevard, the street is oddly empty apart from a lone shade standing in front of a Christian Church. The spirit of a middle aged Latino man nods to her as she walks by. "All I wanted was a cold beer. Now the Silver Dollar Bar is a church. No chance I'll ever get that beer, I suppose."

"Not here anyway." She shrugs. She wonders if the spirit is tied to this spot. She doesn't even consider who he is until she realizes that she's passed that church before and there's a plaque on the front wall honoring the memory of journalist, Ruben Salazar, killed at the Silver Dollar Bar by the L.A. Sheriffs.

She turns back and watches as he fades away. "Nothing has changed. Nothing will ever change again." His image is gone before his words dissipate to silence.

Her tia's door is open when she gets there. At first she worries that the shadows have beaten her here, but then she catches the first whiff of incense and hears 70s punk playing on the jukebox, and she knows the old woman is home, enjoying the night.

Light flickers from the twenty-three candles stacked on the ofrenda between the foyer and the entryway to the living room. Five candles on the bottom shelf, ten on the next, three with the pictures of Yolanda's mother and grandmother. Five more on the next shelf, and ten in front of the pictures of the two people most important to her tia. In place of the traditional Virgin Mary or saints, the top shelf holds pictures of Frida Kahlo and Alice Bag.

"Why are you here? This is the one place you cannot find what you seek."

She hadn't counted on this. It hadn't occurred to her that the woman who has helped her the most in her life wouldn't be receptive to aid her now, but maybe she should've known that when her tia had given her the recipe for the rite, but hadn't offered to help her perform it that she's meant to do it herself. "But I need help."

"Once you started the quest, what more help can I offer?"

"They're after me. I think."

It's clear her tia knows which "they" she means without her having to say so. Or did she? Yolanda's not sure which words came out of her mouth. Her tia frowns and winces as she thinks aloud. "You've been warned not to empower them with such thoughts."

"I didn't think that I did."

Her tia moves past her toward the door. She shuts it and locks the deadbolt first. The next lock is a clockwork mechanism. A five pointed star sparkles over the face of it when she finishes winding it. "They've followed you here. We only have a few minutes."

Yolanda steps into the kitchen to peer through the window.

A similar five-pointed star is etched into the glass. The smoky wraiths, black as the night, trace back and forth in front of the star, occasionally darting at it before reeling back again.

"The rift wraiths are an ever present danger when we approach the barriers. But there is worse. They serve much worse. Now, why have you come?"

Gravity comes and goes in waves under Yolanda's feet. She could graph its intensity versus time and it would be a perfect parabola or maybe a cosine. She looks back to her tia and realizes that she hasn't answered the question. "I can't find them. I've looked for mom and dad everywhere I remember being with them, but they're not there."

"The goal of your ritual still eludes you?"

"Unless you can answer for them. What do I do? Do I leave the city? Take the job I don't want because it pays better? Or do I take the job I want, stay here where it costs more, but I'll earn less?"

"If I had the answers you want, you would not have gone through the trouble to see through the barriers between worlds."

"But they're not here and I still need an answer."

Her tia looks over her shoulder as the glass on the windows rattles. "We have so little time. Three cards of the tarot? Past, present, and future?" She moves to the kitchen table. The table cloth is covered in scattered ash from the incense, beeswax from candles, and coins from a ritual that Yolanda does not recognize.

Her tia clears a space on the cloth and hands Yolanda a small bag containing the cards. "Ask your question and shuffle the cards."

Yolanda does as she says. She takes the top card and places it in front of her.

"The Queen of Wands. The black cat symbolizes her protector. She is passionate, she is accomplishing her goals."

"But that's my past."

"Yes, it could be that these are what you find lacking in your life. Are you without passion, mija? Is that why you dwell on the past? You've lost your path and are looking to find where you went off it?"

Yolanda shakes her head, though she's not so sure. It's hard enough for her to think about these things without a head full of mushrooms, not to mention the weird mathematics, and the collision of worlds from both the holiday and the magic of Los Angeles. She tries to put the lid down on the million separate thoughts firing through her head as every stray neuron attempts its own unique investigation, and she flips the next card.

"It would appear so. The Hanged Man. A life in suspension. You may just need to let go. To let yourself fall so you can set about achieving what it is you want."

"Maybe that's the problem. I've always wanted to find out all I can, but sometimes I get stuck. And I just want to ask them why? I just want to hear them once more tell me that I can do anything if I set my mind to it."

"Child, how can you not know that they would say this if they were here? Don't you know that they're proud of everything you've accomplished?"

Yolanda understands but she can't accept it. She wants to see the future. She wants to see the last card. As she starts to flip it, glass shatters from the kitchen and the temperature in the house drops twenty degrees in the blink of an eye.

The black smoke sweeps in accompanied by a howl so loud, Yolanda's ears sting despite her attempting to muffle them with her hands.

Her tia tries to rise from her chair. She raises her hands and starts to chant, "En el nombre de Kahlo y Bags salir de este lugar!" Before she can say it a second time, the shadow blast hits her, and she's knocked back into the wall so hard her chair bursts and her head dents the drywall. A tempest swirls through the living room, picking up and twisting the debris. Yolanda backs away, but the shadows pick her up and swoop her towards the mirror over her tia's couch.

It draws her in at what seems like thousands of meters per second.

Yolanda puts her arms over her eyes to protect her from the glass that's sure to break when she hits, but instead she and the shadows go right through, and blackness surrounds her.

When her eyes focus and the world stops swaying around her, she finds herself in a place she does not recognize. Desert? It's rocky around her with dry brush leading to a clearing. The hills on either side are riveted with ruts eroded by fast moving water in the distant past. The smoky shadow wraiths swarm and swirl into a cyclone and then dissipate revealing a man in a black tuxedo and carrying a cane.

"Mr. In Between?"

He smiles revealing teeth so white that they glare in the darkly lit vale and reflect off the pool of inky blackness in front of him. "I see you already know me. Introductions, I suppose, aren't necessary."

"Why have you brought me here?"

"I think you know that, too." The darkness around her vibrates and shimmers into a deep purple. The temperature drops and rises again, matching the cadence of his words, and causing Yolanda to sweat and shiver in rapid succession.

"No. I don't."

"You've been here for ages. You didn't start out here. But lately more and more of you resides here. I'm starting to think it's time to charge you rent. Or to begin your apprenticeship."

"Apprenticeship?"

"The way you're going? Or rather not going, I can't think of a better Mrs. In Between."

Yolanda realizes her jaw has dropped. She starts to giggle, can't believe who she's giggling at, and then starts to laugh all the harder. "This is the weirdest proposal I've ever had."

"Oh I know you won't accept. It's too big a change. But you won't go anywhere either. You can't. You'll just linger here until we both wither away in the wind, sun, rain. Your indecision will be measured in geologic time."

"You're wrong." She shakes her head and tries not to lose focus, but there's a light in the distance, a lone spot of white in all the darkness around her. It pulsates and then explodes into a thousand separate lights before contracting, withdrawing back to darkness. Yolanda worries she's forgotten something, and then realizes all this has taken place in no time at all, it's just the mushrooms. She's only just stopped telling him he's wrong.

"Oh, please. I recognize it when I see it. It's like staring into a mirror."

"Didn't you have to change to become who you are now?"

"Probably. But who can remember if there was another Mr. In Between. As far as you're concerned, I have always been here before. And you've always been here. Always in this action state. Whether you realized it or not."

"No. If I've learned one thing about the past, it's that I was different. I was always changing. I was always improving. If I have to go back to move forward I will."

He twirls his cane, tosses it in the air and catches it like a drum major leading a parade. "Ha! You will? All you're going to do is stay uncommitted and uncertain. Look at you, you're already rationalizing that if you can't go back, you'll stay right where you are."

Yolanda shakes her head. "No. You're wrong. I've had

enough." She feels like she can't breathe. She wonders if it's the air here, panic, or more likely the mushrooms giving her stomach problems.

"You've had enough for a long time. It hasn't done you any good." The smile curls up and then back down into a frown. "Why are you so sure it's different this time?"

"Because I'm ready to take the plunge." Yolanda dives into the black pool. It's icy as hell, and for a moment she thinks she'll sink forever and drown, but she bobs up in the surf, and catches a wave, bodysurfing to the shore at the beach where she started the evening.

She's sat on the beach so long the sun's come up again. She wonders if she ever left the beach, if the whole night has been a hallucination-fueled trip on the sands until she ended up in the water, but that's probably too rational, and she doesn't want to give into reality just yet, even if she's definitely coming down.

Coming down. With the dwindling effects of the mushrooms, so goes the potential of the ritual. There still is Dia de los Muertos, but without the accompanying rite of the drug and the shared belief of the Halloween celebrants working in conjunction, she doesn't have much hope that the rites will last.

Yolanda shivers and hugs her knees. "It's not like people get that second chance to talk to the dead," she says to no one.

"But you were always special."

Yolanda whips her head around, not having expected the answer, particularly from the voice of her mother.

Her mother and father are standing in the sand behind her, holding hands. They're half-faded, half-transparent. Their image flaps in the wind like it's painted across a sheet of paper held by one upper corner.

"I'd given up. I thought I went through that all for nothing."

Her mother's arms flash from translucent to opaque, just long enough to wrap around Yolanda's shoulders.

"I don't know what to do. I don't know how to move forward."

The wind brushes past her ear. Her mother whispers, "We love you. You'll choose the right way for you."

"I don't want to have to make the choice. I want to do both things, take both jobs. I want to do neither. I want to know what you think."

Her father's spirit doesn't fully materialize, but she hears his words come across and echo on the wind and reverberate with the sound of the waves crashing into the shore. "My child, you came to us for what? For wisdom? What wisdom do you think the dead have that the living do not? We are in the past. You have surely discovered more? Better yet, you are still discovering more. If we have any wisdom, it is this: we have lived our lives and they are over. You still have the time that is left to you. Do not dwell on our lives. Find a way to make your life what you want it to be."

The sounds of his words fade, and her parents are gone again. The trip is over, as is the power of the spell.

Yolanda wanders along the shore until she finds the integral ∫ she drew, somehow not faded from the surf or the wind. She reaches down with both hands and erases it. Finding the stick right where she dropped it, she replaces that integral with the delta. The past is past. What's ahead of her is change.

Yolanda inhales a large breath of air coming off the Pacific, turns and leaves the beach in search of breakfast and coffee to fuel the start of the change she will make for her life.

THE FRIENDLY MAN

Thomas Vaughn

THE FRIENDLY MAN planted the last of the heads then studied the sky. The forecast called for a slight chance of rain, but the clouds were receding and it looked more and more like they would have a clear night. A smile spread across his face because Halloween was the most important evening of the year for the Friendly Man. He looked down the street where the children were playing in their yards, showing off their costumes before they began circulating through the neighborhood. The girl across the street was watching him intently. She stood at the end of her driveway with a plastic pumpkin container rocking on her heels. His smile broadened.

The Friendly Man's house stood at the top of Main Street where it came to dead end. Most of the Victorian homes that lined the street had been remodeled, making it one of the most desirable real estate locations in the city. The Friendly Man's home was one of the few that had not been remodeled since the day it was built. Down in its bowels the open flame gas furnace was coming to life and the noxious warmth began drifting to various rooms through the metal tentacles which branched from the iron hull. The window glass was occluded by age and the trim was cracked. He had been offered a lot of money to sell the house so that new, more industrious owners could replace the dark green paneling and ancient black shingles. But the Friendly Man would never sell. This was the street that attracted the children on Halloween.

Almost all of the homes had decorations. Some were half-hearted while others were more spirited. There were the usual witches on broomsticks and cats with their backs arched. Some displayed pumpkins which had been so elaborately carved they bordered on obsessive genius. But the Friendly Man's house stood out among the scarecrows and pillow ghosts. Every child viewed the street as a gauntlet and at the end of the road you had to get by the Friendly Man.

He turned and studied his decorations. There was a row of heads planted on sharpened sticks along the walkway. The Friendly Man made them himself using his own special process of brining and plastination. Most bore expressions of profound terror or sadness. He could still call each one of the donors by name. Along the gutters hung various hands, legs and torsos—all of which had been subjected to the same technique. The Friendly Man had no patience with rubber prosthetics. He was a man that prided himself on the authenticity of his display.

Sometimes he would see the uneasiness on the faces of his neighbors as they pondered the verisimilitude of his ghastly display, but the plastination gave off just enough sheen in the colored spotlights to make the objects look like they could be artificial. Every so often someone would ask him in an indirect way if he ever thought about "toning it down". This idea never occurred to the Friendly Man who always had an extra surprise waiting for the kids when they got to the door.

He went back inside the house and initiated the power to the display and his house came to life. Some of the heads he had preserved before his technique was perfected had that sleepy look heads get after they have been cut off. But soon he had learned how to pose the faces in ways that were more to his liking. He tried to remain true to the individual's expressive inclinations in life. Recently he had discovered that working from photographs taken during their last moments worked best. The lighting this year was red because it activated the fear responses in the children. In addition, his yard echoed with the sound of buzzing bees. This was a deviation from last year when he used a recording of pigs being slaughtered. He hoped that the unconscious fear of angry insects would heighten the children's cortisol production. It was important that they were in a peak state of agitation by the time they reached the door.

Once he was satisfied that everything met his meticulous standards, he went to check on the surprise. His name was Jack. He had come to visit the Friendly Man about buying new gutters for his house. That was when the Friendly Man had a moment of inspiration. He hollowed out a portion of the bushes that grew alongside his house and there he placed Jack on a wooden platform next to his front window. The kids would never see him until they were right at the door. His arms were tied behind his back and one of his legs had been amputated and tied-off with a crude tourniquet. The Friendly Man came around to the window next to Jack's head and opened it.

"Hey Jack! You hanging in there?"

The man did not stir. The Friendly Man was worried he had used too much morphine.

"C'mon Jack, we only have a few minutes." He reached out and patted Jack's cheek. He moaned softly and the Friendly Man smiled. Jack would be fine. The five-thousand volt cattle prod would see to that. The Friendly Man placed the bowl of candy by the door and began to pace about his living room. He always got very excited right before the fun commenced. He rubbed his hands together and smiled like an expectant father. Soon there were distant sounds of laughter in the street.

He peered outside his window and waited. The first people to approach were a young couple who had just moved onto the street. The child was very young. The young ones always came out early. This one was a little boy. His parents were trying to drag him up the walkway.

"Noooo!" he screamed.

"Come on. I am sure it's all right. Don't you want some candy?"

"Nooo! I'm not going! I'm not going! I'm afraid!"

The Friendly Man giggled and wrung his hands together in delight at the child's distress. The sound of the little boy's wails were like sweet angelic harps to his ears. Finally the parents relented and they went to the next house.

"Maybe next year," the Friendly Man muttered under his breath. It was always a good omen when the little ones wouldn't even attempt an approach.

The next parents who came to the house were pushing a stroller. The Friendly Man frowned. He did not particularly like the ones that were this young. They did not understand fear. They were just innate blobs of protoplasm. The genius of his surprise would be lost on them. Before they could ring the doorbell he intervened by opening the door and greeting them with a smile.

"Happy Halloween!"

The parents seemed young and energetic. The Friendly Man could not tell if it was a boy or a girl in the stroller, though it was dressed as race car driver. It stared uncomprehendingly when he offered it the candy.

"What would you like Cole?" asked the woman. The child looked up at the Friendly Man who waited impatiently. "How about some M&Ms?" the woman prompted. The Friendly Man navigated the candy bowl so that the M&Ms were directly beneath the child's hand and to his relief the fingers closed reflexively. As he retracted the bowl the child maintained his grip while the father took a picture.

"This place is a trip," he said. "I am pretty sure I have never seen anything quite like it. It's totally Texas Chainsaw Massacre. Those bones look totally real."

"Thank you," said the Friendly Man.

"Where did you buy this stuff? It's really high quality."

The Friendly Man beamed. "Actually, I have a little shop downstairs. I make everything by hand."

"No kidding," said the woman. "Every time we meet one of our neighbors, we are always amazed at how many talented people live on this street. We had no idea that we were neighbors with a special effects artist."

As they departed the Friendly Man noticed it was finally getting dark. No sooner had he closed the door than he heard voices approaching from the other direction. These were older kids running in a pack. The Friendly Man held his breath in anticipation. This was his target audience.

There were seven of them. He listened to their voices through the door. "Holy crap! Look at this place. This is freaking awesome," said one.

"This place always rocks," said another. "And he gives out full-sized candy bars."

They got to the door and paused.

"You knock."

"I don't want to. You do it."

Then a girl's voice piped-up. "What is wrong with you guys? Nothing is going to happen. Besides the sign says ring the doorbell. You want me to do it?"

"No, I'll do it."

One of the children pressed the doorbell, activating the floodlight in the bushes along with the cattle prod. Jack began thrashing and screaming. The sight of a bloody, partially dismembered man jerking spasmodically sent the children running. The Friendly Man flung the door open and yelled "Happy Halloween," to his astonished congregation. Half of them had actually darted back into the street. The Friendly Man felt an indescribable joy swelling inside of his body.

The girl who had spoken held her hand to her chest to calm her heart. "Oh my God. I think I nearly died."

"I told you this place was freaking awesome," said another as they lined up to take their candy. "Look at that guy's leg. You can totally see the bone. That looks so real."

"Hey, I think that's a real guy. He is trying to speak. Is that a real guy?"

The Friendly Man winked. "Remember, death is always standing right behind you."

This is what he said every year.

As the children dispersed the Friendly Man closed the door and dashed over to the window. "Jack," he whispered. "That was great."

The man was now conscious, though confused. "What's happening? Why are you doing this?"

"Why? Because it's Halloween. Oh wait . . . Here come some more."

This time it was a group of four.

"This is weird," said one.

"Can you hear the buzzing?"

"Yeah . . . And I heard something else. I think there is someone in the bushes."

"Just ring the doorbell."

Again the floodlight activated and 5000 volts surged through Jack who jerked and screamed. Again the children panicked and one fell off the porch. The Friendly Man beamed at the chaos through the peephole, then opened the door.

"Happy Halloween!"

"Man, that was over the top!"

The one who had fallen off the porch came back up the steps. "I think I just crapped myself."

"Remember, death is always standing right behind you."

As the children ran to the next house one of them was visibly limping. The Friendly Man sighed contentedly. He closed the door and returned to the window.

"Look, Jack. It's better if you don't make any noise until they ring the doorbell."

"What? What happened to me? Where is my leg?"

"It's hanging from the gutter over there. Now listen, they can hear you moaning when they come up the walk. I mean it still works, but it's better if they don't know which direction it's going to come from. Understand? Okay, here's another group."

As the Friendly Man ran back to the door Jack was saying "What? That's my leg hanging over there?"

The kids rang the doorbell and the Friendly Man danced to the sounds of their mayhem. It was beautiful. This time there was a parent nearby.

"Wow," said the man with the filtered flashlight. "That was intense. You really aren't pulling any punches here." It was clear he was even more rattled than the kids.

"I think Halloween is a special night. It gives them something to remember."

"Well I know I am not going to forget it," said the man.

"Help me," said Jack who was again shrouded in darkness. "Call my wife. Call the police. I need a doctor."

"Is that guy okay?"

"That's my nephew. I paid him fifty bucks not to break character. You know he's got a scholarship to study acting in college next year. Pretty good, isn't he?"

"Sure had me fooled," said the man. "Well goodnight and enjoy scaring the socks off of the whole neighborhood." He turned to the bushes. "Good luck with the acting there, Buddy. I am putting you in for an academy award tonight."

The Friendly Man waved. "Remember, death is always standing right behind you."

"Yeah. Tell me about it. I think I married her." The man laughed awkwardly then continued up the street to catch-up with the kids.

The Friendly Man checked the candy dish to make sure there was plenty then returned to the window.

"You're doing great, Jack!"

"Please stop shocking me. I'll do anything if you stop shocking me."

"I'm not shocking you. You're hooked to the doorbell. The kids are shocking you."

"You have to stop this. You have to stop doing this to me. Can't you just try to be reasonable?"

The Friendly Man stared hard at Jack for moment. "Jack . . . Do I seem like a reasonable man to you?"

Before Jack could answer the Friendly Man rushed back to the peephole. It was the little girl from across the street. She was by herself and dressed in an angel outfit with wings. She was a little young to be out by herself, but he had noticed she was becoming increasingly insistent about approaching his house alone. The Friendly Man cackled as she cautiously made her way to the door, a steely eyed veteran of his tricks. He watched her look to one side when Jack began his entreaties.

"Dammit Jack," whispered the Friendly Man to himself. "If you screw this up you are really going to pay."

After she pressed the doorbell, he watched her visibly flinch as Jack began his electrical histrionics, but it was nothing close to the panic he had induced in the other children.

He opened the door. "Now that is what I am talking about.

You are one tough cookie my little friend. I am going to have to start upping my game."

She smiled with pride as she selected her candy. "I was scared for just a second," she admitted.

"But you held your ground, and that's what counts. Just remember, death is always standing right behind you."

She nodded and then impishly pressed the doorbell again and watched with delight as Jack writhed, spit flying from clenched teeth and his gruesome stump convulsing. It was not wise to let Jack take two jolts like that. It wasn't like he was going to last the whole night, but the Friendly Man couldn't help but indulge the little girl. He watched as she dashed into the night and breathed the cool autumn air, enjoying the smell of decaying leaves. There was a great sense of release in his body—a feeling of well-being he rarely experienced. Listening to the street he sensed a lull in the action. He went inside and got a bottle of water and returned to the window.

"Here's a drink of water Jack. You're starting to lose your voice. We can't have you getting dehydrated now can we?"

The man gulped the proffered water greedily. His eyes were bloodshot and it was clear that he was only partially conscious of his surroundings. The Friendly Man frowned and retrieved his flashlight, shining it into Jack's eyes. "You are about to go into shock again. But, don't worry. The electricity should wake you up. I am not certain how much longer your central nervous system will last, but you are holding up pretty well. You must workout. Do you jog or something?"

Jack nodded while his mind drifted in and out of focus. "Bicycle."

"Biking! I knew it had to be something like that. You know it is a good thing you took such good care of yourself. All of these people who just exercise and eat organic vegetables disgust me. It's like they want to live forever or something. At least this way all that hard work you put into caring for your body hasn't been a total waste of time. Did you see that one kid fall off the porch? He will never forget that. You are really making an impression."

"Can you please turn off the current?"

"Jack, the idea is to scare the kids, not put them to sleep. You have to create a climate of sustained agitation in their minds, then shock their systems with massive jolt of fear. Mortal terror is an essential part of childhood development."

"But I can . . . I can pretend."

"No can do, Jack. Look, these kids are already spreading the word. We have set a high bar here tonight. Some things cannot be done in half measures. Here comes another group. Get ready."

The doorbell chimed and the gruesome cycle repeated itself. This time one of the kids fled the house without getting his candy. The Friendly Man clapped his hands in victory then returned to the window.

"Now what were we talking about?"

"In the name of God, I beg you to stop. You have got to stop."

"Religion? Don't even get me started on that one. Those Christians are the worst. I've got two of them on stakes out front there. I guess they came peddling their Bibles to the wrong house. They flounce around telling everyone who will listen that God loves them and they are going to live forever in magic-land. I mean what kind of an idiot would believe that? And the worst part is they pour all of that crap into the heads of their kids. These poor children have few defenses against that sort of nonsense. You see, that's where I come in."

"You're insane."

"I'll tell you what's insane, Jack. Pyramids."

"Pyramids?"

"Yeah. Why did the Egyptians build the pyramids? Because they were afraid of death. Think about thousands of people dragging those giant granite slabs up the side of those ridiculous artificial mountains. And for what? It's just one big condo for your mummified boss. You can't take it with you. What an enormous waste of resources. One look at my yard and you see there is no ambiguity here—no delusion. This is the end of the line. You cross the threshold of my front door and you are not getting out alive."

The Friendly Man paused and listened to the sound of laughter on the street. Jack moaned and tensed in painful anticipation.

"Okay. They are on the other side of the street. False alarm. Anyway, all these kids nowadays are told they are special and that their opinions matter. Let me tell you what. You don't matter. Nothing that you say or do or think matters. When you die, that's it. The universe slams shut behind you and it's like you were never here. All you leave behind is a stinking corpse on a meat hook. That's all we are."

The doorbell caught them both by surprise. There were more shrieks of terror from the yard. The Friendly Man went out and greeted his guests in his usual manner. As the children left they began chanting the Friendly Man's reminder in unison.

"Death is always standing right behind you! Death is always standing right behind you."

He returned to the window. "What's burning over here? Oh . . . I wouldn't think 5000 volts would do that. You still got a few more in you?"

"Please, stop doing this to me." For Jack, the pain was more than just physical. There was something humiliating about having his torment take place right out in public with no one lifting a finger to stop it. It reached a level of sickness that he thought unattainable.

"That's the other problem with today. Everyone just thinks about themselves. Have you ever thought about what it's like for guys like me? You know, guys who do this sort of thing." The

Friendly Man gestured to the array of body parts hanging around the house. "Look, nobody is throwing me a parade on my special day. You know how often I get to come out of the closet? One night a year. I get to be myself in public for one night a year. The rest of my life is spent in that damn cellar. You talk about injustice."

"Am I going die?" whispered Jack, tears forming in his eyes.

"Well, of course. Oh . . . you mean tonight? Well, yeah . . . that too. Frankly I don't know how much more you can take. I am actually surprised you are still with me. Hey look, I know it sucks that this is your last night on Earth and you have to spend it listening to me go on and on. But I am simply telling you this so you understand your death is serving a higher purpose."

As the night wore on the children came and went until Jack's body was at an end. Each time the terrible pain coursed through his system he could hear their cries of horror mixed with delight. It was so strange that people could take pleasure from this terrible spectacle. But even through this haze of suffering, he began to perceive that there was a sick logic to it. It was as if this brutal ritual was teaching a valuable lesson—that the mastery of something as inevitable as death could only be achieved through its acceptance. But even as this thought took shape in his mind, he rejected it. He thought about all of the things he wanted to do with his life and he knew one thing. He was going to live.

As the crowds turned into a trickle, the Friendly Man shut off the lights. The candy bowl was almost empty. Jack pulled at the ropes, but was too weak to free his hands. He knew that there was no way to reason with his captor who was clearly insane. Little bits of half remembered prayers tumbled from his lips. As he searched his mind for a plan he felt a small hand on his shoulder.

"Be really quiet." It was a girl's voice. "I'm gonna cut these ropes, but you've got to be really quiet. He can hear good. Okay?"

Jack nodded, a glimmer of hope piercing this endless nightmare. He did not know who his savior was, but all he could do was whisper, "Thank you."

He felt the knife cutting through the nylon cord and after several seconds his hands were free. When he could move them, he reached around and pulled the cattle prod from his flesh. He winced at the pain because the electrodes had fused to his skin.

He heard a distant voice say "You have to crawl. Don't go to the front or he will see you. There is a way out around back. Come with me."

Following the voice he rolled to his side and began pulling himself through the bushes, dragging his ruined stump across the ground. "I'm going to live. I'm going to live. I'm going to live," he said over and over again.

"Just follow me," said the voice. Jack's field of vision was blurry, but he could see enough to realize that whoever was saving him had wings. Then it came to him. He was being rescued by an angel. God had heard his prayers and sent an angel to rescue him, just like he had read about in all of the books and seen in all of the movies. Silently he gave thanks to his protector and picked up his pace, keeping sight of the luminescent wings under the feeble glow of the street lights. All Jack knew was that he had to follow his angel.

Meanwhile the Friendly Man was straightening his house. It was important to bring in the decorations first thing. He couldn't have anyone stealing one for a souvenir. When he went out on the front porch and peered into the hollowed spot next to the bushes he noticed that Jack was gone.

"Now where did you go?" he asked. He dashed to the street and looked in both directions. "Nope. This is not good," he said to himself. He knew this year's plan was risky. If he did not find his decoration, it would mean no more Halloweens for him. That would mean villagers with torches and pitchforks. Then he heard a few dull thuds coming from the back of his house. Trying to look casual he jogged around to his backyard where he found the little girl from across the street standing over Jack. She was holding an aluminum softball bat. The man at her feet was inert.

"I see," said the Friendly Man. "I guess the prank was on me this year."

"Yeah," said the little girl. "You had a funny look on your face."

The Friendly Man laughed. "I guess I did. You had me going there. Let's take a look at your handiwork. You didn't hit him in the head did you?"

The girl twisted on one foot, the bat dangling from her hand. "Maybe."

The Friendly Man was too relieved to be angry. "Yeah, you bashed him pretty good. He definitely has a fractured skull. You must think you're Babe Ruth."

"Who's Babe Ruth?"

"Never mind. I think I can repair most of this. There is nothing like a good challenge."

"You're going to put him in your yard?"

"Well of course. You can't go wasting things like this. Actually, he wasn't a bad guy. I think maybe he was right about the gutters come to think of it. It wouldn't do for him to go through all of that suffering for nothing." Then he looked at the little girl. "You promise me something?"

"What?"

"You wash that bat when you get home."

The little girl nodded her head and started to cross the yard. The Friendly Man took the body under each armpit and began to drag it around the side of the house. When he looked up, he saw the little girl was watching him again. She was smiling as a breeze came through the trees and a cluster of dead leaves dropped at her feet. There was something in her eye. It was more than just the gleam of a budding predator. It was a measured stare—almost a challenge.

"Remember," she said. "Death is always standing right behind you."

A chill went up his spine. The glitter from the wings of her costume shown in the moonlight.

"Yeah," he replied. "I guess you're right."

MANY CARVINGS

Sean Eads and Joshua Viola

"**L**IGHT THE LAMPS, Alaster," the boy's mother said, lifting her needlework to squint at a stitch. Alaster lay on the floor, so obsessed with his brother that he didn't even notice the chill of the wooden planks through his night shirt. The month-old infant cooed from his crib and his kicking feet made the most delicate thuds, a noise that pleased Alaster. It reminded him of pulling carrots from the ground and wiping away the dirt and hearing the earthen clumps break on the ground.

"Alaster."

He pushed himself to all fours and then went to light the lamps. An October gale gusted against the house, speeding him along. He liked to think of each wick as a person with an oval flame of hair. The fire always seemed to bow toward him at first, like a curtsey to thank him for life. Then it stretched with fuel like a person waking in the morning, arms up, back arching. When he was a little younger, he gave each flame a name and pretended they were all family members. But those memories embarrassed him now.

He knelt by the crib and smiled. "I think William wants to eat."

"He'll cry if he does, Alaster. None of my boys were ever shy about their hunger, you least of all. Your father warned me when

I married him that appetite is prominent among all Cheverus men."

Alaster asked if he could have honey then, but his mother smiled and shook her head. "It's much too late for that, child."

"Would you read to me then, like Father does?"

His mother paused a moment, then her hands worked faster. "Aren't you too old for stories?"

"Father reads me different stories now."

"Does he?"

"About generals and soldiers and—"

"I must speak to him about that."

Alaster looked up to see if his mother was cross. She didn't seem so. But there was something in her expression he didn't understand. Did she not like stories? Why had she never told him one from a book?

"Your father will be back soon enough. He'll have stories from the market, I'm sure."

"I wish I could have gone with them. It's not fair that Benjamin gets to go."

"Benjamin is fifteen. You'll go with them soon enough. But now you have little William to watch over."

Alaster couldn't help pouting. He'd never been to the city, and this was Benjamin's third straight season helping Father at the market with the other men. He always came back with tales of wonder. People singing and strange animals wondering here and there, and drinks and candies found nowhere else. The tastes Alaster's imagination created always turned to sour envy on his tongue.

He looked down at William and thought, *When I'm older, I'm going to go to the markets while you stay behind, but I'll bring something back for you.*

Alaster kissed the baby on the forehead. Drowsiness overtook him shortly thereafter, and he had little memory of his mother turning off the lamps or picking him off the floor. He did remember a sleepy protest that he was too big to be carried, but his mother was very stout, like most of the village women. It would be a few years before he truly became too heavy for her.

He woke to the sound of a fierce hammering from the front door and the baby wailing in his parents' room. Alaster heard his mother up and on the move. He left his bed and instantly shivered in the night's chill. The banging gained urgency. Alaster thought there must be an army outside demanding shelter.

As he came to stand beside his mother, Alaster heard a voice shouting to be let in.

"It's Benjamin! But why is he here, Mother? What could have happened?"

Each question engraved a new line upon his mother's face.

"Go tend your brother."

"But my brother is—"

His mother's expression shut him up. He'd only seen her look this way once, a few months before William's birth when word arrived of an accident in the field. Mother simply said, *"Jonathan,"* in the same hushed way she said *Jesus* in church, and took off running despite her condition. But Father ended up not being hurt too much, and Ms. Sibley came to tend his injury.

"Thank you for coming so fast," Mother said as she, Alaster and Benjamin gathered to watch Ms. Sibley apply a poultice to Father's ankle. Alaster fixated on the old woman's hands, so big at the knuckles, so slow and careful with Father's bandage—and then so swift to touch his mother's stomach.

"A shame the accident, if it had to happen, couldn't have occurred two months from now. What's the expression? Kill two birds with one stone?"

But it'd be three more months before William was ready, and then Ms. Sibley delivered him just as she'd delivered Benjamin. She'd wiped her hands clean on a rag, smiled at Alaster and said, "Easier than your brother, but not as eager to arrive as you."

"Alaster—go to William. *Now.*"

He blinked back to the present as the door rattled and Benjamin again begged for admission. Alaster retreated to his parents' bedroom and knelt by the baby's crib. "Hush," he said, stroking the infant's sparse hair. But William went on wailing, drowning out all other sound. After a few minutes, Alaster couldn't stand not knowing what was happening with Benjamin and left the bedroom to see. He found his brother holding a sheet of paper before his mother's face.

"But why would Jonathan write when he knows—"

"He told me to read it to you, Mother."

Alaster crept closer, keeping close to the wall. William's cries became distant to him.

"Dearest, a great illness has struck at the market. More people are ill here than well. It is a devilish thing, but with God's help we will persevere. Already I am feeling better just writing to you. I return Benjamin to you since he remains healthy. I know you will disapprove of the decision, but he is a capable boy and I did not send him back alone."

Mother said, "Who did you return with?"

"Cameron."

"Martin Huntley's oldest? Is Martin ill, too?"

"Yes, Mother. We traveled the entire way back together and—"

"Where is Cameron now?"

"At home, talking to his own mother, I suppose," Benjamin said, adding a laugh that Alaster thought almost mocking. This drew him closer and his presence caught his older brother's attention. Benjamin fixed him with a bold, assured stare. He seemed even taller than before, though that couldn't be possible. He and Father had been gone not even a full week.

"What sort of illness was it, Benjamin?"

"How should I know?"

"Was there coughing?"

"Yes."

"How was your father's appetite?"

Benjamin shrugged. "He was eating."

"And keeping it down?"

"Mostly."

"There's that, at least," Mother said, gathering her gown around her as she turned. Alaster thought she looked miserable. In most times of trouble, she'd say, "It's in God's hands now." But she hadn't said that when she thought Father was hurt. And she didn't say it now. Alaster figured she wanted to consult Ms. Sibley, but there was nothing to be done at so late an hour. And the market was so far away.

"Are you hungry, Benjamin?"

"No, Mother."

"Are you sure? You must have traveled for hours."

"Our fathers gave us bread for the trip."

"Then go to bed. You too, Alaster."

But Benjamin went straight to his parents' room. Alaster and his mother exchanged looks before following.

"What are you doing, Ben?"

"I've missed my brother."

He picked William up and cradled him. Alaster's face went hot when the baby's cries turned into contented coos.

"He missed me."

"Settle him back into the crib, Benjamin. It's time for all of us to sleep. In the morning, I'll visit with the Huntleys."

"You don't believe me, Mother?"

"What sort of question is that? I only want to find out more details."

Alaster watched Benjamin slowly return William to the crib.

"I told you —"

Mother reached forward and grabbed him by the back of his neck. "I'll assume this defiant tone comes from being exhausted. Go to bed now—both of you."

In their room, Benjamin flopped upon the mattress and was asleep at once. Alaster didn't realize how quickly he'd become used to having the bed to himself. Now his brother's large, sprawling body reduced him to the left edge. He couldn't sleep on the verge of teetering.

"Ben, give me room," he said, prodding his shoulder.

A drowsy, distant tone came from Benjamin's lips. "I will . . . I will . . ."

"Then do it."

"I will . . . I will . . ."

Alaster rose up to peer at his brother in the dark. Ben's lips moved but a different voice came from his mouth. A whisper like the dry rustle of wheat fields and as scratchy as winter bramble. Then it was Ben's voice, clearly saying, "I will, I will." Then the whisper again. Alaster wondered if his brother was dreaming of talking to someone.

"Yes, Mother."

His brother let out a short burst of laughter with an even meaner edge than the laugh he'd given earlier. Alaster settled back onto his little slice of mattress and clutched himself. He did not sleep even after Benjamin went silent and his breaths came and went at the slow, steady pace of dreams.

But drowsiness stole upon him at some point. He woke with the bed to himself again and a feeling like *he'd* been the one dreaming. Ben was still at the market with Father. There'd been no midnight return, no news of illness.

Alaster tossed the blankets off him and changed clothes before leaving his room. He heard his mother's faint voice calling for him.

Entering his parents' bedroom, he found her in bed, still dressed in her gown. She lifted her arms as he rushed to her.

"Sick," she whispered.

So last night was not a dream.

"Could you have what Father has? Maybe Benjamin—"

"He took . . . took . . . "

Alaster leaned closer. "Took what, Mother? Where did he go?"

"Huntley . . . William . . . "

She rose an inch toward him, beseeching with a fervor that lasted seconds before she collapsed back onto the bed and turned her face to the wall. Alaster saw sweat pooling at the base of her throat. He drew back and his heels struck William's crib. He turned and gasped at the empty box.

"Benjamin took William?"

She nodded.

Alaster thought he understood. Father sent Benjamin back to avoid being sick, but somehow Mother became ill too. Now Mother wanted them all to go to the Huntley farm. But why would Ben have left without him?

"Mother—"

She tried to speak but her voice didn't reach a whisper. The sound of her struggle made his chest hurt. He went to Father's desk and took out a piece of paper and a pencil.

"Write out what I should do and I'll do it."

Mother's eyes shifted to the pencil and paper and she began to cry. She made a pushing motion, shooing him away. He felt certain staying here brought her pain, and he took off running without another thought. His feet slapped at the single dirt path leading to the main road. Once there, Alaster turned left. Not the direction of the neighbor farm families like the Huntleys and the Mastersons.

He went on without a conscious thought until he arrived at Ms. Sibley's little cottage.

SEAN EADS AND JOSHUA VIOLA

No smoke came from her chimney, but Alaster heard sounds from within. He knocked on the door. "Ms. Sibley, it's Alaster. Can you come and see my mother? She's sick."

A sound like many mouths stifling laughter came from the other side. Alaster stepped back. He felt the sunlight's gathering heat on his narrow shoulders. It wasn't strong enough to thaw the ice creeping up his spine.

"Child, why are you here?"

He spun around to find Ms. Sibley standing there, wrapped in layers of warm garments. She must have started the day early, venturing forth when the temperature was far less comfortable. She carried an open basket in her left hand, overflowing with mushrooms and roots and sticks and fallen leaves, as if she'd collected according to random fancy. But the pumpkin cradled in the nook of her right arm drew most of his attention. He'd never seen one so perfect, its unblemished orange skin blazing in the daylight.

Ms. Sibley came closer. "Alaster, I see, and not long out of bed from the looks of it. What's wrong?"

He fought to draw his attention off the pumpkin. "Mother—she's sick. Father too. At the market."

"How do you know about the market?"

Alaster explained about Ben's return and the letter Father wrote.

"I know," Ms. Sibley said, moving toward the door. "Many doctors have been summoned, and I've heard there are road signs posted now warning travelers away. I fear it is plague."

He gasped. "Mother and Father have the plague!"

"Don't fret, Alaster. After all, fall is upon us, and that's the season for many maladies."

"Will you come?"

"Yes. I have business at the Whitmore farm anyway. Mrs. Whitmore's baby is due next week, but I have a feeling it will happen today. I always have a sense about these things, and I've only been wrong once. My error stands before me."

She placed the basket and the pumpkin down at her door. Its orange skin seemed to brighten and deepen by the moment. Alaster stared at it until Ms. Sibley cleared her throat. "Does something vex you, child?"

"Where did that pumpkin come from?"

"My patch, of course."

He looked around. She had farmed only the most modest plot of ground, enough to sustain herself. There was certainly no pumpkin field.

They started walking back the way he'd come. "So why are you here and not Benjamin?"

"He was gone when I woke up. He took William and I guess went to Mr. Huntley's place."

"Without you?"

"I'm sure he was rushing to please Mother."

Ms. Sibley's pace quickened and Alaster found he had to run a bit to match it.

"How are things between you and Benjamin since little William came along?"

"Benjamin isn't less mean."

She laughed. "No, I daresay not. But is there jealousy? Do you fight for the child's affections?"

"He's only a few weeks old. He doesn't know us."

"For the last sixteen years, I have been the first to greet the children of this village—except for you, of course. A newborn's eyes are so tired, like they already understand the miseries in store for them. The wisdom of infants surpasses all of us."

Ms. Sibley's pace grew even faster, so that she seemed to glide over the ground. Alaster did not see how her old legs carried her like this and had to run to keep up.

They reached Alaster's home and he started for the door, but Ms. Sibley seized his shoulder. "No. Your mother sent you away to protect you. Honor that wish. I'll go in alone."

A piece of paper on the floor caught his attention. He bent to pick it up as Ms. Sibley went past him, heading toward his parents' bedroom.

Alaster felt certain he held the note Ben read to Mother last night, but as he turned it over he found only gibberish. Why would Father write *this*? And how could Ben have read it like it made sense?

Ms. Sibley's footsteps drew his attention. She wasn't gliding now.

"Alaster," she said.

"How is Mother?"

"Sleeping deeply—and cool to the touch. We should let her rest."

"But I brought you here to help!"

"Sleep is often the best doctor of all."

He cast a longing glance toward the bedroom door. As he did, Ms. Sibley pinched the paper between her thumb and forefinger.

"What is this, Alaster?"

"Nothing," he said. "I don't know. Something Benjamin had."

"May I see it?"

He let go of the paper with more reluctance than he could explain to himself. It felt like surrendering a secret. Ms. Sibley's eyebrows rose.

"I don't understand. It's just letters and symbols," Alaster said. "But Ben said Father wrote it and he read from it. It said there was a sickness in the market and that's why Ben came back with Cameron Huntley."

"Cameron," Ms. Sibley said, clasping her hands together. "How well I remember delivering him. My first, I think. I knew he'd be a sharp lad. His mother bled like she'd given birth to a razor."

Alaster just stared as Ms. Sibley walked past him to the door. "Come along," she said like an afterthought. "I will take you to the Huntley farm where you can join your brothers. Then I'll continue on to the Whitmore home. That baby is coming within the next ninety minutes. I feel it in my marrow, and I don't want to miss the birth of a *second* child."

The promise of seeing Ben coaxed Alaster to go with her. Their walk took only twenty minutes at the old woman's aggressive pace, with Alaster's side aching as he worked to keep up. Only the sight of the farmhouse gave him a second wind. He dashed ahead of Ms. Sibley, calling Ben's name, certain it was his brother coming around the corner. He stopped cold, realizing it was Cameron. Stocky, a year older than Ben and a little larger, Cameron had always seemed a friendly giant. Alaster remembered being much younger and begging rides on his back. Cameron never refused him.

"Stay back," he said now, and Alaster stopped.

"What's wrong?"

"There's sickness here. My ma is sick."

"Is that so?" Ms. Sibley said, stepping to join them.

"Yes, ma'am."

"Mine is too," Alaster said. "She sent Ben and William here to stay with you. She told me to go, too."

"They're not here."

"Where are they, Cameron?" Ms. Sibley said.

"Ma thought it best they didn't stay so they kept on going."

Alaster spun towards Ms. Sibley and bit his lower lip as a tremble overtook him. But the old woman kept her attention on Cameron.

"May I see your mother?"

He nodded. Ms. Sibley told Alaster to stay outside. He hugged himself and waited—but not for long. Ms. Sibley returned looking very pleased.

"Cameron's mother is sleeping as well, and likewise cool to the touch."

She started back toward the road.

"But what about my brothers?"

"Likely they too went on to the Whitmore house. It would be the next practical place. Might as well continue with me."

Alaster looked back in the direction of his home. How nice to be there when Mother woke up feeling better. But how long would that be? Imagining a wait of hours, alone and lonely proved foul water for seeds of hope. It'd be much better to find Ben and return together.

They set out for the Whitmore residence, a mile south of the Huntley farm. Ms. Sibley did not hurry now. Perhaps she knew time was on her side.

"Have you given much thought to your future, Alaster?"

No one had ever asked him such a question, and his immediate thoughts embarrassed him with their frivolity. He'd imagined himself a pirate, a soldier, or an adventurer. So many beanstalks climbed, so many giants bested. But he knew these weren't answers to an adult's question.

"I'll be a farmer, like my father."

"Nothing else?"

He frowned, knowing only one other profession. Old Reverend Peterson's face flashed through his memory.

"Maybe a preacher?"

Ms. Sibley grunted. "Stay with farming."

Her tone confused him. Both his parents considered Reverend Peterson to be an important man, though Alaster had never felt much comfort in the man's craggy features. Perhaps he was not so prominent after all. Wouldn't Father have sent Ben straight to him? Wouldn't Mother have sent her boys to seek his help first?

They reached the Whitmore home. Ms. Sibley did not bother knocking before opening the front door.

"As I suspected," she said with clear delight.

He looked around Ms. Sibley and saw Mrs. Whitmore on the living room floor, undressed in a way that made him blush and turn his head, though he lost to the temptation to give her several quick, fascinated glances. Mother had been concerned for her. He remembered her saying so last week. "I worried that William might delay until your father had gone to the market. But I have two strong boys to help. Mary has no one. At least she's young and very healthy."

She didn't look so now. Her body rippled with strain.

"How did you know?" she said through moans and gritted teeth.

"Just a sense of the season."

"I thought I was going to have to bear this alone. With Adam at market—"

"Is he sick, too?" Alaster said.

Mrs. Whitmore seemed to become aware of his presence for the first time and tried to work a blanket over herself. Ms. Sibley soothed her.

"The child is assisting me. I take it his brothers are not here?"

"Brothers? What? No—no one. Sick? What does he mean? What—"

A sudden scream overtook her as her body convulsed. For all Ms. Sibley's talk of assistance, Alaster found she needed none. Her hands slid along the young woman's thighs as she settled into a position that blocked much of Alaster's view. His stare alternated between the floor and Ms. Sibley's back. His heart beat very fast, almost like he had two in his chest. As Mrs. Whitmore's screams became piercing, as her voice bled into so many frantic pleas and prayers, Alaster found his hands clenching. Something was wrong. Something had to be. He'd not been allowed in the room when Mother gave birth to William, but he'd listened and there wasn't nearly this much agony. Ms. Sibley liked telling

Alaster he was too eager for the world, hence his early arrival. Could a person be the opposite? Could a baby be reluctant to breathe the air? Could it be afraid or perhaps think the time, the moment, not right?

He stepped closer and to the right. The baby was halfway out, its head like a slick, shiny gourd in Ms. Sibley's hands. The rest of the body belonged to a mysterious place Alaster could not understand. He watched Mrs. Whitmore writhe as the baby kept coming. A terrifying, fleshy string was attached to the infant's stomach, and as the feet came through the cord brought with it a purple mass that reminded Alaster of calf's liver sewn up by a drenched skein of yellow and red yarn. He pointed at the deformity, thinking it must be some dead twin.

"It is the cord, and the rest is called afterbirth. It is nature's way. Now go to the well and bring a pitcher of water."

He left but saw the cord in his imagination. He lifted his shirt and looked at his belly button. Had there once been a cord there? Had there been one on William? The questions distracted him so much, he spilled most of the water on the way back and had to refill the pail.

When he returned, Ms. Sibley was cleaning the baby and gathering the afterbirth for disposal. Mrs. Whitmore's eyes were shut in obvious exhaustion.

"Alaster, go to the kitchen and bring a knife."

"What for?"

"To cut the child free of its cord, of course."

He left and came back with the only thing he could find, a heavy butcher's knife. It seemed light enough in Ms. Sibley's grasp, though. She smiled at the blade, then brought it down on the cord. Alaster winced, convinced the baby would scream. But it seemed to feel no pain of separation. Ms. Sibley wrapped fresh linen around it and put the child into its mother's arms. Mrs. Whitmore offered the faintest of smiles.

"Adam will be so pleased. He thought he might be too old to become a father."

Ms. Sibley only turned to the window and said, "The day has lapsed more than I realized."

"I'm very cold just now," Mrs. Whitmore said.

"Alaster, start a fire."

He did, bringing wood from a pile just outside the door. As the blaze caught, he turned to see Ms. Sibley gathering the afterbirth and the cord into the bucket.

"I will dispose of these for you."

"Thank you for everything," Mrs. Whitmore said. "But do you have to go already? I am very tired and worried. What will I do if something goes wrong tonight? Without Adam here ..."

"I cannot stay, unfortunately. But Alaster can."

He flinched. "I can't. I have to find my brothers. I have to—"

"You need to stay where you can be both safe and of use. Your parents would want this. Should Mrs. Whitmore need anything, you'll be able to help."

"I would feel much better about it," Mrs. Whitmore said.

He looked between the two women. His mother *would* have him stay here and be of use. But where were Ben and William?

He turned toward the door—

"Please," Mrs. Whitmore said.

—and pivoted back.

"I'll stay."

"Good lad," Ms. Sibley said, patting his head. "I'll go now. Come and find me should anything go wrong here, though I'm sure all will be well."

"Tell Benjamin where I'm at if you see him. And will you stop in and check on Mother on your way back?"

"Yes to both, Alaster. Such a good, brave boy you are. It would have made me so proud to say I helped bring courage such as yours into the world."

He beamed at her and was still beaming as he watched her leave, full pail in hand. As soon as she disappeared, Mrs. Whitmore called for him.

"The fire needs more fuel."

"Yes, ma'am."

Then she needed more water.

"Alaster, will you help me sit better in this chair? Can you bring a pillow for my back? Alaster, fetch my quilt from the bedroom. Can you see if the chickens look like they've eaten today? And the pigs?"

The evening found him exhausted.

He sat by the hearth, clutching his knees against his chest as he stared at the fire. How were his father and Cameron's father and Mr. Whitmore? Was Mother still cool to the touch? Was she awake? What if *she* needed more water, more fuel for the fire and a pillow for her back and a quilt for her lap?

"Mrs. Whitmore, I think I should go. Just to check on my mother. I can come straight back."

She didn't answer. Alaster rose and found her asleep with the baby cradled at her breast. The baby's eyes were closed, its mouth slightly open. Neither would realize he'd left.

He tiptoed to the door.

"Womb to earth, and earth to womb, I bind thee to new skin and new sires."

He turned and took a cautious step toward the mother and child. "Ms. Sibley?"

The words continued in her voice. Alaster peered through the dark and listened.

"Soon your true heart beats within another chest."

He crept closer and let his sight confirm what his ears told him.

Ms. Sibley's voice came from the baby's tiny mouth.

"And you'll receive my milk through a foreign breast."

A sharp, familiar laugh came from the sleeping baby. Alaster turned and ran through the cold night. He passed the Huntley house, which was entirely dark and cold, and finally came flailing toward his house. He collapsed against the door, wheezing and gasping. His fingers failed on the latch several times before he fell through and crumpled on the floor.

After a minute, his lungs began reclaiming air. Alaster got to his hands and knees. "Mother," he whispered, crawling forth. By the time he reached her bedroom, he could get to his feet. He stepped through and saw her in the dark. It did not seem like she'd moved since the morning.

"Mother."

He reached her bedside.

"Mother?"

Alaster gripped the edge of the mattress to steady himself. Then he leaned forward and touched her face.

He kept his hand against her cheek determined to melt away the ice he found there. Ms. Sibley had called her cool to the touch. God, for a fever now! Her stiff fingers clutched nothing but time, and time had escaped her grip. Alaster grabbed her shoulders and shook her and wept. "Wake up, Mother. William's here. I've got William. And Father's here. Mother! Father says you have to wake up!"

There was no mad flight from the house, only a dazed stagger as he retraced the morning path that took him to Ms. Sibley cottage. As he neared, the sound of voices singing gave him pause. They belonged to children and the sound echoed from the forest behind the house.

No one stood at the front, though light showed in every window. He snuck up to the nearest one and immediately clapped both hands over his mouth to stifle a gasp.

The window looked in upon a cramped kitchen. A black stove blazed in the corner and Alaster felt its heat on the glass. Several knives of different sizes and shapes lay upon the table. Mrs. Whitmore's pail and the pumpkin he'd seen this morning were there too. The gourd's waxy skin caught the firelight and made it seem like a ball of flame.

Ms. Sibley entered. Alaster's eyes widened at her appearance. She wore no clothes, and her naked body seemed split in two, one half younger than her years, the other half far older. The youthful breast, firm and round like a pumpkin, caused a stirring in him. But just as quickly the ancient breast soured the feeling like milk left out to curdle.

She held the cord from Mrs. Whitmore's baby stretched between her hands and spoke nonsensical words to it. As she began to writhe, Ms. Sibley placed one end to her own stomach as she touched the other end to the pumpkin.

The fire in the stove flared and suddenly the cord came alive like a wriggling snake and held its attachments on its own. Now Ms. Sibley stepped forward and took up the longest of the knives. Brandishing it in both hands, she drove the blade into the pumpkin and sawed until she could pull the top off like a hat. Setting the piece aside, she dipped her fingers into the gourd, scooping the wet innards of seeds and guts into a mushy pile. She worked fast, still chanting, a sound like a flock of black birds cawing in a mown field. Once the gourd was hollow, she reached into the pail and took up the purple afterbirth, contorting it between her fingers like a baker with dough. After several squeezes, she crammed the fleshy mass into the pumpkin.

As soon as she finished, the cord connecting them burned like a wick. Ms. Sibley showed no alarm. With a single sweep of her hands, the fire rose up and entered the pumpkin. Alaster saw a glow rise out of it, a light that ceased only when Ms. Sibley put the pumpkin's cap back into place.

She took up another knife.

Alaster's fascinated horror kept him in place. He did not hear the noise behind him until it was too late. Fingers seized his shoulders and tore him away from the window. He wilted under the grip and whimpered until he saw Ben staring down at him. But it was Cameron Huntley who'd seized him. Ben's arms were occupied with a baby. Alaster blinked, certain it must be William. But the child was much smaller.

Mrs. Whitmore's newborn.

"Ben, why—"

Ms. Sibley came out the door. "Trouble, my children?"

"Yes, Mother," Benjamin said.

"*She* isn't Mother! What's the matter with you, Ben?"

Ms. Sibley now stood before Alaster, who averted his eyes with a fierce turn of the head. She pinched his chin and forced him to lock gazes.

"Benjamin is no longer your brother, Alaster. Like the other children, he has answered to the call of his true mother. Long have I waited to bring my sons and daughters into my arms, and then into the arms of their Father."

She had Cameron bring him into the kitchen. Alaster kicked against him to no avail, stopping only when Ms. Sibley picked up the knife again.

"Place the baby on the table, Benjamin."

"Yes, Mother."

"No," Alaster whispered, frozen inside at the sight of the helpless baby surrounded by so many blades. Ms. Sibley must have guessed his anxiety and laughed. "What concerns you? Do you see scars upon my children's faces?"

She put the pumpkin beside the infant, took up the knife and brought its tip against the shell. Another chant came from Ms. Sibley's lips. The knife's tip glowed with a brilliant silver light as she stroked it across the pumpkin like a painter. Several minutes passed, and when she finished the chanting also ceased. Alaster saw a perfect duplication of the newborn's face carved into the gourd. Its features blazed with orange light.

"Now he too is mine—like the others. Like everyone but you, so quick to come into the world. Tell me, Alaster: are you equally as eager to leave it?"

He craned his neck toward Ben. "Mother's dead, Ben. Do you hear me?"

"Mother's here."

"Our real mother!" He turned to Ms. Sibley. "You're a witch! Did you kill her?"

"All of them," she said.

"And Father?"

Ms. Sibley looked piteously upon him. "Poor Alaster, of all the children born in the village since I came, you alone are not mine. Which means you alone are now an orphan."

"Father's not dead!"

"Yes, he is," Ben said without emotion. "I killed him."

"As I killed mine," Cameron said.

"As all the young men who accompanied their fathers to the market did," Ms. Sibley said. "It was my wish. And my children follow my wishes."

She motioned Benjamin forward and he came to suckle briefly from her decrepit left breast.

"May Alaster have some too, Mother?" he said, pulling back.

"My milk is for my children alone. Take the baby to the nursery and place it next to William. Both will want a feeding soon."

Alaster watched his brother obey, then glanced at the pumpkin.

"You did the same thing to Will?"

"Yes," Ms. Sibley said. "Would you like to see? Earlier you admired that pumpkin very much. But I will show you something far more wondrous. A last glance at the world before your eyes close forever to it. Bring him, Cameron."

Cameron forced Alaster forward. They left the cottage and started into the woods. Ms. Sibley carried the infant's gourd under her arm. The voices of other children rose again in their strange hymns, growing stronger as they penetrated the dense forest. From the sound, it might really be every boy and girl he knew. Dozens and dozens.

They came to a glade filled with a vast patch. There must have been several hundred gourds scattered across the ground, all attached to their vines. A frost had come over most of them, a touch of gray on the otherwise vibrant orange shells. Ms. Sibley led them into the patch, stepping around the orbs. Many of the pumpkins looked entirely normal, but here and there Alaster found one with carved features glowing in the dark. He recognized so many faces.

Then he saw Ben's pumpkin, perfectly capturing his face as it was now.

Alaster shook his head and looked away.

"Benjamin wasn't a day old when that carving was done," Ms. Sibley said.

"How can that be? How do you do it?"

"Alaster, don't assume I'm the carver just because I hold the knife. My Husband works through me, and His art is so much more subtle and skillful than mine."

"Your husband?" Alaster's voice barely registered.

"I'm sure you can make a guess, good Christian lad. Unfortunately another in the village was starting to make a guess as well. Poor Reverend Peterson, muttering his suspicions out loud. My hand was forced, and the plan had to begin earlier than desirable. I would have preferred an army of adults. But obedient children will do."

Alaster's throat went dry. He just hung his head and watched Ms. Sibley kneel with the freshly carved pumpkin in both hands. She brought the stem against one of the many vines and spoke unrecognizable words. Another flash of light and then the pumpkin became part of the patch.

"Now he is my child *forever.*"

Alaster began to sob. "I want . . . I want to see William's."

"You needn't look far," she said, gesturing to a pumpkin only a few feet from Ben's. "No point separating blood brothers, is there? Yours would have been here as well."

She knelt and held up a pumpkin with his baby brother's face cut into it. She lifted it as high as the vine would let her, almost chest level.

"He can't belong to you . . . not William . . ."

"His heart is mine."

"*No.*"

Ms. Sibley gave him a smile of gleeful sympathy. Then she went back to Benjamin's pumpkin and cupped it in her hands. "Bring a knife," she said.

Minutes later, Ben appeared, blade in hand. Moonlight cut itself on the edge.

Ms. Sibley's fingers closed around the handle. She plunged the knife into the top of William's pumpkin, and a sickly, wet sound commenced as she sawed. Alaster's scream was stifled by Cameron's large hand smothering his mouth. Nothing stopped Ms. Sibley's knife. She tossed the cap aside, drove the knife into the soil with evident satisfaction, and reached within the gourd.

"Mine, all mine," she cooed, lifting a small beating, human heart. Blood ran down her boney white forearms like ink as she held the heart above her head. She stood and spun around, gnashing her teeth at the pumpkins all around her. "All of you are mine! All of you are His! Rejoice in your *Father!*"

The children of the village, boys and girls of all ages, began to leave the dense forest and enter the glade. They did not sing now. They stood in solemn expectation, heads bowed just a little in submission.

Alaster's head bowed too as bitter resignation filled him. Through tears he saw Benjamin's pumpkin almost at his feet. Part of him wanted to kick in the face. The flash of violence shocked him. Why blame Ben? He'd been under the witch's command since birth, unaware of his dire state until the witch brought her spell to fruition. What did she want? The town? Power? What would she do to the children if not send them forth to spread her vile plans to other villages?

He stomped his foot in powerless frustration, his sole coming down on the vine that connected Benjamin's pumpkin to the patch. As he did, Ben gave the faintest grunt. Alaster looked over and saw a strain on his face, a brief clarity in his eyes. No one else seemed to notice, and his eyes clouded back to submission a moment later.

Alaster stomped again. This time he pressed his foot against the vine as hard as he could and twisted his ankle.

Benjamin blinked. Then he looked around.

Then they made eye contact.

Alaster would have done anything to bear down on the vine with all his weight. Cameron's grip kept him from that. He twisted his foot again. His movements now caught the witch's attention. She seemed startled, unsure.

Benjamin shouted. He launched forward and seized the knife from the ground in one move, then stabbed it into Ms. Sibley's ribcage. She howled like a wolf and dropped William's pumpkin as she staggered. A frantic wave of her hands brought the other children to her defense. Cameron threw Alaster aside and headed toward Ben, who started retreating. Alaster began tearing at the vines, even biting them as he tried to break the pumpkins free. Each separation freed a corresponding boy or girl.

Ben was gaining allies.

The witch came at Alaster now, bounding across the patch, blood dark as lamp oil flowing from the stab wound. Alaster scrambled, knowing he had to find Cameron's pumpkin. He was the oldest boy and the only one stronger than Ben.

He saw Cameron's carved face glowing like fire and clawed his way toward it, wrapping both arms around the pumpkin, shrieking as he twisted all his weight against the vine. Cameron froze in the distance but it wasn't enough. Alaster saw the witch's dark shadow falling over him.

Then he heard Ben shout his name. Alaster and the witch both looked to see him charging across the patch, slashing as he went. The witch chanted and the pumpkins began to explode around his feet like cannon bursts. Ben screamed, losing his balance. He threw the knife as he went down. The blade went over the witch's head and struck the ground a few feet from Alaster's right hand.

He seized it and cleaved the knife into Cameron's vine.

The pumpkin fell heavily to the ground, and Cameron staggered, squinting like someone waking from a long dream. He moved toward the witch, who now straddled Benjamin, both hands around his throat. Alaster rose to attack.

"No!" Cameron said. "Cut the vines! All the vines!"

Alaster worked with the knife, moving faster than he thought possible. He slashed everywhere, at every pumpkin both enchanted and ordinary. More children became free by the second. Cameron meanwhile had knocked the witch away from Benjamin and the two older boys stood shoulder to shoulder against her.

The freed children gathered at their backs.

"You'll all die," she said. "Without your connection to the patch, the hearts within will wither soon. Poor children. Come back to your mother and Father."

"We'd rather die," Ben said, "and be with our *real* parents."

The children fell upon her.

TRICK 'EM ALL

Adam Light

TRAVIS RAINES COULDN'T believe it. He had been stuck with the menial task of pushing the sweets out the door when the trick or treat festivities got under way. At sixteen, he was considered too old to go out and take part in the real fun, but his parents refused to allow him the honor of escorting his brother and sister around while they went door to door collecting their booty.

Staring down into his bowl of corn flakes, he muttered, "Why can't I take them out?"

He had known it was pointless to ask the question, but he was not known for his tactfulness. And he was pissed.

A troubled look passed between the two adults.

"We don't feel you're ready for that kind of responsibility. You're manning the candy dish, and that's final. We shouldn't have to explain all of our decisions, anyway."

"Maybe next year you can chaperone, kiddo," his mom added.

He looked first at his dad, then at his mom, his breakfast forgotten. "I know what it is. You can try to bullshit me all you want, but I get it."

"Watch your language, young man," his dad warned, brow

furrowed. "And if you already know why we don't want you doing it, you shouldn't have to ask."

Travis imagined how good it would feel to lunge across the table and scoop out his old man's eye ball with his spoon. His stomach squelched like a giant fist had squeezed its contents into his upper intestine with malice, and he excused himself from the breakfast table without another word.

Honestly, he had no desire to drag those little shits around the neighborhood anyway. What irritated him was the lack of trust his parents had for him. He saw himself as mature for his age, and the fact that they still treated him like a child was what really got his blood boiling.

He marched upstairs and set to work carving the massive pumpkin he had stored in his closet. He was supposed to do it outside, but he didn't care. Yesterday, he had drawn an evil face on it with a magic marker. As he chiseled out the demonic features and emptied its gooey innards, he focused all of his hatred on it. He imagined the knife sliding in and out of his father's chubby body, gouging holes in his mother's makeup caked face. It felt good to get his aggression out like that. It was liberating. After he finished, and the wicked face had been crafted just to his liking, he lit a candle, lifted the top off the pumpkin and set it aside, lighting it up. He knew that if he got caught with a jack-o'-lantern in his room, it would only illustrate his parents' point in regard to his immaturity, but fuck 'em. They could rot for all he cared. He was beyond caring about their opinion of him.

Travis had never been fast to make friends; in fact, he had never been involved in a meaningful relationship with another kid, or even his own siblings. He glanced at his carved jack-o'-lantern and silently lamented his lonely existence.

Finally, he sighed and cleaned up his pumpkin mess, tossed everything into the trash, and checked over his work.

"And you shall be called Jackass, my friend," he said.

A moment later, the pumpkin replied.

So you want to be friends, huh, Travis?

Travis blinked.

He shook his head and laughed. Yeah, right, dumbass. The jack-o'-lantern is *alive.*

Once again, it spoke, its soft voice mellifluous, inviting.

I'll be your friend, if you want, Travis. How about it?

This time he thought he actually saw the jack-o'-lantern's mouth move.

Not completely convinced he hadn't imagined it, he still answered. "Sure, I'll be friends with a talking pumpkin."

Good. Thanks for that, young man. I knew you had good taste. And so do I. We're going to get along just fine.

There was no denying it. The thing was talking. What craziness is this?

I've sought release from the darkness for so long, Travis, Jackass said. *You've brought me into the light, and I am more grateful than I can put into words.*

Travis was floored. This couldn't really be happening. He had finally lost his mind.

"This is just great. I'm such a loser, I'm having a conversation with an inanimate object. Jesus Christ."

You made me, Travis. I'm here because you wanted me to be. This is real, and you're not a loser. I think you're pretty terrific.

Travis sat in stunned silence, his mouth hanging open. He watched the pumpkin's features, the mouth and eyes he himself had cut out of the thing, come to life and move in an almost exaggerated mockery of a human face.

You created me, but I fear the job is only halfway finished. I'm just a head! A low throated, mischievous laugh erupted from the candlelit mouth. It made Travis's flesh crawl. *I need to be whole. I'm in a pretty compromised position right now. I need you to complete me. And I know how to make your problems go away, too, by the way.*

Jackass winked conspiratorially at him, and Travis grinned. It was like watching a live cartoon. Even though his mind was unable to grip what was happening, it was certainly a delightful experience. No one would ever believe it. But he wouldn't tell anyone. This was his secret.

Travis's mom called him downstairs, and though he had no desire to move at all, he figured he'd better go find out what was going on. The last thing he needed was for one or both his parents to come storming in to find a lit jack-o'-lantern in his room.

"I'll be back soon, Jackass," he said, and ran out of his room, still unsure whether Jackass was real, or if he had simply fallen down the rabbit hole. Maybe he'd had a nervous breakdown, and was really sitting in a padded cell right now, hallucinating the whole thing. He hoped not.

Regardless, the wicked witch waited, and he had to find out what she wanted.

It was time for dinner. They had tacos, which were good, but Travis could barely concentrate.

The twins were not at the table. His dad revealed that one of the neighbors, whose kids were friends with the twins, was going to do the chaperoning, and had come over and gotten them a little while ago.

And they still insisted that Travis pass candy out to the trick or treaters.

Travis's bitterness about being relegated to such an asinine job on this wondrous night rekindled, and though his attitude was acrimonious, he kept his temper in check. A plastic smile pasted across his mug, while he thought about what waited upstairs for him, he endured the pain of sitting with his parents. Jackass consumed his every thought.

Unfortunately, his mom and dad prattled on and on, over

explaining the reason Travis was not old enough or responsible enough to walk his younger siblings around the fucking block. As far back as he could remember, they had treated him this way. As if he didn't understand them the first time they said things.

And they had already started drinking.

The old man and the witch had been out to get him for so long. They treated him like shit right to his face, showing him no respect at all. He knew how they talked about him behind his back, too. He had overheard the talks they had when they thought he wasn't able to hear them.

Like the time he found the Golden Retriever in the woods behind his school playground. The dog had been old and sick, and he'd done it a favor, put it out of its misery. Then, he'd been inclined to see what made the animal tick. So he'd taken it apart. He thought back on the day with a mixture of emotions. Touching the organs and bones he'd pulled from the animal's furry flesh had been so exciting, his penis had bulged excruciatingly against the inside of his jeans. He hadn't understood why that had happened at the time. He only knew that it was exhilarating, and the urgent throbbing in his loins had been his introduction to sexual arousal.

He'd been caught by some teachers who had been dispatched to find him when he didn't show up for class after recess.

His dad had come to get him from school, but had barely spoken.

When his mother had arrived home after work that night, they had discussed Travis behind his back. Thinking he was asleep, they spoke openly about their disdain for him, how he made them sick and afraid to sleep in their own home.

"Jesus Christ, Tom. Where in the hell did this come from? Because it certainly isn't from my side of the family."

"Now, Judy, I don't think that's necessary. Sometimes people are just born . . . different."

"We're perfectly normal, and we made a psychopath and brought him into the world, then? Is that it? Jesus Christ."

Travis had heard them loud and clear. It was awful. His own parents hated and feared him.

His father had beaten him within an inch of his life the next day. It had been a savage thrashing, and Travis had, for a frightening moment, thought his dad had meant to kill him. Amazingly, his dad had avoided leaving any obvious marks on him.

"You tell your mom what just went down, you sick little fuck, and you can kiss your ass goodbye. This'll seem like a day trip to Disneyland, got me?"

He had nodded, tears still streaming down his face, swearing vengeance on the bastard.

"Seriously, Travis. Your ass is headed for boarding school if you fuck up one more time." His face flushed, sweating so profusely he looked like he had just finished a marathon, and he had not waited for a reply. He just stormed out of the room and Travis had heard the tell-tale sound of the liquor cabinet opening and slamming as his father retrieved a bottle of something strong.

Travis had been kicked out of grade school after the incident, at the tender age of ten. His mother had quit her job, too, so he could be home-schooled. He had seen a therapist for a while, and was given a clean bill of mental health. But mom and dad were never convinced. They spoke about him in hushed tones behind his back to this very day.

Those thoughts weighing heavy on his mind, Travis unceremoniously excused himself from the table, mumbled "fuck both of you" under his breath, and went on his way.

He hurried up the stairs, but slowed down as he neared the top, and stopped altogether when he reached his bedroom door.

Back in his room, the sun drooped low outside the window, casting a blinding glare through the dusty glass as it crept closer to the edge of the sky. He turned on his mp3 player, cranked up the speakers, and filled the room with the sounds of death metal. He then sat cross-legged on the floor in front of Jackass, and shoved his glasses instinctively up onto his nose with a forefinger.

"Sorry to make you wait so long, buddy. I had to deal with those assholes who brought me into this world." The pumpkin seemed to gaze straight through him. Its mouth twitched, though, its evil grin expanding.

It's time for us to help each other, Travis.

"Okay. But, um, how does that work, exactly? What else can I do for you?"

We both know how you feel about those two fools you call your parents. Do we not?

"I guess."

I need to ambulate. I'm not meant to sit here in this little patch of bum-fucked-nowhere for the rest of eternity. I need your help with that.

"Okay. It would suck to be just a head. I feel for you."

I know what it is you need. You need to be free from your parents' iron fist. They only cause you pain. I can help you get rid of them for good, Travis.

"How do you propose that I get rid of them?"

I think you know the answer to that, Travis. I will not suffer a fool for a companion. You need them out of the way, and I need them to make me whole again. It's that simple. I can't exist inside this rotten gourd for very much longer. In order for me to come fully to life, I need some of their . . . parts.

It had all been true. Every second he had spent carving Jackass, he had fantasized about his parents meeting terrible fates. The pumpkin had been his outlet for the rage he had felt. And now it was encouraging him to get rid of them. It was insane.

"What exactly are you saying, Jackass? You want me to . . . kill them?"

It was your hatred for them that fueled your creativity when you made me. I am born of your rage. You know that this is what you want.

"Tell me what you want me to do."

Jackass explained what had to be done, laying it out in detail for the boy so he could understand. As the explanation spilled forth, Travis grew anxious, his alarm growing every minute.

Finally, the pumpkin said: *I'm the only friend you've got, dear boy. You will do what needs to be done, and if you prove you're worthy of taking a most esteemed position at my right hand side, I can give you so much more than freedom. You'll know what it's like to be somebody. To be really important.*

"I just don't think I can do what you're saying. I don't particularly like them, but I'm no killer."

Time runs short, even now, dear boy. If you don't act soon, all will be lost. You'd be crazy not to take this opportunity.

"I hate them, I really do. I'm just not capable of doing anything like that," Travis answered.

Travis knew that he shouldn't be taking any of this seriously. He could just stomp the jack-o'-lantern into the floor and it would all be over. But the damned pumpkin had him mesmerized.

Do as I say, or you may as well kill yourself, Travis. Those fools have wanted you dead all along. They wish you'd never been born. Look at your pathetic little life. Yours is a soul yearning to unfurl its beautiful wings and fly free. Don't you want to soar free, Travis? You're in prison. You're nothing. Nothing! They'll see you into an early grave and laugh the whole time, the dying breath choked out of your fragile little lungs.

Though it was insane, the pumpkin made some good arguments. His family had been against him all along. They had never tried to understand him. They didn't care if he lived or died.

A rush of conflicting emotions had overcome him, nauseated him.

In a moment of panic, Travis dashed out of his room and charged headlong into the bathroom, slamming the door and locking it behind him.

Jackass was in his head, waiting for him. *No more running, my friend. The world is ours. Just set me free, and the world is ours.*

Finally, Travis could not stand it anymore, and screamed out, "Please just leave me the fuck alone! Why are you doing this to me? Why, *Goddammit*?"

Then he broke down, head in hands, sobbing loudly, incoherent words churning like gravel in his mouth.

Immediately following Travis's outburst, his dad's footsteps rumbled up the stairs. Travis felt the first cracks appear in his sanity, and knew he was teetering too close to the edge of a chasm that was so deep that if were to slip over that edge, he would never stop falling.

He knew, as the pounding footfalls approached the bathroom door, that his only option was to get the hell out of the house. Just run away, hide out in the woods for a while. Otherwise, there was no telling what might happen. He was surely going insane.

You can't run away from me, my dear Travis. You and I are forever bound to one another. And we have so much work to do. Gather your tools, and let's get on with it. No more bullshit.

Travis's brain suffered a vicious cramp and panic seized him, and he feared he was having an aneurysm.

Through his anguished pulsing headache that gnawed on his skull like a pack of rats, Jackass's soothing voice coaxed him, encouraged him to kill for him.

Travis composed himself as well as he could, splashed cold water on his face at the sink, and slung open the bathroom door at the exact moment his dad was preparing to open the door and walk in.

Father and son stood speechless for a moment, staring at each other, silent in the awkward moment. Finally, Travis edged past his dad and hurried down the hall before his dad had a chance to say anything to him.

He took the stairs at a gallop, sprinted down the hall toward the foyer, and slid to a stop upon the wooden floor mere inches before he would have plowed into the front door.

Outside, trees swayed to and fro, the gusting winds denuding branches; orange, yellow, and crimson leaves swirled along through the crisp autumn twilight. Running around the sides of the house, he unlatched and flung wide the privacy fence gate, launched himself into the backyard and headed for the tool shed.

Everything he needed was there. He grabbed a small hatchet, a machete, a vicious looking filet knife with a razor sharp blade, the heavy duty battery powered jigsaw, and an assortment of other large hunting knives his dad kept in a locker, which was conveniently unlocked. All of it went into one of his dad's old weather-beaten rucksacks. On the way out, he spotted a large, gleaming hacksaw with a nearly two foot blade. He took it, too.

Hauling the sack of tools into the house and up to his room proved easier than he had figured. His parents were nowhere in sight. The television in the family room was turned up too loud, so he couldn't hear anything else, but there was no doubt they were lounging on the sofa, getting soused, probably unaware that he was even still around. Travis had been certain that his dad would be waiting for him to come back inside after his outburst.

He carried the rucksack into the bedroom, and emptied the contents on the bed.

Travis sorted the tools out and advanced the plan to its next phase. The sky was darkening outside, and there would soon be kids streaming through the neighborhood; he had to make the best of the precious little time remaining before then.

"Mom!" he yelled. "Can you come up here for a minute?"

Despite his intentions, he felt unusually calm. His palms were dry. He hefted the hatchet, and ran the blade lightly across his thumb. It was sharp enough.

The television volume lowered and his mom called up from the bottom of the stairs. "Everything all right up there, Travis?"

"Yeah, it's all good, mom. But can you come up here and look at something for me?"

His voice was steady, but he felt nervous and hoped his mom didn't detect anything threatening in his voice.

After a moment, she came up the stairs.

Do it quick, Travis. If you hesitate, all is lost.

He ignored Jackass, and stood just at the side of his bed with the hatchet held behind his back, gripping it fiercely. When his mother walked into the room, he blinked a couple of times, while she stood swaying a little on her feet, glancing around the room. She spotted the jack-o'-lantern and frowned at him.

Before she could speak, Travis made his move.

He swung the hatchet up and lunged at her, swinging the hatchet down with all the power he could muster as he closed the distance between them.

She never suspected a thing, just stood there, her mouth opening up in a little puckered "o" right before the razor-sharp hatchet punched through the top of her face and nearly split her head completely in half.

His mother convulsed horribly and then went limp. Gravity claimed the lifeless body, and she hit the floor like a sack of flour, pulling the hatchet handle out of Travis's hand as she went.

Travis gazed at the sight of his mother sprawled on her back, murdered by his hand, but Jackass's voice interrupted right away.

Quickly, Travis. Get your dad up here, now.

"I know."

Travis dragged his mom's cooling body over to his walk-in closet and pulled it inside, then shut the door.

He had to get his dad up here without arousing his suspicions.

One down, one left to go.

"Fuck it," he muttered.

He yelled to his father.

"This better be important, Travis," his dad bellowed from below.

"It is! Something's wrong with mom," he answered, hoping he sounded panicked enough. "I don't think she's breathing!"

The telltale footsteps thundered up the stairs. Travis pushed his bedroom door until it was nearly closed.

Travis pressed his back up against the wall just to the right of his open bedroom door.

His dad came barreling into the room, slowed down only slightly by the door.

"Judy, are you all rii—"

The fish knife slid viciously across his dad's throat before he could finish his question.

Blood jettisoned across the room with incredible force. It splashed onto the walls and Travis's bed before his dad's hands went up to the ragged, gaping gash in a desperate bid to keep the rest of the blood from escaping.

Gurgling, he turned and saw his murderer standing there, a sadistic grin on his face, brandishing the knife at him. His eyes were shocked and wide, but also confused. There was no doubt in that look that he couldn't believe his son had done this. Blood was sheeting down his front like water from a faucet. He went down within a few seconds, and thrashed violently around on the carpet as he drowned in his own blood. It took an eternity.

The hour of resurrection is nearly at hand. Jackass was quick to assert his will.

Do it all exactly as I told you, Travis. Our destiny depends on your ability to carry out my instructions.

Travis nodded at the jack-o'-lantern. "Okay, okay. I've got it together."

He had to drag his mom's body out of the closet. He laid her out beside her husband, who had curled up in a fetal position as he died, and went to work on her with the jigsaw. When he had the chest cavity chiseled out, he used the fish knife to cut out her heart. It was bigger than what he had expected, but still went into the top of the jack-o'-lantern easily enough.

Ah. Yes, that's it, Travis. Keep going. You're almost there.

The next part was the real bitch. The jigsaw battery died halfway into the first cut he made in his father's skull. He had to resort to using the hacksaw. It took him too long, and he began to grow panicked, but the body had to be flipped over three times in order for him to cut all the way around the head and remove the skull cap while causing as little damage to the brain as he could help.

While we're young, Travis, Jackass quipped. Travis was not amused. This was awful. He had finally managed to detach the brain from his father's cranium, but it was slippery, and kept sliding out of his hands.

At last, he stuffed the brain into the top of the pumpkin, and collapsed onto the bed, exhausted from the exertion.

He watched Jackass carefully. Waited for something to happen.

When nothing changed after several minutes, he stripped and got in the shower.

Refreshed after a good scrubbing, Travis was back in his bedroom. He ran his fingers through his stringy wet hair, a few locks falling back over his glasses, blocking out the view of his hideous creation sitting in the corner below the bedroom window for a second.

A crushing black metal dirge poured forth from speakers hung around his room, vocals like demons conjured forth from the very bowels of the deepest hells, several down-tuned guitars laying down thick stuttering riffs. It was perfect. The gore-soaked clothes Travis had changed out of were balled up atop his bed. He had changed into his favorite outfit. Black leather pants, a Marilyn Manson t-shirt, leather jacket with jingling zippers everywhere, combat boots.

He had gone back to the shed after he finished with his parents. The gas in the five gallon can had sloshed around at the bottom, but he figured he would not need a whole lot. It would be enough.

In sixteen years, Travis had never felt more isolated, helpless, or doomed. He sat and brooded, flinching every time he looked around him. Tears of madness leaked from his eyes. A few candles strategically placed on the windowsill and headboard described otherworldly patterns on the otherwise night-darkened room. The bloated jigsaw smile of the jack-o'-lantern sat dark and oozing beneath the window. For the last fifteen minutes, Travis had contemplated his next move, but he had been unable to stir himself into action. His ass simply refused to detach itself from the carpet in his spot in the opposite corner of the room, no matter how badly he needed to act.

He stared fearfully at Jackass as it leered at him, its demonic grin causing a fit of chills to coruscate through his spinal fluid.

It was Halloween night, and darkness had fallen. In his neighborhood, trick or treating had just begun, and droves of children would come knocking at the front door any minute. Time had run out. The night was already alive with the laughter of so many children. The shouts of joy and wild abandon, as the children made their merry way through from house to house, dragged like fingernails across so many blackboards in Travis's brain.

He wished more than anything that he could trade places with one of those kids. He longed to know their innocence, for his was lost.

Somewhere out there, the twins would be roaming around with their friends, unaware of how their lives had been devastated while they had their night of fun. Travis had taken their parents from them.

He was aware of how everything had gone horribly wrong, but he actively attempted to convince himself something could be done to reverse time and put everything back the way it was.

Everything that has happened, I've brought upon myself.

He peeked out the window. The arc sodium street lights buzzed to life as twilight changed to dusk. Smaller lights further illuminated front porches of the homes whose residents participated in Halloween festivities. The wholesome sounds of children finally freed to gather their treats filled the chilly night. They capered about out there, blissfully unaware of the atrocities that happened every day in the sick twisted world around them.

Travis thought about the acts he had committed. He was a murderer. Not only had he killed his parents, he had mutilated them, stuffed their pieces into his jack-o'-lantern. And what had it all been for? Had that really been him? He wasn't a good guy, as far as he knew.

Am I evil? He could not believe it, but he knew it was he who had brutally destroyed these two bodies strewn over the length of his bedroom carpet. Their fluids were spattered from one side of the room to the other by his hands.

In the midst of this human wreckage, he had waited for something that was never going to happen. He didn't know for sure what he had expected to happen once he had done the things Jackass had bid him do, but he knew now that there would be no triumph tonight. He had been promised a new lease on life, a grand new existence, but the only world opening up to Travis was one in which merciless convicts raped little guys like him in the shower every day for the rest of their lives. Jackass had lied.

But had he? Or had Travis just been lying to himself. He supposed it didn't matter in the end.

Jackass had remained conspicuously silent ever since his dad's brain had gone into its hand-carved cranium.

Had it ever really talked to him at all?

He glanced furtively around, seeing the aftermath of the evening's carnage as if for the first time.

Bile filled his mouth, and he stagger-stepped around his parents' corpses, ran down the hall into the bathroom. After the contents of his stomach had been expelled, he felt a little better. His throat burned, so he stuck his head under the bathroom sink and drank greedily for a few seconds.

On trembling legs, he returned to his room. He didn't want to go back in there, but he had to. The end of all this was coming at him like a tidal wave, about to crash into him and deliver him to his fate.

The smell of gasoline burned in his nostrils.

After he had doused his bloody clothes and bed, there was a little bit of gas left in the can. He now opened the lid and poured the remaining fuel on his head.

An eerie hush had descended, like the room itself had been sealed inside a mausoleum deserted for centuries. Travis sat at the foot of his bed, in his newly christened kingdom, and consciously averted his eyes from the mirror that adorned the inside of the bedroom door. The sight of his reflection shocked him. He quickly looked away. Then he picked up his television remote control, averting his eyes from the carnage he had wrought, and swung it violently into the mirror, sending thousands of pieces of glass showering down onto the floor around him.

He'd found a pack of wooden matches in the shed when he retrieved the gas can. He pulled one of them out of its box now and looked around at his room one last time.

Then a peal of laughter boomed through his head like thunder in a mason jar. Travis cried out, the pain driving him to his knees, his resolve dissipating like so much smoke.

Foolish boy. What are you doing? You won't be ruining it all now. I still need you to complete the ritual, Travis. You're the last piece.

Jackass laughed like a crazed hyena. When the cackling finally came to an end, the jack-o'-lantern began to vibrate. It looked bigger than before, and there was a tangle of green vines sprouting from underneath its bloated, bloody face.

The jack-o'-lantern was raised off the floor by the new growths erupting from its every surface. The vines twined around each other, tighter and tighter, until they formed a thick stalk-like formation upon which the pumpkin was lifted higher into the air, growing taller than Travis before it finally stopped.

New offshoots grew outward from the stalk, one sprouting from each side, like arms.

Come to me, Travis. I need you to finish your job.

Travis understood something in that moment. This thing he had created, it was not his friend. It wasn't going to do anything for him. He would have to stop it.

Stepping over his dead father, he reached down and pulled at the hatchet that still protruded from his mother's face. It wouldn't budge.

What are you doing, Travis? I have plans for you, boy.

The thing was laughing again. Its improvised arms stretched toward Travis, but they had not grown long enough to reach him.

Travis tried again to free the hatchet's lodged blade, but it was no use. He would have to tackle Jackass and take him apart with his bare hands. He whirled around and tried to step over his mom's prone form, but his foot caught on her blood-streaked abdomen, tripping him. His arms flew out in front of him as he fell, but it was too little, too late. His face smacked the bedroom window, cracking but not shattering it, and his jacket met the fat black candle sitting atop the sill.

An explosion of agonizing pain ripped through his head. Travis didn't notice when the fallen candle ignited his jacket, but he felt the sudden concussion of the gasoline catching light, setting his entire body aflame.

He screamed, windmilling his arms wildly as he ran right into the waiting embrace of his monstrous creation.

Jackass embraced the burning boy, smothering some, but not all, of the spreading flames. The boy screamed and screamed as his flesh cooked; his head burned like a roman candle. The bloody, viscera-packed jack-o'-lantern face loomed in front of him as his eyes melted out of their sockets. Its laughter was the last thing he heard as the darkness took him.

The fire spread fast. Within minutes, it had completely engulfed the top floor of the house, and soon the shocked trick or treaters standing around on the street, watching the house burn up, had to clear a path for the first responders, who arrived, sirens blaring, twenty minutes after a neighbor had called 911.

The firemen bravely battled the leaping, crackling flames, hoping like hell they could rescue anyone who might be trapped inside the burning house. As they focused their attention on the front of the house, the back door creaked open and, through it, something crawled out into the chilly October night. Dozens of zippers jingled as it crept across the ground. Its jigsaw smile broadened as it emerged from the burning house into the October night.

It was alive, and it was free.

OFFERINGS

Joanna Koch

BLAINE'S HEAD HURTS at the sight of Amelia shuffling up the block. Hot from raking leaves, Blaine stretches as she admires her new house in her new neighborhood. The cold pinch of October air and brisk setting sun anticipate kids pouring in tomorrow at dusk. This is prime candy territory, nothing like the streets where Blaine grew up. Children don't trick or treat in Blaine's old neighborhood, not with the fires and gunshots. Down there, they call it Devil's Night. Blaine's worked her way up and out, from dishwasher to sous chef to culinary manager. She's hosting her nieces and nephews at the new house tomorrow, and she expects to show them the flawless picture of safety and charm she's paying for. Being a member of this community doesn't come cheap. Looking down the block, it's a perfect Norman Rockwell until Amelia enters the frame.

Amelia is the neighborhood chimera. Big moist eyes, throbbing temple bones and a perpetual brood in tow mark her as an anomaly. Maybe she runs some sort of daycare. Low cost, out of her home. The couple across from Blaine points her out as *Amelia Something—do you think she even has a license?* They raise their eyebrows in knowing distaste. Fiftyish and dressed for golf no matter the day of the week, they interrogate Blaine. By the time they spot Amelia, Blaine's relieved to shift the critique to the other woman's childcare credentials. She feels wrong about it later when Amelia shambles by. Nervous and harried, Amelia wanders the upscale streets like a restless spirit locked in a magic circle of misbehaving mongrel children.

Blaine watches Amelia push the cumbersome double stroller with its side-by-side compartments for twins. It's an old design, less streamlined than the front-to-back models used by jogging moms. Amelia's posture recalls street people pushing shopping carts full of god knows what in Blaine's old neighborhood. When Blaine was a child, she shunned the faceless figures covered in rags. She'd cross the street when she saw one coming. Moving away isn't only about leaving behind the fear and filth. It's about finding a place where it's safe to be a better person, the kind of person Blaine wants to be.

Blaine hushes the hint of a headache and waves to Amelia, "Hi!"

Amelia's profile passes unaware. Her eyes face front. Sundry children scamper behind. Tomorrow morning is curbside pick-up. The children grab loose garbage from waste bins and pull recycling out of neatly bundled stacks. They drag and kick their finds down the sidewalk, inventing games as they go. After exhausting the entertainment value of an empty bottle of bleach or a discarded pizza box, they fling it onto the nearest lawn.

Amelia plods onward as cans and cartons and odd bits of trash spread through the street in her wake. She's like a tanker spewing oil.

"Hello there," Blaine calls out.

The rotten brood swarms around Amelia like flies. Although there are only three, they create the chaos of a full-blown horde. The children stop and look at Blaine, then glance at each other and continue their moving massacre.

Blaine heads down the sidewalk after them. The three children, all girls, peek back at her with feral eyes. Amelia nears the end of the block. Before she disappears around the corner, Blaine jogs to catch up and shouts, "Hello there!"

Amelia startles and turns. Her eyes are wide and glassy, her hands clutch the stroller, and her sunken face suggests nights of wakeful trance in lieu of sleep. Amelia bares her teeth and says, "Hi. How are you?"

Moments ago, half the neighborhood toiled outside under autumn's vaulted light. Now it's getting dark. The birds don't chirp. Houses are barren and hushed behind festive haunted facades. Blaine does her best to return what must be Amelia's smile and says, "Good. How are you today?"

Amelia's brow furrows. Her watery blue eyes darken. She says, "Fine," without conviction or irony. The horde has spread, triangulating the two women in their sites. One girl tears apart layers of cardboard from a warped packing sheet by peeling off thin strips and waving them in the air to be taken up by the breeze. The other girls fan the air with smaller sheets of cardboard, too far away to have any effect that isn't imaginary. To Blaine's surprise, a long cardboard curl bounces on the wind, rises aloft, and then snags in the high, bare branches of a deciduous shrub.

Blaine nods at the tangle and says, "Someone's going to need a ladder to get that down."

Amelia looks baffled.

Blaine speaks up in case Amelia is hard of hearing. "They've been scattering things all over the street behind your back. I don't mean to be rude." Blaine maintains a deferential smile as Amelia stares at her wildly. Blaine gestures at the nearest shred of cardboard and then points to one of the girls. "I'm sure you want to talk to them about littering."

"Oh!" Amelia says. Her eyes bug out and zig zag around the perimeter of the triangle. Her voice is harsh. She punches out her words: "Don't do that! You're bad! Clean it up!"

The girls don't react.

Blaine stutters. "Oh no, I didn't mean—I'm so sorry, I didn't mean you should—"

On an impulse to evoke warmth, Blaine leans down to look in the stroller. Amelia blocks her. She swerves the stroller away and starts firing out questions: "Do you have a job?"

"Yes," Blaine says. "Of course."

"Where do you work?"

"A hotel."

"Which one?"

"The Kentwood Astoria."

"What do you do?"

Blaine wants to lie to Amelia but has no reason other than the urge to cross the street when confronted with a shopping cart person. Blaine acts like an adult and tells part of the truth. "I work in the kitchen."

Amelia's eyes have the dark, desperate plea of a cornered animal. Her fingers twist on the stroller handle as though they can't break free. Blaine wonders if the stroller is empty. There's no movement or cooing under the blankets, no crying or kicks, and come to think of it, she's never noticed Amelia tending to any passengers in the double compartments.

Amelia smiles again, but she looks more like she's in pain. She says, "I wish I had a job like that."

"It's great. I love to cook. Always have." Blaine doesn't tell Amelia she's the culinary manager of both restaurants in the hotel. She doesn't offer Amelia a job. "Planning, making everything just right. You know what I mean." Amelia stares. The girls amble in closer. Blaine chatters. "You'd think after fifty, sixty hours a week I wouldn't want to do the same thing at home, but I love it. In fact, you know, I really have to go. My nieces and nephews are coming over for trick or treat tomorrow." The girls saunter up behind Amelia like cowboys challenging Blaine to a draw. Blaine clears her throat to cover up an inappropriate laugh at the absurd image. In the silent intensity of their stares, Blaine says, "Why don't you drop by?"

Amelia says, "Oh. Okay."

The girls remain inscrutable.

"I'm sorry," Blaine says. "I have to go. I didn't mean to be rude earlier. I can't imagine. It must be hard for you, with so many."

Amelia's eyes seek the horizon like a shipwreck victim. She looks over Blaine's shoulder and speaks to the vanishing point in the distance. She says, "They're not mine."

Blaine can't lie to herself. She's relieved when Amelia doesn't show up.

The house has been silent for at least an hour when the doorbell rings. The house is too quiet with the party over and the kids all gone, or maybe for Blaine, it's just quiet enough. Blaine's not sure she'll ever be ready to have children, not after what she saw in Amelia's eyes last night. She's been savoring the adult version of the witch's brew punch and contemplating her goals when the doorbell interrupts. It's ten-thirty.

Through a sliver in the curtains, Blaine spies Amelia clutching the stroller handle. She's at the end of the walkway near the street, almost out of range of the porch light. In the dark, the stroller looks more like a shopping cart mounded with hoardings of homeless life than it does in the daytime. Amelia's eyes jump from Blaine's front steps to flutter moth-like at the motion in the window. Her mouth stretches into a desperate leer. Blaine sighs. A headache threatens. Placing her cocktail on the mantel, Blaine grabs a handful of good chocolate. The kiddie stuff is all gone. She wonders why the hell Amelia has the children out so late.

The three girls present pillowcases faded and tattered from too many wash cycles. Frayed edges sag in tiny, expectant hands. The children wear the same clothes they had on yesterday when they plundered the garbage. Their only costumes are their masks. Blaine forces herself to say, "Well, aren't you cute," as she drops chocolate into each threadbare sack.

The masks look realistic, like expensive theater props. Blaine appreciates the quality, but not the content. The first girl wears an Inuit style bird head with spiraling hypnotic eyes and blood oozing from its beak. As the blood accumulates, it drips on the girl's clothes. The head is plumed with what appear to be authentic feathers that rustle when she receives her candy. The second girl has the red face of a devil with hairy ears, gnarled fangs and a long forked tongue that lolls out of the side of her mouth. In place of a nose, the devil face sports a fully formed miniature devil with arms, legs and tail that dances and gestures. The tiny devil double mutters and drives at the air with a pitchfork. The third girl is a faceless, pink, flabby thing with several soft, rounded horns that protrude from the top of her head. The horns are more like knobby tentacles or snakes that stretch and enlarge at the ends. They bob and pulsate with engorged veins along the shaft like a vulgar pseudo-medical device. When Blaine gives her candy, the horns throb and lilt.

Amelia grins.

Blaine does her best to keep smiling at the masks. She's given away all the chocolate and the girls don't move to go. Neither does Amelia. Blaine turns her palms outward and then clasps them together. "Well," she says, "Trick or treat."

Amelia yells, "Say it!"

"Wik yur ree," the girls mumble under their masks. Then the

smallest girl, the one with the flabby tentacles on her head says, "I gotta go potty."

Amelia doesn't respond. Her teeth are clenched like a fiend and her watery blue eyes are frozen into hard, round marbles. The little girl bends her knees and bounces, pressing her hands between her legs. Her flabby horns wobble. "I gotta go now!"

"Okay, hon. Come on." Blaine grabs the little girl's hand and takes her to the guest bathroom. The protrusions nudge Blaine's forearm. Blaine isn't sure if she's more disgusted by the physical sensation of the soft horns or by the behavior of the girl's mother. Or whatever Amelia is supposed to be. Blaine kneels, eye-level with the eyeless face. She asks, "Do you need any help?" The little girl giggles and slams the bathroom door.

Blaine wonders how the child can see anything from inside the mask. She hopes she can take it off on her own. After several minutes of quiet, Blaine says, "How are you doing?" There's no answer. Blaine tries the door handle. It's locked. Blaine taps a few times. "Is everything okay?" The toilet flushes and the girl bursts through into Blaine's arms. Blaine catches her and asks, "Did you forget to wash your hands?" The girl shakes her head, jiggling the mask's rubbery horns. She squirms out of Blaine's grasp and runs away.

Cold air and scraps of leaf litter from the street tumble into Blaine's living room through the open front door. The girls sprawl on Blaine's Persian rug sorting mountains of candy. Their tattered pillowcases drape the room. A statue of Kuan Yin sticks her sutra out from under a worn floral pattern. Soil and rocks spill from a houseplant trampled by a herd of threadbare unicorns. Pink polka dots clash with tasteful earth tone upholstery. Blaine rushes past the disaster to fetch Amelia from outside.

The walkway is empty. The street is deserted. Blaine looks up and down the block and jogs to the corner, passing plastic gravestones and cardboard skeletons. She runs to the opposite corner, searching by the orange glow of jack-o'-lanterns with wicked smiles that share an inside joke. Heading back up the other side, black cat decals mock Blaine's panic with cartoon anxiety in their eyes. Swaying effigies of an old green-faced witch nod wisely, warning Blaine to be mindful of the historical fate of unconventional women. The same black-cloaked dolls with pointed caps hang from every porch except for Blaine's, as though marking her lack of affinity with some unspoken tradition. Amelia is nowhere in sight.

"Damn her," Blaine whispers.

Returning to the brood, Blaine crouches on the living room carpet. All three girls wear their masks. They sort candy in silence. Starting with the largest piece, regardless of flavor, color or type, they arrange stacks to achieve an even distribution of mass. Little hands weigh and move the candy each time the job appears done. Blaine guesses it must be a game with rules only the girls understand.

The dissimilarity of the girls with other children leaves Blaine unsure how to act. Earlier, when her brother's youngest spilled red pop on her pants, Blaine improvised a new costume bottom with a pair of patterned leggings. The girl stopped crying, the others quit teasing, and all of the children got curious about the hidden treasures in Aunt Blaine's closet. Blaine raided her wardrobe for accessories and ended up hosting a side party in her bedroom and dressing up with the kids. Her siblings looked at her askance, but it was more fun than listening to her brother-in-law pontificate about current events.

Blaine breaks the silence. "That's quite a haul. Looks like you guys hit the jackpot tonight."

The girls continue their candy game with the gravity of old men playing poker. They don't eat any candy. They don't battle or bargain for favorites. They measure and sort.

"Which one do you like best?" Blaine asks.

None of the girls says a word.

Blaine takes a small cellophane bag of candy corn out of the middle pile and tears it open with her teeth. "You don't mind if I have this one, right?"

She's got the girls attention. They stop playing and turn toward Blaine while she chews the sugary tidbits. The candy is so sweet it's almost painful to eat. Blaine says, "Did Miss Amelia tell you where she was going?"

Facing Blaine, the girls don't answer or resume their game. They sit still except for the unnatural movement of the masks.

"Can you tell me where Miss Amelia went, or make a guess for me? Did she say anything before she left?"

The bird mask rolls its spiraling eyes in exasperation. The devil nose smirks. The flaccid horns quiver.

"Has she done this before? Where does she go?"

The autonomous devil nose can't contain itself any longer. It blurts, "She can go to Hell!"

Blaine keeps chewing as the nose does a little dance and the face around it glows a deeper shade of red. Blaine's amazed by the craftsmanship. She can't see any wires or strings. She says, "You look like you'd know the way there."

All three girls burst out laughing.

Blaine isn't sure if laughter is progress, but it's better than weird silence. She addresses the autonomous devil nose. "Excuse me, sir. We haven't been properly introduced. My name is Blaine. What's your name?"

The miniature devil raises its pitchfork. The girls chant in happy unison like a squad of cheerleaders: "We are Legion!"

"I see," Blaine says. "So you're little demons tonight."

The masks nod with enthusiasm.

Blaine rises and gathers the discarded pillowcases from around the room. "Being supernatural and all, I know you're not tired, but it's getting pretty late." She picks up candy and drops it into the bags. "I'm sure all of you know that if demons don't get back to Hell before midnight they turn back into regular boring girls."

The masks confer quickly. Blood-beak points her hypnotic spiraling eyes at Blaine. "That's not true! You're lying."

Blaine shrugs off the accusing stare. The eyes make her dizzy if she looks for too long. "Find out for yourself then." She shovels candy off the floor with both hands and fills up the sacks. The girls try to stop her and pull the candy back out. Blaine is bigger and faster and competitive by nature. She pins a full pillowcase closed with her knee and uses her elbows to block the girls' assault. Hands slap and bump and grab. Wrappers tear and candy colors smudge under fingernails. Blaine's breathless as she presents each girl with a full pillowcase in triumph. "Okay. Come on, let's get up and go."

Blood-beak says, "Go where?"

"Home," Blaine says. "Lead the way."

Devil-nose is the biggest girl. She cocks her head to one side and says, "We are home, dummy."

Blood-beak concurs, "You'll get used to it."

"Nope," Blaine says. "You're evicted. Up and out."

Devil-nose lifts her pillowcase as high in the air as her arms can reach and turns it upside down. Candy bounces across the carpet, rolls under the chairs and coffee table, and lodges between the end tables and couch. Detached wrappers drift and scatter into every corner. The other girls follow her lead and do the same. Then they count to three and toss their empty pillowcases into the air and clap. The sacks parachute over the room like jovial ghosts at play.

"Fine," Blaine says, taking the smallest girl's arm, the shy one with the wobbly horns on her faceless head. "You can go without your candy."

Horn-head's body goes slack. Her arm is dead weight in Blaine's grip. She wails, "No, Mommy, no. I don't like this game." Blaine tries to hold her so she'll stand up, but the child collapses in tears and rolls as if she's in agony, crushing warm candy into the rug.

Devil-nose rushes to comfort little Horn-head, clutching her tight and rolling along with her. "Look what you did. You made her cry!"

Blood-beak flings her feathers at Blaine before she joins. "You're supposed to be nice!"

Something slick splatters Blaine's face. The girls wrestle in a confusion of animal parts and totem heads. The smallest one cries: "Mommy, mommy, don't make me leave you!" The others scream the same words in repeated torment and mocking laughter. The miniature devil on the biggest girl's nose brays and squeals. Blaine feels dizzy and insane, like she's watching a pen of cannibal pigs mangle each other on her living room floor.

The cacophony of laughter and piercing wails from the girls stabs Blaine's temples. She says, "Stop it" uselessly. The roiling mass expands and engulfs her like a migraine. Her head pounds until she realizes that the pounding is outside her skull, on her front door, where a fist demands an answer. Blaine lunges and almost falls into a blinding light. It's the police.

Two officers stand on the threshold. One shines a flashlight inside and says, "Excuse me, ma'am. Is everything all right here?"

"Oh no, no it's not," Blaine says. "Please, come in."

The officers exchange a look and step inside. Behind them the deserted street has come to life, not with roaming ghosts but with peering neighbors, open storm doors and illuminated porch lights. The black witch effigy dolls are lit from behind, casting shadows. They sway on their brooms, titillating lurid whispers up and down the block.

The girls cling to Blaine's legs like baby marsupials cowering from a threat. Blaine gestures at the creatures with open palms. "Their mother left them here. Or babysitter. This is so terrible, the poor things. Please, can you get them home?"

"What's the address, ma'am?"

"I don't know."

"Have you called their mother?"

"I don't have a number. Her name's Amelia."

"Amelia what?"

"I don't know. Everyone knows her. Ask one of those people." Blaine points over the crush of the girls at the peeping faces outside. The officer with the flashlight lowers it, and then turns and shuts the front door. The last thing Blaine sees outside is the neighbor couple in matching bathrobes pulling their witch doll down from the rafters.

The second officer buddies up next to Blaine and the girls while Flashlight scans the scene. The girls press into Blaine. Devil teeth snag holes in Blaine's sweatpants. Blood drips from the beak and dampens her thighs. Flabby horns writhe on her like hungry worms.

Blaine pushes back at the girls. Her fingers sink into the horns like chewed bubblegum. The bloody beak nips at her wrist. "Jesus," she says, "Get them off me."

Flashlight says, "Calm down, ma'am."

Buddy admonishes, "You shouldn't talk that way in front of the children."

Blaine knows she's got blood from the bird-beak spattered across her forehead and her pony tail has fallen halfway out. Smeared candy sticks to the carpet, Kuan Yin lies prone among used pillowcases and shredded wrappers, and watery dirt from the house plant spreads a black stain on the hardwood floor. Blaine tries to act more reasonable than she appears. "Please," she says, "Can you take them? Their mother must be worried sick."

From the mantle, there's a loud *chink* as the ice melts in Blaine's cocktail glass.

Flashlight says, "Have you been drinking?"

"I made punch," Blaine says. "For my family."

"Is that a yes, ma'am?"

Blaine says, "It's not like that. It was mostly children."

"Where's your husband?"

"I'm single."

"Three kids and not married," Flashlight says to Buddy.

Blaine starts to protest and Buddy comes to her defense. "Things are different now than when we were coming up. You can't judge girls these days, what with women's lib and them having to work and all. Be glad it's not the drugs."

Flashlight shakes his head at Blaine. "I guess I'm just old-fashioned."

Blaine struggles against the girls. "Look, you don't get it. Listen—ouch, stop it!"

Flashlight kneels next to Blaine and speaks to Blood-beak. "Hi, sweetheart. You look really scary tonight. Did your mommy help you with your costume?"

Blood-beak says proudly, "No. I made it all by myself."

"How about that?" says Flashlight. "What's all over your mouth?"

"Candy."

"Is that what you call it? It looks pretty messy. Did you eat too much candy tonight?"

"No, sir."

"What about mommy? Did mommy have too much fun and get messy?"

Blood-beak says, "She invited us, sir."

Blaine says, "What does this have to do with—get them off me!"

Flashlight says, "Do you think you can be good for mommy tonight?"

"For Christ's sake," Blaine says. "I'm not—"

Flashlight cuts her off sternly. "How much have you had to drink tonight, ma'am?"

"Two glasses of punch. Who cares?"

Buddy explains: "See, honey, if you blow point-oh-eight it's a mandatory report. We have an obligation."

"Report what? This is my house."

"We have to call protective services. It's mandatory."

"Are you crazy?"

Flashlight stands and puts his hand near his holster. "Just relax, ma'am. There's no need for talk like that. Answer the question. Are you the sole caretaker of these children? Is there anyone else here?"

"No, but—"

"Seems like she lives alone, then," Flashlight says to Buddy.

Buddy shrugs. "Yeah. Too bad she didn't drink much. It's gonna be rough."

Flashlight checks the scene once more and moves toward the door. He declares: "The only substance I see being abused here is sugar."

Buddy says, "You got that right."

"Wait," Blaine says. "What about them?"

"Mommy, you're so funny." The girls laugh and hug Blaine's legs like a Chinese finger trap. The more she struggles, the tighter they grip.

Buddy tells Blaine, "I'd try to relax more if I were you."

The girls join their small hands and close the ring tighter around Blaine. They spin Blaine against her will as they circle and begin to sing a nursery rhyme. Blaine cries out, "Wait. Report me. Take them away. Please."

Buddy's eyes follow the counter-clockwise motion of the girls spinning Blaine around and around. He frowns at Flashlight. "I hope she can handle them better than the last one. What do we tell the Connors about Riley?"

Blaine shouts: "Hey. Arrest me. Get me out of here."

Flashlight says, "I don't think we need to make a big deal out of a few extra treats on Halloween. Everyone knows the risks."

"True," Buddy says. He turns to Blaine once more. "We'll let it slide this one time. We know it's hard being a single mom, especially when you have so many."

Blaine's voice succumbs to the sing-song chant of the girls as Buddy and Flashlight lock the door behind them. Blaine mouths the muted words: *They're not mine.*

The chant pulsates around her. The song is a nursery rhyme Blaine doesn't recognize in a language she can't understand. Her head throbs in cadence with the repetitive melody as she spins. The girls distort and expand, forming a membranous skin. Blaine punches at the elastic mass enclosing her. It absorbs her effort and warps back into place. She tries to aim for their faces and fails. It's impossible for Blaine to single out the individual masks in the spinning swarm of devil laugh, razor beak and warm flesh. Blaine can see everything clearly, but her mind can't process what she sees. The girls have sloughed off their street clothes. Their bodies are the same as their faces. Their faces are not masks.

At the edge of an empty ballpark, a baby stroller waits outside in the dark. It's a cumbersome double stroller, the type with side by side seating compartments for twins. An autumn frost coats the bulky shape, highlighting it under the glow of the Hunter's moon against a backdrop of pines.

If a curious passerby stops, they breathe easy to notice no

sound or motion from the abandoned stroller. Coming near, they worry about what they'll find tucked underneath the blanket. The worn coverlet appears to be decorated with alphabet blocks, but upon closer inspection, the symbols look more like ancient runes. Thinking twice about using their bare hands, the curious observer searches the ground for a fallen branch. They lift the weather-stained blanket, revealing a vacuum of darkness inside the stroller compartments blacker than the surrounding night. A flash of deeper, greater darkness from within startles them. They drop the branch, and it's sucked away. There's a crackling sound, as if something unseen is trying to eat the branch.

Another crackling sound resonates across the park. At the crest of a hill, the neighborhood is gathered around a bonfire. It's the end of October again, the transitional time between fall and winter. Until the New Year begins on the morning after Halloween, the fate of the community hangs in the balance. The veil is thin, and everything can change tonight. With equal reverence and revelry, the neighborhood residents wait for the cutty black sow to show her face and give herself up as an offering.

Blaine doesn't hear the bonfire or the crackling of the branch from the double stroller compartments. She hears the hungry crying of its passenger. Blaine experiences the crying as a direct bond, as her own insatiable need. The rest of the world is barely audible. As Blaine practices leaving the stroller unattended for longer and more agonizing stretches of time, the sound of crying never stops. When Blaine grasps the handle once again, she's flooded with a sickening relief. Then she's compelled to push. The giggling girls encircle her, swarming and weaving in a chaotic orbit. One full year of Blaine's life has passed this way.

Near the bonfire, Blaine's neighbors watch with orange faces, lit by flame. The couple in golf clothes gropes one another with weird delight. Flashlight and Buddy stand at attention, solemn in their fire safety gear. Other familiar faces leer, faces Blaine can't associate with names, joggers and gardeners and pedigreed dog walkers. All grow hideous with grotesque laughter, spitting and popping like logs in the fire, grinning like jack-o'-lanterns sharing an inside joke.

Blaine's exhausted from a year of service, a year of keeping the girls well fed with scraps and travelers from the hotel, a year of constant need and no rest. Blaine sees an easy answer in the beckoning flames.

Lucky for her, the girls are good at keeping secrets. Blaine's primed them as much as she can. They're excited she wants to play dress up and they've been rehearsing every day. Tonight is their big chance. The girls leap as the stroller hits the bonfire. Blood-beak jabs her maw deep between Blaine's thoracic vertebrae and into her spinal column. After a rupture of pain, powerful wings emerge from Blaine's back. Blaine feels stronger and lighter. She begs her hands to release the stroller. Gravity helps them comply. As Blaine rises, Devil-nose plunges down her throat. Blaine feels like she's choking until a long, fiery tongue snakes its way over her esophagus and out of her mouth. She sprays fire on the crowd below. The last girl, faceless and soft-horned, clings whining around Blaine's waist. She's the youngest of the three and needs a little push. Blaine coaxes her gently and reminds her of the plan. They merge, and a glorious Leviathan unfolds beneath Blaine's wings.

The stroller rolls down the hill, unmothered and ablaze. The crowd chases it in frenzy. Blaine lays them to waste. No one remains to save the stroller from burning. No one is left to hold the maw of the portal open and allow the unseen occupant to gape into a world where it doesn't belong. The passenger is banished. The crying abates. The October sky glows amber and red, and the mythical beast Blaine has become circles the neighborhood and pumps its majestic wings. It rises higher and higher in an ascending orbit above the trees and wraps itself in wisps of cloud. It folds its wings and settles into the sky. Drifting across the moon's silhouette in a chimera-shaped nest, the beast slips into an unspoiled sleep.

MASKS

Lisa Lepovetsky

A S DON QUIXOTE and Sancho Panza emerge from the red Plymouth, Sancho Panza straightens out the goose feather pillows creating a large gut behind the scuffed leather belt. The sun is trying to disappear behind the tops of white pine trees surrounding the small brick house at the edge of town, staining the sidewalk from the curb a deep burnt orange. The two are silent as they stroll the block from the red car to the house, and Sancho Panza pulls a Kleenex from a hidden leather pouch when the wind picks up.

"Damn. I always have trouble with my contacts when the wind tosses the dust like this. Everything's kind of red and distorted. It's as though the world were at the bottom of a pool of diluted blood. I'm glad we didn't have to park farther away, like last year. Remember? We had to duck Halloweeners the whole way up the block."

Don Quixote says nothing, but they walk faster past the parked cars, and hurry out of the cold, mean evening when the door is answered.

Joan of Arc ushers them in with a flourish, waving the foil-covered sword behind her. "The others haven't all arrived yet. Michael's still making the punch in the kitchen." She gestures though the archway, with its string spiderweb, and they glimpse a short man with large wings hovering over a cauldron. He pours in something green from a bottle.

Saint Joan grimaces. "Damn. Now it'll taste like melon." She turns her attention back to her two guests. "I think I know who you two are, but I won't make my guess until the unmasking, after everybody's here." There's a knock on the door. "Excuse me," she says. "More haunts are here. Make yourselves at home." She hurries off.

Music throbs around the strange figures like an invisible tide, ebbing and flowing around the pier of voices. The soundtrack from the film *Halloween*. Their hosts have thought of everything, as usual. Orange and black crêpe paper streamers sag from the ceiling like the legs of a huge, desiccated spider. Paper skeletons and witches peer from windows and walls. Candlelight and smoke create a warm fog. There is not enough room in the small den, and the overflow is in the kitchen, around the temporary bar set up by the refrigerator, where the archangel Michael serves drinks.

The music from the stereo is very loud. Sancho Panza nods toward the sofa, but Don Quixote shakes his head. "Let's find somewhere quieter," he shouts, "where we can be alone and talk."

Sancho Panza points toward the ceiling and says, "One of the bedrooms. Come on." They make their way to the carpeted stairs and decide to open the first door they come to.

Halloween. I watch children wandering in frightened packs, disguised with rubber, plastic and painted flesh. Some wear sheets in a vain attempt to emulate spirits. If they only knew. Unsuspecting doorbells are thumbed by sticky digits, hooked protectively around twisted handles of paper bags also masquerading as pumpkins or ghosts. On the Eve of All Hallows, nothing is as it seems.

Cruel lean cats, black as libido, balding in uneven patches, cross my path as I shuffle through ankle-high piles of moldering leaves. More of the dead and dying, the color of blood and sunsets, drip silently from naked branches to rest in my hair or on my hunched shoulders. I hate to be touched and whirl, clutching uselessly at the empty air, my heart thudding against its bony prison.

Halloween. Distorted macrocephalic squash glare at me— imbeciles perched on weathered porches and peeling fences. Their hollow eyes watch and carved mouths open in silent shrieks. I imagine the long knives, reflecting the clenched teeth and narrowed eyes of the assassins, plunged deeply into the tense burnt ocher flesh. They saw steadily, lobotomizing the pale pulp within and replacing it with gobs of melting wax. Their flickering faces taunt me. Toothy grins and silent circles of mouths beneath triangular eyes. A few are more complex, with glowing swirls and letters.

Halloween. Even the weather is infidel, sultry and sensuous one moment, seducing me to remove my clothes, to bathe in her crackling, musty warmth. Then, with a casual snap of barometric fingers, I am chilled to the depths of my soul, shivering in the unblinking stare of a street lamp. Who can I trust? I shake my head, trying to clear it for the celebration to come.

I learned early that trust and faith are fleeting things, as ephemeral as mother love and safety.

LISA LEPOVETSKY

An owl-headed woman leans over to shout into the shoulder of a headless man. "God, I can hardly hear myself think over that damned music." His torso bobs in agreement, and he places a bloody severed head on the ashtray and stuffs some potato chips through an opening in his shirt.

"I hate Halloween parties," he yells. "You spend weeks planning your oh-so-unique costume and some jerk shows up in the same thing. Then you have to spend an hour stuffed into it, sweating, until everybody decides to show up." The severed head is tucked back under an arm and the hand disappears under the cape.

The owl-headed woman nods. "I know what you're saying. These damned feathers are driving me mad. They constantly tickle my nose and get in my eyes. I keep sneezing, and I can hardly see anything without my glasses. I can't wait until the unmasking at midnight."

A red satin demon holding a martini enters the conversation, moving around the iced keg. "You know what I hate the most? Until the unmasking you really don't know who everybody is. I mean, some people you know. They just wear half masks like this." She points to the red fabric molded around her eyes. "Or maybe you recognize a voice or two. But there are always a few who won't talk and lurk someplace, watching . . . waiting. I don't know, it gives me the creeps. I know that's the idea, but I'm afraid that when that mask comes off, the face underneath it will be even worse—or maybe it's not a mask at all . . . "

"I know exactly what you mean," says the owl-headed woman, blowing a feather out of her face. It's like that person dressed like a clown, sitting in the armchair in the corner. He doesn't say anything, just sits there, watching everybody else. He doesn't even have a drink."

"Or she," the demon says. "It could be a woman. You can't tell with all that makeup and the yellow wig. It could be anybody."

"I tried talking to him—or her—earlier, offering to get a drink, but he wouldn't say anything," the headless man says. "He wouldn't respond, just turned his head to look at me with those weird blue eyes. If you ask me, I think they're tinted contacts. And I don't remember anybody I know having eyes that color. I don't mind saying, it gave me the heebie-jeebies."

The owl-headed woman shudders and finishes her martini in one gulp. "I'll stay 'til midnight, but not a minute longer."

A spasmodic wind coughs around me, clearing brown leaves from the cement gutter of its throat as I struggle against it. Filthy gauze ghosts with oversized Styrofoam heads dance madly, blindly beneath branches and electric wires. How thin those wires, how dark and slender in the twilight. Electric umbilicals connecting each solid brick embryo to the invisible womb of the night. Watching the wires, I can see pulses of power swell and swim into the houses, promising safety, security, comfort.

Safety. I laugh, thinking of what is safe for them and what is safe for me. My safety is here in the night wrapped around me, in the voices whispering in my mind, in the familiar hunger gnawing at my gut. My comfort is in the things that make children afraid of this night: revenants, witches, the "things that go bump in the night." But also the more concrete things that their parents fear: the poisoned popcorn balls and the apples with bits of razor blades embedded in them, waiting for the unwary, the less vigilant. I shudder deliciously at the thought.

No one knows to fear me, though I am the living embodiment of all those terrors, the one who holds their future in my hands, at least for tonight. I've learned to love the pain and terror this night can bring. The delicious tears of their anguish. This is my night for retribution.

My hand drifts to my pocket, easing along the smooth metal, stroking the blade. Long thin steel, colder than my icy fingers, colder than hate. Colder than the endless empty years until tonight. This is what it's all led up to. I feel blood surging through my blue veins, my red arteries, pushing past the pliable valves of my heart, filling its hungry cavities, satisfying its need. For the moment.

The doorbell (hooked to a recorded gong, just for the occasion) rings three times in quick succession, and Saint Joan struggles through the crowd to the door, her sword parting the merrymakers like Moses at the Red Sea. A papier-mâché frog croaks angrily as she knocks him out of the way with her shield, and Don Quixote and Sancho Panza duck quietly out of the way before she reaches them. They know there are doors upstairs, hiding quieter rooms and make their way silently up the carpeted steps. Sancho Panza opens a door marked with a homemade sign: ABANDON ALL HOPE, YE WHO ENTER HERE. The bathroom.

"Very funny," Don Quixote mutters as they back out.

There's another door at the end of the hall. This door is partially open, and they can see it's a bedroom, with a flowered silk bedspread and matching drapes pulled to the sides of the windows, over sheer curtains. When their eyes adjust to the dark after closing the door behind them, they sit together on edge of the bed. Sancho Panza is the first to speak.

"I'm sorry I dragged you here, Charlie. I thought it might cheer you up. I guess I was wrong—again. I never was very good at reading you. It's my timing or something. We can make a graceful exit pretty soon, when all the guests have arrived. It's almost midnight."

Don Quixote is silent, rising and crossing the room to the window. He looks through the sheer curtains to the few mottled leaves on the branches outside. A group of Halloweeners passes below, shrieking and laughing and rattling candy in their plastic pumpkins. "For some reason," he says, "those kids in their masks and costumes make me sad."

"I'm the one who should be sorry," he continues. "I'm being a shit. You were considerate enough to invite me at the last minute, even if it was just a gesture because Sibyl left. God damn it. Who'd have thought . . . I suppose that's always been my problem, hasn't it—acting without thinking. It was nice of you to ask me, and if I'd been thinking then, I'd have realized I wouldn't have any fun, ruining the night for you. I shouldn't have come."

"We need to talk about Sibyl," Sancho Panza says. Don Quixote starts to speak. "No, don't interrupt me, Charlie. Some things have to be said, unpleasant things, even things you couldn't know. Sibyl's changed, she's . . . I don't know, wrong, somehow."

Sancho Panza's voice drifts up to evaporate in the polyester canopy, and they sit in silence a while, both deciding how to continue the awkward conversation. The heavy bass of the music rhythmically vibrates something on the wall across from them, and a woman shrieks in laughter or fright near the bedroom door.

Sancho Panza starts at the sound, then laughs self-deprecatingly. "I wish they wouldn't do that. It always sounds like someone's being killed or something. I guess this party isn't the best place for me, either."

Don Quixote says, "It sounds like neither of us is in a festive mood. Let's just go down and tell Michael and Carolyn that we can't stay."

"Not until we've finished talking."

A dog barks hoarsely in the yard beside me, exorcising the Halloween spirits in his own way. Maybe he's lonely or frightened, or hungry. I turn on him, my eyes glowing hot with ancient passions, and he tucks his ragged tail and backs away, a snarl deep in his chest. He quivers, then slinks through a tattered privet hedge. He can feel my quest, my desire my hunger.

I slowly approach a house. Its white pillars and wrap-around veranda valiantly attempt to emulate the great Southern plantations. But the fading clapboard house is dwarfed by its own façade. A rake and push lawnmower, both rusting, rest against one wall. A tasteful straw wreath wrapped in orange and brown ribbon hangs on the door above a brass knocker shaped like a lion's head. It sports smiling skeletons and colorful spiders. A comfortable, safe home. Safe—there's that word again.

I remember another home and child alone in the dark, waiting, listening, crying, and the stern voice of a man: "I'll give you something . . . " But memories are unimportant now, distant. All that matters is the night stretching out before me like a corpse and the silver song in my pocket. My hunger speaks a language of its own, and something laughs deep inside me, something growing like a dark light. A light I never knew was there before tonight. This is my epiphany.

Caressing the white wooden siding, I watch small chips of paint snow to the dry brown grass. I touch my tongue to the boards and savor the heavy metallic taste of lead. In only a moment I know this house and its kind, but it is not what I'm looking for tonight, what will fill the emptiness inside my gut. Maybe after. Reluctantly, I turn back to the darkness.

Sancho Panza tugs at the pillow stuffing behind the leather belt and speaks in a low voice. "I'm glad you're here, but I was so surprised you came. I didn't think you'd want to . . . be with me after everything that's happened between us."

Don Quixote is still staring out the window. He doesn't blink. "Sibyl's living with you now, isn't that enough? I had hoped . . . but I always knew she'd end up with you. It's you she loved. Me, she feared, even pitied. If it hadn't been for that, she would have gone with you right after the split. She said as much when she left. She has your sense of tact." He chuckles mirthlessly.

The door opens a crack for a moment, and the music swirls loudly around them. "Sorry," mumbles a ghoul, holding the hand of Goldilocks. "I didn't know anybody was in here." He laughs. The door closes again before Don Quixote or Sancho Panza can reply.

Sancho Panza takes off the large hat and runs her red fingernails through the graying curls. A sigh escapes her shadowed, trembling mouth. The lips open to speak, then press together again, and her head shakes slowly. A pickup truck rattles past and glass shatters on the sidewalk below. "Devil's night," she says, shaking her head. "I hope they didn't soap the car." Don Quixote doesn't respond.

Finally Sancho Panza speaks again in a near-whisper. "It's so hard to talk to you when you get defensive like this. And I don't think pity has anything to do with it. Sibyl . . . well, I can't imagine her doing anything out of pity. Or love. Not anymore."

Don Quixote clears his throat. "God damn her. How can she

just pick up and leave like that?" His voice breaks and his eyes glitter in the light from the street.

"Charlie, don't do this to yourself. Or to me. I should have called, I know. But she begged me not to, and you know how persuasive she's always been. Please don't turn away. We have to talk about this. You have to understand."

"Oh I understand. Always have. You were never able to say no to her. She chose to live with you and you let her. Never considered turning her away." Don Quixote sniffs and straightens his collar needlessly.

"She was living with me, yes, for a while. But now she goes off by herself for days at a time. I don't know where she goes or where she stays. When she comes home, her clothes are a mess, and her eyes . . . I just don't know what's going on with her anymore."

Don Quixote's voice is loud, hoarse. "I suppose that's my fault now, too. You'll want to blame all this on me. Well, why should I care where she stays? I don't need this, Amanda, I just don't need this."

Moonlight suddenly glows on the silver strands combed carefully across Don Quixote's scalp, and Sancho Panza looks away, down on her pale hands clasped tightly around the wooden sword. She rises and slowly, almost imperceptibly, reaches over and touches his arm.

"Things—and people—aren't always what we want them to be," she whispers in the dark. He nods and they sit in silence for a while, letting the heartbeat of the music pulse around them.

"Hall of the Mountain King," she says. "It always sounds to me like someone going mad."

MASKS

I'm getting close; I can feel it. My very skin is electric with anticipation. Every hair on my body stands out rigid, aching. My breath ghosts around me, mingling with the cold fog like steam from a locomotive. I zero in on the emanations of my targets. Their desire to continue to live is almost as strong as mine to prevent it; our connection is unbreakable at last.

Some late Halloweeners pass on the far side of the street, laughing and counting their take for the night. They pause in their revelry, looking across the dirty, pitted pavement toward me. I know they are not able to see me—I am very still deep in the shadow of a yew tree. Yet the children become silent for a moment, then run down the street shrieking, costumes whipping out behind. Children have that extra sense. I love children.

I love their innocence and recognition of truth. They know what is real and what is an illusion. Adults lose that, to their detriment. I love children's recognition of the dangers abroad in the night, dangers not always visible to the naked eye. I love to hear their screams.

I want to chase them now, but my quarry tonight waits farther down this street. The voices of the night are growing louder. They demand to be obeyed, and I will not deny them. I grind my teeth and answer them with my pain. The two who call themselves Charlie and Amanda will be the first to feel my wrath, and their hearts will serve as a gift to the Eve of All Hallows. The rest are mine.

Sancho Panza touches Don Quixote's faded shoulder gently. "Sibyl has problems, Charlie. There's something terribly wrong with her, ever since she left that drug cult or whatever it was. She's filled with emotions I can't begin to understand, or even recognize—hate and rage, and something more frightening than those. She seems . . . changed."

"Changed? What does that mean, 'changed?'?" Don Quixote snorts and shuffles his feet in the shag carpet. "I can never understand you. You speak in riddles. You never say what you mean."

Sancho Panza starts to pace. "I'm not really sure what I mean, I guess. But I worry about what's going on in her mind. She won't eat at home anymore and she rarely sleeps there, no matter what I say. I don't know who her friends are—or if she even has friends, for that matter."

Don Quixote stands, straightening his shoulders, turning away from her. "She's an adult now, got her own life to live. I know better than anyone else that she has problems. If you remember, I raised her most of her life while you were out . . . " The unfinished sentence hangs like a cobweb in the corners of the room.

"Anyway," he continues more softly, "she claimed there were no drugs involved in the group she joined a while back. They just prayed or chanted or something innocuous like that. She claimed she's been away from it for almost a year, at any rate." He still doesn't look at Sancho Panza, but has to lean toward her slightly to hear her when she speaks.

"There's more." Sancho Panza's voice is like a thin wire. Her teeth clench as she speaks. "When she is home, Charlie, she talks in her sleep. I can hear her through the wall. She says things . . . awful things about us and people in general and mumbles strange names I can't make out. I'm afraid for her—and for me, if you want to know the truth. I lie awake in the dark waiting. I don't know what for, but sometimes I wait all night." A tear glistens on her cheek and the doorbell gongs hollowly in the hallway as another reveler arrives.

Sancho Panza reaches out in the dark and grips Don Quixote's hand.

MASKS

Stopping on one deserted street corner, I run a finger along the thick shaft of the knife handle, savoring its ridges and curves. Hesitantly, I test the cold thin metal on my wrist, rewarded by a tiny splitting of skin as one warm drop of blood eases into the coarse fabric of my coat. I continue, following the thin diamond wire to my destination. The streets are empty now. The children are all tucked safely in their beds. The children . . . oh yes, the children. Later.

I imagine the perfect chaos to come. I can taste the sweet-sour fear already, hear the thundering of twenty hearts beating in panicked unison, smell the metallic odor of blood and sweat pulsing through desperate pores. It has been so long and yet no time at all. The dark night will be clothed in scarlet sheets.

I finally arrive. The house is a small brick cage, electric jack-o'-lanterns grinning happily from the windows. They are there—I can sense their sweet foulness already, and I want to retch with the nearness of them. They want to escape, but I am God tonight.

I stare in for a moment, letting the fun-fright, the playing at fear, trickle around me. Shortly the farce will end, and I will wallow in their truth. My knife slices through the copper lifelines and the house blinks its eye and holds its breath.

Don Quixote sighs. "All right, I guess we are her parents, even if we haven't lived together for five years. If it's as bad as you say— and somehow I believe it is—we have to do something. We'll find her tonight and make her get help. Maybe if we approach her together . . . "

Sancho Panza mutters, "I only hope we're not too late." Louder she says, "Let's skip out the back door. Neither of us wants to be here anyway."

Making their way through the crowd of bodies, like salmon swimming upstream, Don Quixote and Sancho Panza finally reach the kitchen. As they push the bar aside and squeeze around it to the back door, the lights and music suddenly go off. Someone mentions a circuit breaker, and Saint Joan begins bullying her way toward the fuse box in the kitchen.

"Let's get out of here before she notices we're leaving," whispers Sancho Panza, and they open the door onto the back patio. As they do, the front door opens and an icy draft rushes past them. Don Quixote pushes the door shut behind them as screams begin growing in the den like a shrill carillon.

Don Quixote grasps Sancho Panza's arm and starts down the back stairs. "Sounds like the last guest has finally arrived," he says. "We're going to miss all the fun."

ABOUT THE AUTHORS

Sean Eads and Joshua Viola are writers from Denver, Colorado. Sean has been a finalist for the Shirley Jackson Award, Lambda Literary Award and the Colorado Book Award. His first short story collection was published in 2017. Joshua is the owner of Hex Publishers. His latest anthologies include *Blood Business* and *Cyber World: Tales of Humanity's Tomorrow*. His upcoming novel, *Denver Moon*, will also be released as a comic book.

Amber Fallon lives in Massachusetts with her husband and two dogs. A techie by day and horror writer by night, Mrs. Fallon has spent time as a bank manager, motivational speaker, produce wrangler, and butcher. Her obsessions with sushi, glittery nail polish, and sharp objects have made her a recognized figure. Amber's publications include *The Warblers, The Terminal, Sharkasaurus, Daughters of Inanna, So Long and Thanks for All the Brains, Horror on the Installment Plan, Zombies For a Cure, Quick Bites of Flesh, Operation Ice Bat*, and more.

Charles Gramlich lives in the piney woods of southern Louisiana. He is the author of the *Talera* fantasy series and the SF novel, *Under the Ember Star*. His stories and poetry have been published in magazines such as *Beat to a Pulp, The Horror Zine*, and many others.

Joanna Koch is a fan of folklore, fairy tales, and anthropology. Her short fiction has been published in journals such as *Dark Fuse* and *Hello Horror*, and included in several speculative fiction anthologies. Joanna is an MA Contemplative Psychotherapy graduate of Naropa University who currently lives and works near Detroit.

Curtis M. Lawson is a writer of unapologetically weird, dark fiction and comics. His work includes *It's A Bad, Bad, Bad, Bad World*, *The Devoured*, and *Mastema*. He is a member of the Horror Writer's Association, and the organizer of the Wyrd live horror reading series. He lives in Salem, MA with his wife and their son.

Lisa Lepovetsky has published fiction and poetry widely in the small press, professional publications and anthologies. Her work has appeared in *Ellery Queen's Mystery Magazine*, *Cemetery Dance* and many other magazines, and such anthologies as *Dark Destiny*, *Blood Muse*, and *HORRORS!*, among others. She earned her MFA from Penn State, and her most recent book is *Voices From Empty Rooms*, a collection of dark poetry.

Adam Light resides in northeast Florida with his beautiful wife and daughter, and their aptly, though perhaps not so imaginatively named Walker hound, Walker. He haunts a cubicle by day, writes horror stories at night, and virtually never sleeps. He is the author of several short horror stories, some of which have been published in his first collection *Toes Up: Horror to Die For*. He also has stories in the *Bad Apples* anthology series and *Dead Roses: Five Dark Tales of Twisted Love*.

Evans Light is a writer of horror and suspense, and is the author of *Screamscapes: Tales of Terror*, *Arboreatum*, *Don't Need No Water* and more. He is co-creator of the *Bad Apples* Halloween anthology series and *Dead Roses: Five Dark Tales of Twisted Love*. Evans lives in Charlotte, North Carolina, surrounded by thousands of vintage horror paperbacks, and is the proud father of fine sons and the lucky husband of a beautiful wife.

Chad Lutzke lives in Battle Creek, MI with his wife and children. he has written for *Famous Monsters of Filmland*, *Rue Morgue*, *Cemetery Dance*, and *Scream* magazine. His fiction can be found in a few dozen magazines and anthologies including his own 18-story collection *Night as a Catalyst*. Lutzke is known for his heartfelt dark fiction and deep character portrayals. In the summer of 2016 he released his dark coming-of-age novella *Of Foster Homes and Flies* which has been praised by authors Jack Ketchum, James Newman, John Boden, and many others. Later in 2016 Lutzke released his contribution to bestselling author J. Thorn's *American Demon Hunter*, and 2017 saw the release of his novella *Wallflower*. His latest, *Stirring the Sheets*, was published by Bloodshot Books in spring 2018.

Josh Malerman is an American author and also one of two singer/songwriters for the rock band The High Strung, whose song "The Luck You Got" can be heard as the theme song to the Showtime show "Shameless." His book *Bird Box* is also currently being filmed as a feature film starring Sandra Bullock, John Malkovich, and Sarah Paulson. *Bird Box* was also nominated for the Stoker Award, the Shirley Jackson Award, and the James Herbert Award. His books *Black Mad Wheel* and *Goblin* have also been nominated for Stoker Awards. *Unbury Carol* is his latest novel.

Jason Parent is an author of horror, thrillers, mysteries, science fiction, and dark humor, though his many novels, novellas, and short stories tend to blur the boundaries between these genres. From his award-winning first horror/mystery novel, *What Hides Within*, to his widely applauded police procedural/supernatural thriller, *Seeing Evil*, Jason's work has won him praise from both critics and fans of diverse genres alike. His work has been compared to that of some of his personal favorite authors, such as Chuck Palahniuk, Jack Ketchum, Tess Gerritsen, and Joe Hill. Jason grew up near Fall River, Massachusetts, the setting for several of his novels. He has lived in New England most his life, currently residing in Rhode Island.

When he is not writing fiction, **Thomas Vaughn** is a college professor whose research focuses on apocalyptic rhetoric and doomsday cults. Most of his writing seems to stray through the realms of literary horror and dark magical realism. He has been fortunate enough to have stories accepted in four different magazines and anthologies in 2018 so far. He wrote the story in this one just for you.

Ian Welke grew up in the library in Long Beach, California. After receiving his Bachelor of Arts in History from California State University, Long Beach, he worked in the computer games industry for fifteen years where he was lucky enough to work at Blizzard Entertainment and at Runic Games in Seattle. While living in Seattle he sold his first short story, a space-western, written mainly because he was depressed that *Firefly* had been canceled. Following the insane notion that life is short and he should do what he wants most, he moved back to southern California and started writing full time. Ian's short fiction has appeared in *Big Pulp, Arcane II*, the *American Nightmare* anthology, and the *18 Wheels of Horror* anthology, amongst other places. His novels, *The Whisperer in Dissonance* (2014) and the Bram Stoker Award-nominated *End Times at Ridgemont High* (2015) were both published by Ominum Gatherum Media.

Gregor Xane is the author of *Taboogasm, The Hanover Block,* and *Six Dead Spots*. His work has been featured in *Stupefying Stories, Dead Roses,* and the popular Halloween anthology series, *Bad Apples*. He is perfectly symmetrical.

WANT MORE?

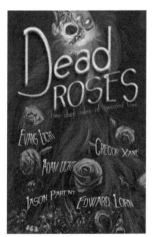

CPSIA information can be obtained
at www.ICGtesting.com
Printed in the USA
BVHW07s0731071018
529496BV00002B/341/P